FRANCOIS
FOUND

Amy Feldman-Bawarshi

For information, contact: feldman_amy@yahoo.com

First print edition: December 2014

Cover Art by Victoria Yeh

Summary: 1837, London: In this story of revenge, redemption, and reunion, Francois and Michael, two runaway orphan boys escape their brutal master and begin a journey to find a stolen letter that will reveal Francois' true identity and family lineage.

[1. Mystery adventure--fiction. 2. Abandonment and kidnapping--fiction. 3. Great Britain--history--Victorian period 1837--fiction. 4. Brothers--fiction. 5. Revenge, redemption, reunion--fiction.]

Printed in the United States of America

To Daliah and Aden, who found me

To Anis, who helped me realize I was never lost

FRANCOIS FOUND

PART ONE

Chapter One: Finding Escape

Saint Mark's Orphanage, Amen Court, London, 1837, Saturday April 22nd, 3:32 am

Francois hid under his broken, metal-framed bed, watching Sledgeham's shadow haunting the halls outside the *shat* room, as the boys called it. He knew certain things about the night unfolding before him. It would be the same unfolding. Served up with a twist. Different night, same night. Yet always a slight twist— whether a rage of blackened blue set into Michael's face, or a whip of red lines into his back, always there was a slight variation of theme. Same, yet different. Yes, he knew things.

Michael was inside the shat room now, no doubt being set with cleaning the wooden shat box as well as the large ceramic bowl underneath that mostly caught the excrement of Saint Marks. There was also the floor to think about. Each morning an unlucky boy was charged with carrying the ceramic bowl of bowels down the rickety stairs to the outside dumping pit next to the outdoor privy. Sledgeham locked the doors at night, so the boys had to rely on the shat box for nighttime emergencies.

He knew Michael hadn't eaten for hours. Was he starving by now or so repulsed by human stench that his own hunger revolted against him? Lying still under the bed, paralysis choking his throat, Francois peered out as best he could into the hall. He couldn't see Michael from his position but the dormitory door opened enough for him to hear Sledgeham bang something hard against the floor.

Francois knew the others must be listening too—to Sledgeham's rants. How could they sleep through it? But they knew the run down. They weren't fools. Helping Michael only brought on their own dose of it.

Anyway, they don't owe him like I do. And I always get to him in time. Tonight's no different.

Master Sledgeham rampaged with a whiskey bottle in his right hand and a belt in his left, but his jumbled words finally slurred to the point of nonsense as he buoyed through the hallway, banging away.

Always the first sign, the banging into things. He'll soon be down.

Crawling mouse-like from under his bed, Francois eyed the eight other beds in the room. The other boys either slept through the ruckus or pretended to sleep, just like always. He appreciated the predictability. He peeked around the dormitory door looking for signs of life in Sledgeham, who was now out cold, his reeking body listless on the discolored wood-planked hallway floor.

The shat room door remained slightly opened, and flickering candle light spilled out from within. Strangely the exact shadow casting itself around Sledgeham looked like a rectangular casket of sorts, and Francois imagined for a moment that the old man was dead.

Gingerly stepping over the creaky floorboards to get to Michael, Francois heard a thump from inside. Suddenly, a rush of dirty water slushed out from the slanted shat room floorboards, trickling into the hallway and down the stairs below. He stepped around the flow, pushed the door ajar, and now stood directly over Michael, who lay on the floor, half of his raw and purple face exposed, his right hand and fingers still tightly grasped around a scrub brush.

"Michael, get up. He's out!" Francois nudged Michael's back, as Michael tried to push himself upward.

"Where's he?" Michael's voice was barely audible.

"Hallway. Come on, I have yeh!"

Francois stood over Michael, looped his hands under Michael's frame, and pulled in an upward motion, but Michael's heaviness caused Francois to stumble forward. Francois stepped over Michael and kneeled next to him.

"Get up, I said!"

"Head hurts."

"Yeh gonna hurt more if…"

The boys heard Master Sledgeham at the same time.

"An' what we got here? Ha'ah twofer the price o' one?"

Francois and Michael went stone cold. Francois stared toward the door, his dizzy thoughts turned to escape, his cheeks flushed, as he saw Sledgeham's stick-like body against the door frame,

~ 3 ~

blocking their exit out. Here came that paralysis again, that dominating rush flooding Francois.

Michael, adrenaline pumping now, found the strength to push himself off the ground. But his efforts were too slow and before Michael could stand completely, Sledgeham stood over him, a meter away, laughing wildly, as he slurred, "What yeh gonna do about this, Francois?" as Michael felt the piss hit his back, heard the hissing snake, smelled the sickly ketone stench of urine spraying him. Francois' mouth took shape into a downward crescent moon, his forehead wrinkled, and he whimpered.

"Get yeh shank bone up and clean this mess, Michael, if yeh smart enough to know what's good for yeh. Then I'll spare yeh little rabbit shiverin' o'er there in the corner, yeh hear me? Move it or I make me some rabbit stew...." Sledgeham slurred.

"Yeh whinge's with me. Leave 'em outta it."

"Or what? What yeh gonna do, eh?"

"Michael, don't...." Francois pleaded, for what he wasn't exactly certain.

"I'll clean, just leave him alone," Michael said, with a renewed but brazen vigor, as he used the bucket near him to stand up, his hand still clutching the scrub brush, his back to Sledgeham.

Francois glimpsed Michael's wild angry eyes for a moment as Michael gave him a quick look of reassurance. Then, suddenly, Michael swung his body around and threw the scrub brush dead aim straight into Sledgeham's eye socket, running full speed toward Sledgeham, swinging the metal bucket and hitting Sledgeham's left side of his head and ear, grabbing with his other hand the key around Sledgeham's neck with such force, he yanked it off with a snap. Francois stood motionless watching in horror, unable to breathe. It happened so fast that he did not see Michael take the key. Michael pounded into Sledgeham, knocking the drunkard down as he yelled, "Run Francois, now!"

Sledgeham lost his balance entirely enough for Michael and Francois to escape through the door into the hallway. Right behind Michael, Francois felt Sledgeham grabbing for him. Francois gained speed down the steps, three at a time, pressing between the bannister and wall like an agitated monkey swinging from twine to twine. He barreled past Michael, which was not only odd, but a first.

Keep up, Michael!

As the boys descended down the steps, which felt to both of them mountainous and interminable, Sledgeham yelled after Michael, "I'll kill yeh boy! I'll beat yeh teh death!"

Francois made it to the ground floor and took refuge behind Sledgeham's desk, in the sitting room adjacent to the stairway and the front door, watching this madness unfold before him. Francois begged for it to stop, wondering why Michael moved so slowly down the steps.

Sledgeham lunged toward Michael down the stairs. He was an old drunk and could hardly walk a straight line most days, but his anger always sobered him, and he grabbed the air as he wiped the spit off his face with his tattered shirt, gaining speed, screaming and cursing. Sledgeham swatted his belt around at Michael's head, the metal buckle making contact, as Michael raised his hands to protect himself, as Sledgeham kept whipping furiously.

Fall, fall, fall! Francois willed.

Francois turned his thoughts to himself.

Coward.

Shame hooked him as Michael took the whip.

Sledgeham slowed down briefly to dismantle a heavy framed picture of Jesus from the wall, still managing to swing his belt with one hand—at Michael's back, head, arms, beating skin and air. But then, Francois' prayers were answered by some divine miracle. Sledgeham lost his balance and slipped; he did not get up so quickly. Instead, he sat on the stairs rubbing his right ankle, moaning and screaming lunatic curses.

Move it, Michael! Faster! Get to the kitchen!

As Michael reached the front door to the orphanage, Francois called out, "No, Michael! Wrong way!" as his gaze turned to the shadows congregating on the stairway above. He saw the other boys—seven marbled statues, their eyes in disbelief, following the extreme violence below.

Michael grabbed at the front door's iron knob. It looked to Francois like Michael was picking the lock below.

Michael's head's not right! He knows Sledgeham's got the key!

"No Michael! It's locked!" Francois screamed from behind his hiding spot.

The key around Sledgeham's neck.

Francois paused, then fixed on Alfred at the top of the stairs. Alfred stared back at him, their eyes locking.

Alfred! Sometimes Sledgeham gives Alfred the key. He's the only one who Sledgeham trusts won't run away. Maybe Alfred has the key!

Michael kept fiddling, his graver than usual situation closing in.

"It's locked, Michael! No use!" called Francois again. Sledgeham turned his head to Francois, whose petite frame stood behind the desk in clear view. Sledgeham grabbed at his chest, and realized he was missing his key; his twisted body rose upward.

He ain't got his key!

Even from over there on the staircase, Francois smelled that sickening whisky odor emanating from Sledgeham's patchy, spotted skin. Francois again turned toward Michael. Though Michael's back was turned, he could tell from the way Michael moved, that Michael's hands vigorously worked, fingers picking and poking. Michael turned his head around, taking into view where the beast was in proximity to himself; his legs buckled from his abrupt turn. For a moment, Michael caught Francois' eyes, he grinned slyly, and held up the dull metal key in his fingers.

In that split second, Francois surged with elation, as he breathed the stagnant air of Saint Marks, and exhaled the unfamiliar but palpable sound of possibility.

Francois called up to Alfred, whose eyes also transfixed on the key in Michael's hand. It was Alfred's job to clean the courtyard daily, and he was the only one besides Sledgeham who knew how to use the finicky lock.

"Alfred! How'd yeh turn the key?"

"Stick it in deep, Michael! Jiggle it til it catches! An' turn left three times!" Alfred yelled directly to Michael.

~ 7 ~

"I'll get yeh feh this!" Sledgeham turned up the steps, his bony finger pointing at Alfred, as he cried out in pain over his twisted ankle, then turned around again toward Michael's direction.

The pewter letter opener on the desk caught Francois' eye, he quickly grabbed it, and ran closer to Michael, hiding this time behind the worn Georgian sofa in the sitting room to the left of the orphanage front door. Francois watched helplessly as Michael's hands shook uncontrollably at the bolt. But then!

Michael did it! He opened the lock!

The metal letter opener cut into his palm, but Francois squeezed tighter as he called out to the boys above, "He's done it!"

Michael lifted the heavy bolt, threw the bolt lock to the ground, as the braver of the boys cheered from above.

Sledgeham slinked closer to Michael, carrying the picture of Jesus, the wooden frame scratched trails as it dragged against floor. Now, Michael pushed the wooden bar up; it raised, fell, and cut the air in two, leaving the front door unencumbered.

"He's comin'!" Francois cried, running closer toward Michael.

Alfred and Farley ran down the stairs, but Sledgeham was now in arms reach of Michael as they split from one another; Farley down the hall to the kitchen, Alfred next to Francois. Francois felt Alfred's shaking body against his own, which warmed him, and made him aware of his own bone coldness.

Francois called out, "Hurry Michael, He's right behind!"

"Faster, Michael!" Farley yelled, running from the kitchen back toward the commotion, flailing a dull kitchen knife in his hand.

Michael grabbed at the door handle and pulled it open, only half aware of the disoriented screams behind him. A burst of cold air flooded the dank, musty entrance.

Fresh air against pale skin, a wave of excruciating pain rippled against Michael as Sledgeham hit him at the base of his neck, then broke the canvas picture of Jesus over his head; he pounded his fist against the piece of wood possessing the nail that held the frame to the wall, mounting it straight into Michael's right shoulder below the blade.

Francois watched in horror, as Michael slumped down to the ground oblivious to the world, with a broken picture of Jesus swinging on his back. Sledgeham grabbed Michael's black mop of hair, holding him tightly as he punched Michael's left side, near the kidneys.

"What's it like, knowing yeh last day on earth, boy? No prayers'll help yeh sorry lot, not now, ain't it a pity? But before yeh leave us, yeh might want'a know my plans for yeh little friend. No more protector around, what's to come of em, eh?" Sledgeham's oily whisper pounded into Michael's head, his words as deadly as his fists.

The attack on Sledgeham came swiftly. Tasting bittersweet vengeance, Francois ran at full speed as he swung the pewter letter opener into the back of Sledgeham's leg, relentless in the twisting and turning of it. His bravery unleashed the courage of Farley and Alfred as they ran to the fallen Sledgeham, kicking at him as he swung and dropped to the ground. Farley stomped on the arm attached to the hand that grabbed furiously at Francois.

"I've been stabbed, I 'ave!" No one stirred. Total silence.

"Don' jus' stand there yeh scum! Go get a watchman, yeh bastards, or I'll blame the bloody lot of yeh!"

Sledgeham's lead-colored skin turned pallid white as he examined his own wound, metal blade sticking straight from his flesh. For the second time that evening, he was knocked out of consciousness. Francois turned to Farley and Alfred.

"Help me get Michael outta here!" cried Francois, as he pulled the picture frame off of Michael.

"Where? Where can we possibly take him? Can't even hold himself up, he can't!" Alfred cried.

"Yeh two can't stay here, that's for sure. It's prison for yeh. I wouldn't be su'prised if yeh hang for this," Farley's head shook.

"Yeh ain't gonna hang, Francois," Alfred softly spoke.

"Well when they get through with 'em, he might wish for it," Farley added.

"Yeh very good in time 'a need, Farley. Can yeh shut up now?" Alfred admonished.

"Look at Michael, nit-wit. Half-dead, but if he lives, Sledgeham'll kill 'em good an' dead. Francois, too," Farley scoffed. "Well, I'm leavin'. Only got a few more months in this vile armpit of an orphan hole on account of me age, so I say freedom from here on wha'ever the cost. And, you, Alfred? What's here for yeh now? Think he'll forget how yeh told Michael to open the lock? *Jiggle it, Michael! Turn it three times!*' Don't be a thick head, Alfred! With Michael and Francois gone, who's next in the whippin' que? Now, seems to me yeh got two choices. Sit here with yeh nickers twisted

~ 10 ~

'round yeh neck, or be a chancer an' go it yeh own. Now make yeh decision an' hurry it up!"

"Jesus help me, weh're sure to get caught. But, seems weh dead, either way, eh? Let's go," Alfred said, resigned.

Farley opened the door further and more spring air scented with hope wafted inside.

Alfred helped Francois lift Michael's lifeless body, each boy holding tightly onto one of Michael's arms that wrapped limply around their necks. His heavy body bore too much weight against Francois' tiny frame.

"Francois, move over, an' get the door," Farley said.

Farley took Francois' place, he and Alfred carried Michael into the darkened courtyard, and Francois opened the courtyard's gate lock, thankful to the locksmith who had fashioned the same key to fit the same bolts—one for the door and one for the gate. As the outer gate swung open, Francois turned back to the five other boys left behind inside—two of them only three years old. He wanted to say something but was without words, and Alfred spoke instead.

"I'll be back for the lot of yeh, I promise."

Alfred's words'll do for now, he thought, as he watched Farley and Alfred drag Michael out the gate, toward freedom.

Chapter Two: Finding Francois

"Did yeh find me what I wanted?" Sledgeham's left brow raised slightly.

Sledgeham took slow pleasure in watching Francois squirm.

Yeh know I didn't. Yeh know I never do.

"No, Sir," Francois' head bent low with shame, his blood slowly reaching boiling point.

"Heh, didn't think so. Then yeh can't get what yeh want, now can yeh?" Sledgeham bellowed, coughing phlegm.

Francois continued washing the dishes, moving his hands silently, not even the dish water stirred. The other two boys in the kitchen stiffened as the master's shrill voice lowered an octave. By this time, after so many taunts, Francois wondered why he still played the master's game.

So much at stake. That's why.

But Francois was getting wearier each year. Another layer of molten anger rose inside his chest.

"I'm talkin' to yeh, idiot! And when I talk, yeh best reply, see?"

"No, Sir," Francois managed to say.

"No Sir? No what, ninny? No to speakin' up or no to my meal of mutton tonight?"

"No to the meat part."

"No to the meat? Yeh can't even beg well enough to get a pasty pie, eh?"

"Tried, I did, but here's everythin' I earned." Francois shifted in his pocket and held up a pence.

"The Church vicars kept careful watch today over us and I stealed away for a moment, but it's all I got!" Francois' voice pleaded. In disgust, Sledgeham hit his fist against the counter.

"No, Sir, no Sir, stupid thing, not even yeh own mother could love yeh, she couldn't. I ought'a burn that parchment, that's what I'll do…." Sledgeham mocked Francois, rambled under his breath, and took a long swig from his flask. He sauntered out of the kitchen, his abrasive, twisted body knocking down a candlestick and some utensils on a nearby table, his incessant mumbling echoing against clank of spoons hitting stone floor.

Sledgeham's mention of the parchment paper made Francois' gut churn, but he managed to keep steady. He closed his eyes. *I'm floatin'*, he thought, trying to reduce the heavy burden in his heart. Lately he began to have thoughts that the letter was long gone, that the secrets it contained about his past were already burned into ashes. The nickel-thick core inside his chest that anchored him to the gravity of his situation began to melt with a rage that pulsed through his veins. He could hardly breathe. It choked him into silence, this bitter violence inside.

The other two boys helping Francois with kitchen duty continued washing and drying the dishes—burden and weight hanging from their necks. They were relieved not to be the eye of Sledgeham's storm. Each knew his time would come. It always did, eventually. But it was never quite as bad for any of the boys as it was for Francois or Michael.

Francois could tell that they felt sorry for him, that they were thankful to be spared his shoes.

Ain't fit shoes to walk in, eh? Well, maybe yeh ain't got nothin' belongin' to this world for him to hang over yeh heads, tis true. But, at least a shred 'a hope, I 'ave. Yeh've got nothin' but infinity—no expectation other than to get through the same old day, jus' like the one that came before, an' the one that comes next. Infinity's yeh madness. At least hope's mine.

The smack against Francois' back set him straight and brought him back from his thoughts.

"Better smarten up or yeh never gonna get that letter, boy," Sledgeham slurred and phlem-laughed his way back into the kitchen. They worked in silent unison. Finished. Went to bed.

That night, like so many others, Francois couldn't get the parchment letter out of his mind. Here is what he knew of his life: He was of French origin, Sledgeham told him that much. It seemed to give Sledgeham pleasure that he was French—an extra reason to exonerate himself from his particular brutality toward Francois.

The rest of the story came from Michael, in bits and pieces over the years. Michael was there the October night Francois arrived at Saint Mark's Orphanage and Michael saw it all. Michael always said that Francois' arrival was like a two-sided coin. If you flipped the coin one way, it landed on Francois' misfortune, but when it landed on the other side, it was Michael's own redemption. This never made sense to Francois, but whenever Michael spoke this, for a reason Francois could not explain, the words calmed his nerves and he felt human.

Francois turned on his side and whispered to Michael.

"Michael, I can't fall asleep. I'm thinkin' about what Sledgeham said tonight to me...about the letter."

Michael, still awake, rose from his own bed, walked slowly to minimize creaking, and quietly lay next to Francois, who moved himself to the right and shifted his shabby old pillow so both heads could share.

"He ain't never gonna give it back. That's why I've got to find it. What did he say, anyway?" Michael asked.

"Same thing he's said before. Said he should burn it. But, it got me to thinkin' that maybe he already did."

"Don't think like that, Francois."

"What does he want with it? So much time has passed. What could he possibly do with the letter now?"

"Sledgeham's a dirty drunk, but he ain't stupid. It's a game to 'em, don't yeh get it? His power over us. I hate 'em, I do. The way he puts on a show for the church, tellin' lies about how good things are here."

"Tell me of the night again, Michael."

The boys heard the creaking of a cot, and some stirring, then a light cough, but it soon quieted again.

"Not again, Francois. It's too long a story. And it always frustrates me," Michael whispered.

"Please Michael. It helps me to remember too."

"Remember what? What's worth rememberin'?" Michael asked bitterly.

"Don't know. That I wasn't born here."

"None of us were," Michael replied, "But, yeh're different. Yeh're from France, the rest of us all bein' English blood. The blood of what, not sure."

"Hounds!" Francois joked, and Michael stifled his laughter. A silent moment passed between them.

"Fine, but the quick version," Michael whispered, resolved to repeat the story Francois needed to hear so often. Francois nodded.

"It was mid-October 1830, the night yeh first arrived. The watchman that brought yeh here said to Sledgeham, *'A priest found this boy at Saint Paul's with this parchment letter attached to his back. The priest who found the boy asked me to take 'em here to Saint Mark's. He'll be on his way soon enough. Said he's got to stop and tell his superior, an' that I should get the boy to yeh as soon as I could. He thinks yeh might be able to shelter the boy while he finds help.'* "

Francois' tense lips eased into a semi-smile, his heart rate slowed, and he held on to every word of his own Grimm tale.

Michael continued, "Like I told yeh before, I can remember Sledgeham's squinty black eyes readin' the note written on the

~ 16 ~

parchment. Sledgeham read the date, which I'll never forget: October 1830. Then Sledgeham read silent to himself. But then, sure as night follows day, he blurted out the name *Claude*...and a lady's name, and...blah, blah...France. Then, Sledgeham stopped readin' out loud again."

Francois interrupted Michael, "Yeh don't remember any other names spoken?"

"Why d'yeh always ask me this same question? I swore on that night to remember as much as I could. I was five years old! Yeh probably wasn't even two yet. But, I remembered as many details as I could. By now, it's the same story, Francois."

The events of the night that Francois first came to Saint Mark's Orphanage became a script for Michael to recite to Francois over the years. And, each time, Francois asked Michael the same questions — but also new ones, writing himself into the lines in hopes of awakening within Michael a new memory.

Francois paused, his lips softening again, "Continue."

"Sledgeham read parts of the letter out loud, like I've told yeh a thousand times before. He definitely said the name *Claude.*"

"And, then the other one?"

"Yeh daft? I don't remember her name!" Michael barked, annoyed by Francois' repetitive appetite and unwillingness to remit.

One of the boys shouted, "Quiet! Yeh'll wake Sledgeham!"

The name. Her name. Michael heard it once. It's in there, somewhere. Just need to unlock it from his memory.

~ 17 ~

Michael waited until the room fell still again, then continued to whisper the tale they both knew so well by now.

"Sledgeham read somethin' about France. And somethin' about care. Sledgeham mimicked the word 'care,' and he spit in the air. Anyway, that's when Sledgeham said out loud the thing about yeh bein' a Frenchie."

Michael's perfect impression of Sledgeham rattled Francois' nerves: *"'We got ourselves a Frenchie here, ain't we lucky? Oh, it'd be too much fun teh let 'em go!'"*

"Is that when Sledgeham spit the tobacco chew next to me, where I sat on the floor?" Francois asked, already knowing the answer. Michael nodded.

Michael shifted his voice to resemble the night watchman who brought Francois to Saint Marks, and Francois always loved this part.

"'Careful! Now, I don' like a 'Frenchie' any more than yeh, but he's just a child and can't help bein' born what he is!'"

Michael quieted for a moment. He cleared his voice and whispered, "I drew close to where the watchman stood, and between the two of 'em, their boozy stench made my stomach turn. That's when the watchman said the priest would be here shortly, and then he exited Saint Marks. With the watchman gone, Sledgeham turned. *'Blahh!'* He jumped as if he were goin' to grab yeh, but Francois, yeh didn't flinch! Just stared at him, like a doe paralyzed by the hunter's barrel. It made me sick to watch. But, yeh just sat and stared."

~ 18 ~

Francois interrupted, recounting his story. "Sledgeham ran upstairs with the parchment. He wasn't gone long. When he came down again, he didn't possess it. That's when the Priest knocked at the door."

"Yea," Michael confirmed, "Sledgeham slicked his oily hair back with his hands, cupped his mouth, like this, to check his own stench—it was awful—and turned to me with his wily black eyes."

Michael's voice turned oily and squeaky, Sledgeham-style. *"'Busy night round here. Who's it now, Michael? Father Christmas?'"*

Michael's impersonation fell away, and his eyes emptied. A cue the priest was entering the story.

Why this shift in yeh mood each time the priest enters the scene of the crime?

"That's when the priest arrived—with his dark brown hair and soft blue eyes that looked kindly and forgivin'. Anyone could see plain simple what the priest thought of Sledgeham. Those eyes of his saw right through him. An' he had that fancy speech like those gentlemen on Fleet Street, too. And thank God he came, because he distracted Sledgeham enough for me to run and pick yeh up before Sledgeham got any more ideas in his head."

"I sort of remember that."

"Naw, you was too young to remember. But I took yeh to the corner by the hallway. Laid yeh head on my shoulder, yeh did, shut yeh eyes, and dozed right off. Tired, yeh were! I was a comfort, first time in my life! I knew yeh was cared for, Francois. The freshness of yeh hair gave it away. And, yeh fingers were so clean, and…."

"We became brothers that day," Francois smiled.

"The priest looked to us. Then he inquired to Sledgeham about the letter he had found pinned to yeh jacket. He wanted to see it again. Sledgeham denied havin' the letter, insistin' the watchman took it. The priest was furious, but he couldn't force Sledgeham to produce the letter. They went in circles about the contents—where it was, what it said, over and over, but no matter. Sledgeham didn't budge. Instead, he twisted his words until they bent outta shape."

"Michael, ain't never come back? The priest's name I mean?" Francois hesitated to ask, but this was to be his new question tonight. His re-write of the story line.

Why'd I never thought to ask it before? The priest's name?

Francois could see his question vexed Michael greatly, but Michael sighed and changed the conversation. He didn't answer Francois' question at all, but what he went on to say satisfied Francois in a different way.

"Still, can't help but wonder, if I hadn't swept yeh up from the floor that night, if yeh hadn't fallen asleep so peacefully, that maybe…what if yeh seemed scared outta yeh wits? Maybe the priest wouldn't 'ave left yeh? But instead, he looked over and saw a babe sleepin' away in my arms. And the priest said—and I'll never forget this—that he wondered if yeh might stay here at the orphanage while he sought assistance from his church elders. He said he was scheduled to leave to York in the mornin', but that bad luck had fallen on yeh, and with some time, he could help…." Michael's voice trailed off.

Blame! Yeh blame yourself for me bein' here. Francois had never considered this before. With intention, Francois changed the course of their whispers. He didn't want Michael to know he knew the reason behind Michael's forlorn silence when the priest entered the story. He didn't want Michael to suffer shame or blame.

"This is when Sledgeham asked him for money?"

Michael nodded. Then came his Sledgeham impersonation.

"*'Jus' so happens a bed here just come open—big enough teh swallow 'em whole. Of course, times are hard—hard indeed. Sure yeh've somethin' to spare in exchange for room an' board?'*"

Francois grabbed Michael's arm, and hushed him, usurping this next part; it was his favorite part to retell, that of the priest, and he practiced his lines to perfection, "And the priest declared, *'I am a man of the cloth, Sir. Not nobility. But I serve a higher form. Feed the boy, shelter him, and abide by the laws of God, Frenchman or not! We must turn this boy's unfortunate circumstances around and bring him justice!'*"

"More or less," Michael smiled warmly, "but yeh've added some trimmin's."

"And he threw the money at Sledgeham!" Francois smirked.

"A good decoy, 'twas. Sledgeham chased after them rollin' shillin's demon speed, and the priest slipped me the satchel of quids folded inside your parchment."

"The satchel the priest removed when he found the letter bound to my jacket. At least he had good enough sense to remove it before he had me deposited here...." Though as for that, Francois wondered if this even mattered since the money never returned him home, and he still didn't know where home was.

~ 21 ~

Michael's tense eyes softened and his face smirked,

"You know yeh tale better than me by now! I'm keepin' 'em in secret for yeh so we can get yeh home one day. And you'd best keep quiet 'bout it. Ain't easy hidin' day in, day out," Michael tousled Francois' hair.

"Still, I wonder who wrapped the satchel inside my letter in the first place."

"We'll never know, unless we find the parchment." Michael corrected himself. "*I* find the parchment. Anyway, it's late. We need to sleep."

"Finish the story, Michael. Promise I'll sleep once I hear what the priest whispered in yeh ear?"

Francois watched Michael's eyes glaze over, like they always did at the priest part, and he despised himself for putting his own needs in front of Michael's, especially after his epiphany tonight. But his desire to finish his story—always to the bitter end—was a great beast consuming him. *Selfish no good boy.*

Michael hesitated, "First the priest dropped the satchel into my hand. Then he whispered to me real quick, '*I believe your master has hidden the parchment letter for reasons I do not understand. Do what you can to find it. If you have such luck, hide it away safely for when the boy is older. The money, too, or all will be lost.*"

Francois thought about a nursery rhyme, and all that was lost.

Finder's keepers, loser's weeper's. Find her keep her, lose her weep her.

"The priest vowed to help, said yeh was a child of God, that yeh must be returned home. Vexed he was, over not rememberin' the details of the letter. Cursed Sledgeham, he did. An' when he left

us, he said, '*Damn this life. Well...make no mistake, God is watching.*'"
Michael fell silent again, deeply boding.

"I wonder what happened to him," Francois yawned.

"I guess he departed to York. Moved on to more important matters. Anyway, vows are hard to keep."

Michael patted Francois' head, carefully rose, and returned to his flat mattress, taking refuge in the contours that fit him perfectly.

Francois closed his eyes, imagining the priest's kindhearted eyes and good intentions. He wondered if God was watching him now. Then, his thoughts floated to the lady whose name Michael could not remember, and imagined her gently tucking him in, gingerly kissing his forehead, as she did every night. This, he told no one, not even Michael.

Chapter Three: Finding Beatrix

Beauchamp's Floral Shop, Hart Street, Saturday April 22nd, 5:02 am

Every day on Hart Street began the same for twelve year old Beatrix. She awakened at 5 am. She slipped her feet into her warm slippers. She dressed herself in her worn-out work apron made from old potato sacks and pieces of scrap fabric she had sewn together. She would find her flint and steel striker in the pocket of her apron, where she always left it. She carefully opened the curtain that separated her corner from the rest of the floral shop, and made her way to the hearth.

On this pre-dawn morning, Beatrix examined the flint's edge in her fingers, holding her tool against the twilight shadows that would soon erase darkness. She decided her flint piece was sharp enough. Beatrix searched in her apron for the metal box containing her fire kit, which she also always kept inside her apron pocket.

She took out a tiny cooked-cotton fabric square no more than an inch wide and wrapped it around her flint, then placed one of her prepared tinder bundles—her bird's nests, as she called them—in the hearth center, and placed dry crisp wood around the nest. She wrapped her three right-hand fingers within the steel striker, picking up the wrapped flint piece with her left hand, and bent down on her knees, leaned into the hearth, and positioned herself over the tinder bundle.

Working her magic, Beatrix thrust steel striker and flint together. Again, and again, until finally she had the sparks needed to catch the cooked-cotton piece. She blew quickly onto the fabric, and set it into the center of her tiny bird's nest, as she blew life into the fire. Soon orange, yellow-streaked flames rose and caught against the crackling wood. Even Mr. Beauchamp couldn't do this as fast as her. She had a way with making fire, and was keenly aware that this power kept a roof over her head and three meals a day filling her stomach.

Beatrix set the kettle and boiled water for her morning tea that she made from old stale tea leaves she collected from the Beauchamp's. The stale leftover bun from last night's dinner satisfied her hunger for now, as she bit, swallowed, and washed down. Down here in the Beauchamp's floral shop, she could hear Mr. Beauchamp's snoring from the upstairs bedroom he and the wife occupied.

She wondered how Mrs. Beauchamp slept through it, but was grateful she did. At least she had some time to herself to think the thoughts she wanted to think. The morning silence contrasted sharply against the noise filling her head when the Beauchamp's were awake.

Outside Beauchamp's Floral Shop, 5:26 am

Francois was the first one to notice the firelight coming from the
floral shop. The floral shop was adjacent to an alley way, where
Alfred and Farley had dragged Michael to rest. They took refuge
while Francois scouted out whether the girl inside seemed a safe
bet. Michael moaned as the boys laid him down onto Alfred's lap.
Exhausted, Alfred and Farley needed rest from dragging Michael
along the silent streets, turning corner after corner, keeping in the
shadowy darkness like thieves in the night.

"You stay down, an' I'll look in the window," Francois
whispered.

"We've been through this three times in the span of an hour.
No one's goin' to help us!" Alfred whispered back.

"Yeh knickers fallen' off again? Calm down. We'll get outta this
mess!" Farley snapped.

"Be quiet! Stop arguin'!" Francois hushed, and looked both
ways before leaving the alley way. Kneeling on the dirt ground,
Francois held onto the wooden Tudor window frame as he peered
inside the shop.

He saw a young girl, about Michael's age, assembling her work
tools. She laid her shears out on her work bench, but then suddenly
turned toward the shop door and windows. Francois quickly hid
below the window frame, hoping she did not see him. He almost

fainted when he heard the shop door unlock, and the wooden door swing open. But, it closed just as suddenly.

Francois breathed deeply and covertly peeked inside the window again, careful not to be seen, though his exhale slightly fogged the window pane. He watched the girl light two candles. She took up her shawl that hung on the coat rack by the back of the shop near her work bench and wrapped it around her shoulders. Again, she turned toward the shop door.

Francois kneeled down quickly and scrambled back to the alley, his face wild, his finger to his mouth—a sign the boys heeded well this time. He waited a moment, then peeked discreetly around the corner. The girl stood outside and turned to her left as if she were expecting a visitor from that direction, as the foggy chill enveloped her face, and from her mouth blew a puff of breath.

The girl waited for the familiar, calming sound of Mr. O'Brien's Clydesdales as they clip-clopped on cobblestones, emerging from foggy midnight grey as twilight broke, two gentle giants pulling the weight of all her troubles behind them, harnessed as they were to the cart that brought her flower load. Francois was careful to hide and watch clandestinely from behind the alley wall as the sound of bells, hooves, and whickering strengthened.

Farley tried to look too, but Francois pulled him back, as Alfred reprimanded, "Don't be a fool, yeh're too noticeable."

Francois, on the other hand, with his thin frame and quiet ways, was a needle in a haystack, neither seen nor heard nor found. But as the horse cart materialized out of the early morning fog, Farley peered out too, ignoring Alfred's admonishment. Alfred remained a pile of frayed nerves, pinned to the ground as Michael lay in his lap unconscious and shivering.

"What is it?" Alfred asked, but neither boy replied.

As the cart drew closer, Francois could hear softness in the girl's speech as she called, "Mr. O'Brien!"

With razor sharp precision, Francois and Farley scrutinized the man as he pulled back the reigns of his horse-drawn delivery cart, took off his cap and greeted the girl.

"Howya, Miss Beatrix! Dia Dhuit."

Mr. O'Brien's Irish brogue and strange words caught and lingered in Francois' ear.

"A fine chilled morn' if I do say. How does it find yah?"

"Well, Mr. O'Brien. Thank you."

Beatrix. O'Brien. Beatrix. O'Brien. Beatrix. O'Brien, Francois repeated their names like his prayers—his things to remember, things of great consequence to call upon during his hour of need.

"Hello Benny and Matilda!" Beatrix patted the horse's noses. "Mrs. Beauchamp requested an extra bushel of flowers today along with her regular order. Have you one to spare?"

Beauchamp? Her master's surname? Francois wondered.

"Benny and Matilda are the horses," Farley whispered.

Francois shot him back a puzzled look that revealed his confusion over Farley's habit of stating the most obvious and inconsequential triviality, especially in dire moments.

Michael stirred and moaned. Francois turned and saw Alfred whisper into Michael's ear, and whatever he said, quelled him as his body relaxed again.

~ 28 ~

Mr. O'Brien dropped his horse reigns to his side, stood up from the leather driver's seat, and stepped down to the ground. Francois noted how gently the man patted one of his horses before he made his way to the back of the cart.

"'Aye, another bushel, lass. But what of? Ahh, some more bluebells will suit nicely! Harbingers heralding spring, they are."

"Bluebells, just fine, Sir. At least, I think so. Mrs. Beauchamp didn't specify her desire."

Mr. O'Brien came from behind the cart holding a large wooden crate filled with daffodils, hellebore, crocus, primroses, irises, hyacinths, pussy willow branches, and bluebells, of course.

"Ah, they are lovely!" said Beatrix, "It is spring once again!"

"Got another crate of bluebells in the back, but let's bring this one inside, first things first."

"The masters are sleeping, Mr. O'Brien. I'd hate to wake...."

"Don't fret, lass. I know the routine an' I know yer masters."

Francois and Farley watched them enter into the shop.

"Wait here, I'll look inside. They'll spot you," Francois said as he ran to the shop window again. Farley knew he was right.

Crouching down, Francois peered into the window, as Mr. O'Brien and Beatrix conversed near the girl's work bench; the girl nodded her head, then Mr. O'Brien motioned toward the door. Francois took the gesture as his immediate cue to get back to the safety of the alley, which he did chop-chop double speed. Sure enough, Mr. O'Brien returned outside for the second crate.

"What'd yeh see?" Alfred whispered, too loud for Francois.

"Shh! Could we hear them? Then wouldn't they hear us? Our voices carry! Say nothing!" Francois mouthed so quietly Alfred relied on lip-reading, as his nervous hand sprung to his mouth.

"I see him!" Farley whispered, "Goin' back inside."

Francois peered around the corner, ever so slightly and caught site of Mr. O'Brien's tweed coat disappear into the shop, as door closed against his backside, absorbing the bang and slam noise of door; all this, to keep the slumbering asleep.

Just as Francois stepped out from the alley to take his position at the shop window, the shop door opened abruptly and he jumped back. He watched Beatrix and Mr. O'Brien step outside into the brisk air, as she handed him a mug of hot something, its witch brew steam rising forth in circles.

"A lovely cuppa, just as always." Mr. O'Brien blew smoky ringlets before he took another sip of his tea.

"It's weak. My apologies." Beatrix lowered her head.

Beatrix's cheeks went ruddy as she cast her eyes down to the dirt ground. Mr. O'Brien's left hand reached into his pocket, he shimmied around, and pulled out a coin. She shook her head with a nod that said no, not necessary. Francois watched Mr. O'Brien slip it into her apron pocket where it clinked against the sound of steel. Impulsively, Beatrix slapped her hand against apron.

"Thank you, Sir. But it's just weakened tea."

"That reminds me, the other mug...," Mr. O'Brien's voice trailed as he went to his cart and retrieved the mug she lent him last Saturday. Then, he tipped his cap, climbed onto his seat, clicked his tongue, which in turn started his horse engines whinnying.

~ 30 ~

"You're a fine lass, Beatrix. Aye, deserving better. Well, I'll be on my way."

"Oh! I almost forgot!" Beatrix ran to the horses and felt inside her pocket for their weekly treat. "Good bye, loves!"

Each horse mouth managed to remove a small piece of sugar cube from her hand, not without scraping their teeth against her open palm, leaving behind horse slobber, which she didn't mind; those two sugar lumps were all she could spare without her masters noticing, but were enough to keep friendship kindling.

Though she was somewhat obscured by the fog, Francois fixed upon Beatrix's delicate facial features, her flushed cheeks now returned to porcelain. Pale skin against ebony hair reminded him of Michael, and he took pleasure in watching her rub their nose bridges, as nostrils blew, as muzzles nibbled her hand.

Eventually, Benny and Matilda clip-clopped away down cobblestone, and Beatrix returned inside the floral shop. Francois waited until Mr. O'Brien's cart was enough out of site, the returned to watching her through the window. She sat at her work bench, carefully clipping diagonally, trimming each flower stem, embellishing it with a thin-stranded lace ribbon. Farley's tap on his shoulder startled him.

"Just thought I'd remind yeh of our situation. Seems yeh've forgotten? What's wrong with yeh? Stare at her all day or get Michael some help, which is it?" Farley reproached.

"I think she's safe. She seems to be alone anyway," Francois hesitated, choosing to ignore Farley's tone. He wanted to chide Farley for his thickheaded impulses.

Can't he see how the wrong move could be the death of us all?

"Yeh goin' in or am I?" Farley snapped.

She's safe... But Francois thought of her masters asleep upstairs.

"She's the best chance we've run into so far. He's in a bad way. Can't carry him no more, and its daybreak if yeh haven't noticed. The whole of London'll be lookin' for us in less than an hour!"

Francois nodded. "Yeh're right, it's time. Go get Michael. You and Alfred bring 'em over."

Francois knew Beatrix had no idea he had been watching her, attracted like a moth to the flame burning inside. He did not want to alarm her. Alarm could bring upon their end. Though Beatrix seemed kind, he knew all about masters, and she had a pair. As for kind, even before he knew how to recite the Lord's Prayer, he had learned early on to be skeptical of all things that appeared too good to be true.

All four boys stood outside the front door of the floral shop now. Francois looked at Michael—head encrusted with dried blood, puffed shut eye like mushed eggplant. Held up entirely by Alfred and Farley, Michael's condition gave Francois resolve to open the front door, come what may. He pushed it open quietly, but it slightly creaked. At her work bench with her back to them, Beatrix spoke as she turned around.

"Mr. O'Brien, you startled me. Have you forgotten something?"

She threw down her bouquet; her smile turned to fright when she saw Francois and the boys.

Farley's voice echoed in Francois' head, "Go on then, speak to her!" Up close, without shadows casting spells against the light of her, or the outside fog painting over her imperfections, this girl had tired eyes which made her feel familiar to him.

Francois couldn't speak with his throat muscles braided around his tongue, but his loss of speech was conveniently timed for once. Beatrix brought her left index finger to her lips disapprovingly, "Shush," and she pointed her right index finger upstairs. Francois and the boys understood immediately what this meant.

Beatrix skimmed over Francois, then Alfred, then Farley, and cupped her mouth when she saw Michael, whose neck hung sloped to the ground, his face down, mop of black hair dangling in tousled strands. Her shallow breathes told Francois that her chest must be banging tight like his own, which somehow gave him confidence.

"What...what is this? What....who are you?" asked Beatrix in disbelief and shock.

"Please help, please...it's my brother, Michael...he's cold...he's been beaten...he's...."

Farley interjected, "Gonna die without help, he is."

Beatrix bit her lip and turned her head instinctively toward the upstairs of the shop. Francois worried who or what could be upstairs that troubled her so; he stared deeply at her with a pleading look, as he choked on his words. Like always, he failed to say what he needed, and he felt a welt of self-hatred fester in the same moment that Beatrix took pity on him.

"Bring him in by the fire, but keep silent—the master and Mrs. are upstairs! They'll throw him out like a dog and send you hence you came!"

Farley and Alfred struggled to carry Michael futher inside the shop; with each passing hour, his weight sagged further, and his heaviness sunk him. Farley knocked into a table as he helped lay Michael onto the floor, Beatrix pleading for them to be quieter.

"Time to say good-bye, Francois. Done what I could. Won't never forget yeh courage. God help yeh, brother. An' God help Michael....Let's go, Alfred." Farley grabbed Alfred's arm but Alfred pulled away, his eyebrows furrowed, his mouth dropped.

"I can't just go...he's still...." Alfred stuttered, looking back and forth between Francois and Farley.

"Yeh clotted blockhead! We've got to split up sooner or later. Come now, or go it alone, all's the same to me."

It was obvious to Francois that it wasn't all the same to Farley. Farley needed to split, but he wasn't quite ready to go it alone.

"I won't leave Michael," Francois insisted.

"But we've got to leave you," Farley replied, "And if yeh knew what was good for yeh, Alfred, yeh'd come now."

With that, Farley sprinted toward the door, unwilling to negotiate further about it.

"What should I do, Francois? I'll stay if yeh want me to?"

Francois fretted but knew what had to be done.

"Go. Farley's right. We'll be fine." His gut told him there was no other way, but he felt sick at the thought of being left.

"Comin' or ain't? Final notice!" Farley whispered too loudly.

Worry crinkled into Alfred's face; his eyes turned sodden.

"I'd better," Alfred said apprehensively. "Yeh'll be alright?"

Francois' approving nod set Alfred free to run to the door where Farley stood; they exited the shop, Alfred taking care to shut the door quietly behind him, so quietly, that it didn't actually shut, and remained slightly ajar. Francois jumped up and ran after them.

Exasperated, Beatrix whispered, "Boy, where are you going?"

Francois realized she must have thought he would run away with them, leaving her alone with Michael. Nonetheless, he ran to the door, but stopped, one foot still remaining inside as he watched them disappear up the street, through the fog, and into the distance like a pair of hungry wolves returning to the wild. He turned back to Beatrix and Michael. Beatrix relaxed and exhaled.

"Michael," Beatrix kneeled beside him, "is that your name?" Beatrix's hands gently pressed into his limp and unconscious body. She ran to the fire, stoked it, and blew more oxygen, cradling the flames with her breath. The fire now roared and Francois could feel its heat. Beatrix returned to Michael's side.

"That's his name. The master tried to kill 'em and we barely escaped. His right shoulder's hurt badly, miss."

Beatrix stared at Michael's crumpled, bloody body. She put her hand to his forehead. "What shameful animal did this to you?"

"Sledgeham."

Beatrix leaned closer over Michael, and with Francois' aid, turned his right upper torso gently to the left, as Michael's blood-matted head fell into her. She ran her fingers gently over his head, and felt several large knots bulging on his scalp. She carefully

~ 35 ~

checked for injuries on the left side of his head. Yes. There, as well. Then, she told Francois that they must carefully turn Michael onto his stomach. His heavy body was difficult to turn and Francois wished the boys had stayed around awhile longer.

Once Michael was laid flat on his stomach, with the left side of his head resting on a blanket, Beatrix ran to get her shears. Back in no time, she cut a square hole around the blood-matted shirt that stuck to his right shoulder blade, and tore away the cloth that stuck like glue. Pulling the fabric reopened the bloody wound which oozed forth a thick yellow pus. Francois' alarm rose at its sight.

"Your name, have I asked you? I've forgotten in this chaos."

"Francois."

"Francois? That's curious. At any rate, please take heed, Francois. I can try to help him, but you must follow my directions and be quick about it. The Beauchamp's will be up sooner than we hope, and though they aren't as fierce as this Sledgeham beast, I imagine they're distant cousins."

"Yes, please, tell me what to do."

"Just do as I say, when I say."

Beatrix got to work. She collected three clean rags. She heated the water kettle over the fire.

"Let it boil, but before the kettle sounds, remove it and pour the water into the pot next to the hearth. And this bowl here, too. We'll need to clean his wounds and to sterilize the sewing needle…and, fetch me that tea mug," Beatrix added, motioning to the table.

Beatrix's command jumbled in Francois' head, yet he was thankful to receive orders; he removed the kettle, poured the hot water into the pot and bowl, and set himself next to Michael.

"You forgot the mug! Pour in hot water!" Beatrix whispered.

Francois responded quickly then returned to Michael's side again. Beatrix hurried over to the Beauchamp's stash of tea, her hand quick to grab loose black leaves.

"I'll worry about the consequences later. The Beauchamp's measure every bit. But he'll need strong tea. Let it cool a bit first," she said, dropping the heap of black tea leaves into an empty pot.

"Use this cup of warm tea for now, until the fresh pot cools," Beatrix said, handing Francois the mug he'd just retrieved.

"Dip this rag into the mug. Squeeze it into his mouth, best you can. Make sure his head is sideways."

Francois licked his dry lips, his own thirst rising up.

"Like this," Beatrix said. She gently stuffed the rag into Michael's mouth, squeezed down, and shut his jaw, which caused him to swallow.

"Keep doing that."

Beatrix handed the rag back to Francois, who struggled to get the liquid into Michael without it dribbling out the sides of his mouth, down his chin, while Francois' transfixed eyes followed this wonderment of a girl, this Beatrix, whose earlier signs of worry dissipated into calm, and she seemed sure of what to do in this pressing circumstance. She pulled from her apron a small wooden box that kept her thread, needles, and thimble. She took out a needle, threaded it, and placed it into the bowl of sterilized boiling water, then rose, retrieved her own tattered blanket from the corner, and threw it next to Francois.

"He's shivering. Cover him."

Francois did as she said, as she removed her own warn socks and rolled them onto Michael's bare and blackened feet. She picked out the threaded needle from the boiling water, wrapped it in a clean rag, and dropped the rag into her smock. Francois closed his eyes for a moment, lost in thankfulness. When he opened them, Beatrix kneeled down beside him and Michael.

"The Beauchamp's will rise within the hour. We need to clean his wounds. I need to stitch this wound below his shoulder blade. Soak your rag first in the boiled water. Start washing his head wounds. Be gentle but firm without causing him pain. I'll work on his back." Again, Francois complied.

"Michael," Beatrix patted his cheek lightly, he began to stir, his bones warming under the blanket, and he opened his eyes. The blurry features of the room began to focus as Beatrix whispered into his ear, "Shush, now Michael, be strong." Francois couldn't shake the irony in her statement. Michael tried clearing his dry throat.

"Francois will give you tea to drink. Bite down on the rag to swallow it, Michael," Beatrix said tenderly.

Francois dipped the rag into the tea and placed it into Michael's mouth, just as she had instructed, and Michael abided her; he furiously swallowed, his thirst too deep to quench. Francois himself was thirsty, and he took several satisfying gulps, hoping Beatrix wouldn't notice. She did notice, but did not seem to care. Francois repeatedly dipped the rag into Michael's mouth as Michael drank in Beatrix's words mixed with lukewarm tea. Beatrix caressed Michael's forehead with her hand and bent down again to his ear.

"Michael, my name is Beatrix. Francois brought you to me. I can help you. Listen to my words, for they will keep you safe."

Michael's face lay still as he stared to the side, fixing his gaze on the worn patterns in the old wooden floor.

"Do as she says, Michael. We can trust her," Francois said.

Beatrix's long braid rubbed against Michael's arm and Francois moved it away as he took in her scent—dried lavender and mint. Beatrix squeezed Michael's hand, and again, leaned over Michael's ear and whispered.

"Don't speak, don't cry, and don't whimper. The noise will wake my masters. They'll turn you over to the constable if they find you. I must clean your wounds and sew you up, Michael. Squeeze my hand if you understand me."

Francois watched Michael's fingers lightly lock Beatrix' own. It was the best Michael could do.

"We're understood then."

Francois gave Michael the wet rag and he sucked the tea dry. Beatrix retrieved the rag from Michael's mouth, dipped it into the hot black tea she had just steeped, tested its heat, and said to Francois, "Use this now. Drink the rest of my warm cup, but save this for Michael."

She reached into her apron pocket, and retrieved the threaded needle wrapped in her clean rag.

"Take this rag to his head wounds now," she said, as she held the sterilized needle tip into a flickering candle flame next to her.

Francois brushed Michael's black hair to the side, away from his face and he felt the first head lump. He began to wash, but Michael cried out.

"Not so hard. Just try to loosen the matted part with water," Beatrix said. "Now bite down on the rag, Michael, but do not make a sound!"

Beatrix took the last clean rag from the bowl of boiled water, and rubbed it against the wound in Michael's shoulder blade, wiping newly formed pus away. Francois could not know that Michael felt hot metal coursing through his arm, back, shoulder, neck, but tears spontaneously surfaced in Michael's eyes as Francois watched, trying to mimic her motions without causing further pain.

Calmly, methodically, Beatrix took hold of her needle.

"The first stitch will hurt the most. There will be four, maybe I can do it in three. Count in your head. Not a sound, Michael. Francois, take his hands in yours."

Michael bit the tea rag hard, jaw-locked, and closed his eyes tight as he grasped Francois' hand weakly; he bit down so hard that he chafed the inside of his mouth on one side, his tongue on the other, tasting blood and black tea. Francois' resolve to watch weakened as Beatrix pierced Michael's thick skin. Michael winced deeply, and Francois' head fell to Michael's ear, "That was the worst of it, Michael, just like Beatrix said. One."

The first stitch felt to Michael like he were a fish hooked, but he did as Beatrix said and remained silent in his deep suffering, his cloth mouth stuffed, his teeth clamped. Francois squeezed Michael's hand, crushing his fingers painfully, to distract him from the second stitch. Beatrix's third stitch laced shut the puncture wound, and patched his quilted skin together again. Michael didn't utter a sound; the pain too severe for him to manage, he slipped away to unconsciousness, which was a much better place to be.

"He's fainted!" Francois cried.

"That does it, all done. Now then, his head still needs cleaning, and I'll do that properly now that he's out," Beatrix said, as she felt the lumps around Michael's head.

"Master whipped him in the head with a studded belt. An' a candlestick! An' a picture frame. An'...."

Beatrix looked out the window, then upstairs.

"Francois, we don't have much time left. You must do what I say. Our lives depend on it!"

"What? Anythin' yeh ask!"

"While I clean his head wounds, you must go for help. This is Hart Street. Yes?" Beatrix waited for Francois to acknowledge her. "Step out of the shop and make a right. Do you know your right from left?"

Francois nodded, yes. She continued, "You'll soon come to Garrick Street...do you know how to read?"

Again he nodded yes. He was particularly good at reading—a rare skill at Saint Mark's, but one he and Michael cultivated in secret. They needed the skill to read because they would find Francois' parchment letter one day. "Yes, I'm quite good," he responded.

"At Garrick Street, turn left. Keep straight several blocks more 'til you reach Bedford Street. Turn right and you'll find Middleton's bakery shop. Mr. Middleton starts his day earlier than mine. His daughter, Bernadette, is usually up first thing, helping her father prepare for the day. You must bring her back here quickly! But, try to do so without her father's knowledge. He's a good man, but who knows what he might do, so it's best to keep it just with her."

Francois' face drained. He did not want anyone else involved. He shot up, and scrambled toward the floral shop door, trying to remember the order of Beatrix' street directions, as she followed.

Beatrix whispered, "A cart! Bring back their baker's cart. We'll need something to transport Michael to safety!"

She pushed him out the door, sharply positioning his body to the right, and he sprinted as quickly as Farley and Alfred had done earlier, but in the opposite direction down Hart Street, feeling more like a lamb than a wolf.

His head raced with screams—Michael awakening with screams, the Beauchamp's awakening with screams, the constable arriving on the scene with screams—all these screams deadened his sense of time and space. He decided to think only of his next steps, as his eyes sought signs of Garrick Street. "Left on Garrick, right on Bedford," Francois bleated, his feet pounding against dirt and stone.

Chapter Four: Finding Bernadette

Middleton's Bakery, Bedford Street, Saturday April 22nd, 6:32 am

On this particular early morning—the first anniversary of her mother's death—Bernadette arose two hours earlier than usual, so she was tired and sleepy before the day had even started. She hadn't slept well.

Longing and sorrow, those twin devils, tightened their fingers around Bernadette's neck, ensnaring her in profound grief so deep it had no beginning or end.

"Mother," she whispered, "send me a sign."

Bernadette pictured her mother's face, but the image she recollected blurred. This was the worst of it—the fading of her—and Bernadette feared the day would come when she wouldn't remember her face at all.

"Keep moving," Bernadette said to herself, as her hands kneaded the dough, freshly-risen this morning.

Regardless of their loss one year ago today, Bernadette and her father made a pact to keep moving, keenly aware of how quickly fates can turn. Neither father nor daughter could bear the thought of losing their home and livelihood to their grief. The day after they buried her mother, they awoke from their own deadened madness before the rooster's crowing and worked silently, furiously side by side, in rote, in step, in saddening syncopation. She remembered that day now, as if it were yesterday.

Though the meaning behind Bernadette's culinary display this morning would go unnoticed today by the usual customers who frequented Middleton's Bakery, Bernadette prepared a feast of baked goods in honor of her mother. The lords and ladies would devour her mother's special recipes, and this filled Bernadette's insides with sweet warmth.

Her jam tarts waited patiently in line to be baked in the brick oven once the apple turnovers were perfectly browned. She would have time later this morning to make her mother's favorite French childhood recipes—onion and cheese quiche and petit fours.

Bernadette baked alone today as her father laid asleep upstairs, nursing a bad cold with bed rest. She tensely kneaded the dried rosemary and thyme into the bread dough. The dough felt too sticky so she added more flour to her hands. Her mother's illness had started out like this—a bad cold. But, there were chores to be done, and a husband and daughter to tend to, a business to help run. She remembered her mother's words: "Rest isn't something I can afford." Then the coughing and fever began. Her mother could no longer stand, so she took to bed. She never left.

*Our Father in heaven, hallowed be your name. Your kingdom come, your will be done, on earth, as it is in heaven. Give us this day, our daily bread...*Bernadette repeated, as her thoughts turned to her own father. She would do things differently this time. She would untwist fate.

~ 44 ~

"Father shall remain in rest until he shows no signs," she said out loud, though there was no one to listen. She would do her father's work, and her own tasks, with obligation and indebtedness, until she could be certain of his health. She was wise to death now. She knew how suddenly he could steal her daily bread.

Bernadette removed the apple turnovers and sprinkled course sugar crystals generously over them. She placed them to cool on her rack. She inserted her jam tarts in the brick oven, waited twelve minutes to be exact, took them out, and then added her first round of freshly baked rolls. Next in line: her coveted cinnamon balls and sugar jam-print cookies, always best sellers. Now, Bernadette mixed flour, sugar, eggs, and milk for the bread pudding.

Suddenly and unexpectedly, the wooden door to Mr. Middleton's Bakery shop swung open, hitting against the wall. Bernadette jumped, her eyes flashed toward the door, her hands spilled loose flour. Her jaw dropped as she stared at the petite sandy-haired boy's cordate-shaped face. His verdant eyes. He looked strangely familiar, and yet he was a stranger to her, though she felt she knew him from somewhere.

Francois scoped the bakery for signs of the girl's father, then turned to the pretty blonde pick-tailed girl in the green dress and white apron edged in red cherry stitches.

"Please…please help me…."

His chest and throat burned against cold morning air, his dogged coughing interrupted his plea, his frustration turned against himself. *Damn me to hell, cursed knave! Too much noise!*

He could not recall the name of this girl. *Beatrix sent me.* He could not remember the direction from which he came. *Michael!* His panic mixed into confusion, his homemade recipe.

Was Michael dead by now? Found out?

Crumpled like a dying spider into a ball, his arms flailing by his legs, he collapsed to the floor, covered his hands in his head and rocked himself. Again, self-reproach. *Idiot. Weakling.* Shame overtook him as he heard Sledgeham's voice mock, *Nameless bastard!*

Astonished by his presence, by his collapse, Bernadette ran and kneeled beside him, gently reaching her hand to his shoulder.

"Who...who are you? Do I know you? Or perhaps you know father? Why are you here so early in the morning? What is your name?"

"Michael....Michael!"

Then he remembered her name. *Bernadette.*

"Why are you here? What is it, Michael?"

"Michael needs help, help me...please! I'm not Michael. I'm Francois!"

At the mention of Francois' name, Bernadette gasped. Dizziness overtook her. It had been a long time since hearing that name. Surely, this must be her mother's sign! She sent him to her!

"What did you say? Who are....I don't understand? Why...who sent you here?" Bernadette stumbled, her face drained of color.

"The girl...with the flowers, over in the shop!"

This was taking too much time. *I have to get back to Michael!*

"Flowers? You mean Beatrix? Is that whom you speak of?"

His water-logged eyes held fast to her bewildered stare.

"Yes! She has Michael. She told me to call on you...for you to come alone...your father might call the constable."

"Constable?" Bernadette grabbed him by his shoulders.

"What is happening? Why do you speak your name to me? And what is this mention of Beatrix? Is Beatrix in trouble? Did the Mrs. beat her again?"

"No, it's Michael. Please! Time's runnin' out! He'll be found! He'll be sent back to the orphanage and master Sledgeham'll kill him this time!"

Bernadette looked over her shoulder toward her father's room upstairs. "My sign!" she muttered. "Mother, guide me!" Francois overheard her say it, though he pretended not to; it was too soft-spoken to have meant to speak out loud.

Bernadette ran to her oven and removed the baked bread. She glanced outside, fixed on the exact shade of light.

"The shop doesn't open until half past nine. Will I be back in time?"

Francois nodded yes, though he had no idea.

"I need to put out the fire. Father's asleep upstairs. He's ill." Bernadette took her hand trowel and threw ashes onto the burning embers.

For Francois, every minute seemed an eternity. Finally, the fire died. Bernadette grabbed her shawl and that of her mother's from the hook by the front door, ran to Francois, put her shawl around him, and wrapped herself in her mother's, cocoon-like. She grabbed

Francois' hand, but stopped briskly at the door. Francois wondered if she had misgivings.

"Please miss, he's in a bad way….he's my brother."

Startled by his word choice, she grabbed inside her apron pocket for her mother's tiny wooden cross, which she always carried with her. Yes, this boy was her sign. This Francois.

"I shall come. But wait! I'll just check on him one last time." Bernadette dropped Francois' hand to run upstairs to her father, who still lay fast asleep. She went to her father's side, placed her index finger under his nose, felt his hot breath against her finger, tucked the sides of his covers in tighter, and ran downstairs as quickly as she could.

"Come then, no time to waste," Bernadette said, as she wrapped herself tighter and grabbed Francois' hand again.

Gratitude gripped Francois' heart, though he was unequipped to handle such sentiment, and queasiness overtook him.

He held on tightly to Bernadette as she ran down the streets she knew so well—shortcuts through back alleys and twisted angles of London. In half the time it took Francois, they were at the florist Shop.

Francois noticed candle light still flickering in the window and measured the indoor illumination against the cyan-pinks breaking through the diminishing grey fog outside. He saw Beatrix rush back and forth, and then, she kneeled down again, out of sight. Francois could see no one else.

No masters!

His queasy gratitude churned alongside his embarrassment over his former panic, as they paused at the door to catch their breath before entering inside.

"I haven't breathed so deeply since mother..."

"Please miss, don't make any noise inside. She has masters upstairs."

"Hush. I know all there is to know about her masters."

Bernadette turned the shop door knob ever so slightly and peeked inside. Beatrix looked up.

Bernadette scanned Beatrix, thankful she seemed in good condition, but Francois watched Bernadette's eyes grow wide as they turned toward the floor where Michael lay.

"God help us!" Bernadette gasped and nodded for Francois to shut the door behind him.

Chapter 5: Finding Mr. O'Brien

Beauchamp's Floral Shop, 7:18 am

Both Francois and Bernadette looked around the shop for signs of the Beauchamp's.

"Shh!" Beatrix held her finger to her lips, but Francois needed no reminders.

Bernadette and Francois tiptoed toward them, both hoping the creaking wooden boards below their feet wouldn't deny them their quiet entrance, wouldn't wake the beasts.

Bernadette took to Beatrix's side, and Francois knelt down by Michael, whose head now lay still on Beatrix's lap as his eyes stared transfixed at the Tudor-framed wainscot wall, and he curled into Beatrix's lap like a wounded dog.

"Has he been conscious long?" Francois asked.

"Francois," Michael sputtered, but they shushed him in unison.

"Get him some more drink, Francois!" Beatrix said, as she handed Francois the mug with the rag tucked inside.

"I'll turn his head slightly this way so he won't choke."

Francois dipped the rag inside the cup, and then put it to Michael's lips. Michael opened his mouth and squeezed down on the rag. He was swallowing much better now.

"He has improved," said Francois, half-smiling.

"Beatrix, what is going on? Who…I don't…?" whispered Bernadette, as her eyes swept over this badly beaten young man.

"I don't know myself!" Beatrix gestured her eyes toward Francois, and continued, "He and two other boys brought Michael here, crack of dawn this morning, torn up and bleeding like a cock in fight! But right now, we have no time for explanations! Mrs. Beauchamp will arise soon. We need to get Michael to safety!"

Beatrix gently touched Michael's forehead, smoothing away loose hairs that fell across his brow, his black hair still matted all over with blood and sweat.

"What do you mean? Where can we take him?" asked Bernadette.

"Did you bring the cart?" asked Beatrix.

Francois heaved his breath inward, not knowing how deeply it affected Bernadette, as it sounded to her like her mother's last breath.

The cart! Forgot! Every stitch of Michael's troubles leads to me!

Francois shook his head, "What of him now? What've I done?"

"There's no time for that! It's not your fault, you poor boy!" Beatrix spoke a calmness that belied her frustration over his untimely outburst and excessive noise.

Just then, a shuffling sound came from above—loud enough to draw everyone's attention. Beatrix, Bernadette, and Francois petrified, as Michael lay still and unaware of his current danger. Beatrix muttered some words under her breath.

Believing himself to be the cause of this stirring upstairs, Francois ossified further into his bone shame, lowered his head,

~ 51 ~

covered his face with his hands and rubbed his fingers over his temples, trying to quell master Sledgeham's voice as it echoed all sorts of insults Francois knew to be true about himself.

Why do I sabotage Michael so? Francois asked himself as he slipped away from his surroundings to mentally prepare for how this bloody nightmare would soon end.

Which master made that noise upstairs—him-brute or her-brute? Whoever it is'll appear soon, find Michael, an' summon the constable. Then what? It's Michael back to Master Sledgeham. Perhaps fleet prison for me? They'll split us up. It's what Sledgeham wants most, ain't it? Me, hanged for stabbin'. An' Michael? Death by Sledgeham.

Francois' hangdog face wore remorse, as his projected future dimmed alongside his pessimistic predilection. So close to escape, luck had run out. Now the hands of fate and time brought this awful morning to closure, and he tasted the familiar melancholy cocktail of desperation and rage until his mouth felt dry. Then, his thoughts shifted to Farley and Alfred. *What of those blokes?*

"I've a thought!" Bernadette jumped, "The bakery shop! Father's ill in bed. Michael and Francois can hide in the back storage room for a day or two until we can think up a better plan. At least this will bide us some time!"

Again, they heard the stirring upstairs, this time more pronounced.

"Mrs. Beauchamp is awake!" Beatrix exclaimed.

Beatrix knew Mrs. Beauchamp's morning routine well. They had only a few minutes to act before it was all over.

In absolute stillness, they listened to Mrs. Beauchamp urinating into her chamber pot, the sound resembling a horse-stream.

"What now?" Bernadette interrupted their silence.

"How we gonna get him there? I forgot the cart!"

"We carry him, like the boys did," Beatrix's calm exterior disguised her own panic, twisting itself vine-like around her. "We have only minutes to do this."

Beatrix slid Michael's head from her lap and laid it on the tattered woolen blanket next to him.

Michael stirred, his chilled bones ached, and his head pounded. In his disoriented confusion, still, he knew his life had been spared by this dark-haired maiden, by Farley and Alfred, by Francois. He would repay them all. He always repaid his debts.

"Francois…" Michael whispered, "Francois, come…come close…."

"We've only a minute!" Beatrix repeated. "We must go!"

Francois leaned over Michael's face.

"Come, Michael. We've gotta leave now! Need to lift yeh…."
Francois hid his moist red eyes, trying to conceal his fear.

"Francois…" Michael continued, "Is this happenin'? Am I dreamin'?"

Francois paused. He looked into Michael's half-moon eyes.

"Tis a very bad dream, Michael."

"How's it end?"

"Don't know, Michael. Not good, I think?"

Francois thought it cruel to give him false hope. The shock of being found—which could happen at any moment—would be too great a blow for Michael against the lie of freedom.

"I know how it ends," Michael replied feebly.

Beatrix spoke quickly, "Michael, the Mrs. is awake! We've got to get you out of here now! We'll have to carry you to safety. It's going to hurt badly when we pick you up! No noise! Your life and mine depends on it!"

Francois and Beatrix each took Michael's side and hurled him upward, both staggering to balance his weight between them.

Your life and mine depends on it. She said it a second time now. Francois flashed his eyes to the jumbling noises upstairs, and imagined Sledgeham's foot-steps descending down on them, a giant beast moving in for its breakfast kill.

"No noise," Michael faintly repeated.

The upstairs floor boards creaked continuously, in rhythm with Francois' quickening heart-beat. Beatrix's cool reserve melted double time into dread. Bernadette's heart stopped altogether. Only Michael remained unnerved, as his limbs hung limply on his two posts that held him up.

The wretched screech of Mrs. Beauchamp exacerbated their current condition.

"Beatrix? Come and empty my pot."

Like a statuette, Beatrix transfixed her gaze upstairs.

"Beatrix? Pot's full!"

With Michael balancing precariously, Beatrix turned to her friend.

"Bernadette, take leave while you can! This might turn scandalous!"

"No, Beatrix! Not today. They came to both of us and they need us equally!"

Beatrix breathed deeply. "Right, then, tally ho, though we be the foxes!"

Trying to synchronize steps, Beatrix and Francois shuffled toward the shop door. Michael groaned loudly as a piercing pain rippled down his shoulder blade.

"Shut up, Michael! Too loud!" begged Francois.

Mrs. Beauchamp's strident warbling voice traveled downstairs.

"What's that noise, Beatrix? Hmmm? Why don't you answer me? Who's there with yeh? Don't make me come down to strike yeh for insolence!"

More rustling and creaking, and then, her bird-shrieks woke up Mr. Beauchamp, who yelled, "Quiet!" to which Mrs. Beauchamp yelled, "Quiet, yourself, ye ole goat!"

The two Beauchamp's exchanged ugly nitpick quibbles, which bought some time, but it was over now, and Mrs. Beauchamp clamored some more as Mr. Beauchamp's snoring resumed.

Francois held onto Michael's left side, and Beatrix his right, while Bernadette opened the door. Held upright, Michael winced as pain emanated from his head, his shoulder, overwhelming him.

"Beatrix, what a fuss you're making! Ain't no right to wake us up so early, little brat! Well, come clean me pot—whew, it stinks— and boil me up some tea now!"

Bernadette held open the front door to the shop as Beatrix and Francois struggled to fit Michael through the Tudor frame at the same time. The crisp April air greeted them, turning their cheeks ruddier.

"You, first!" Beatrix demanded, and Francois abided her. Then, right before she stepped outside into the foggy mist, wearing Michael like a half mink coat, Beatrix called up to Mrs. Beauchamp. Francois stopped moving, Bernadette too.

"Yes, Ma'am, it's just me. I cut myself, is all, I'll be fine...Your fresh tea steeps. I shall bring it to you immediately so you might remain warm in bed, if you please. Mr. O'Brien has delivered our flowers. I'll bring them inside, and then come right upstairs to empty your pot, if that be suitable?"

"Hurry up! I don't wait well!" Mrs. Beauchamp seemed settled for the moment.

"Now Francois!" Beatrix stepped fully outside as her head butted twice to the right, her eyebrows lifted. "Turn right!"

Bernadette shut the door behind her. They would take the twisted short-cut back to Middleton Bakery Shop: six pairs of feet, and two more dragging, down the cobblestone street, hobble-wobble.

Francois found his fleeting courage return again, and anxious to get to Middleton's bakery, his empty stomach grumbled.

He felt ashamed to think of food at a time like this, but for the first time that morning, his thoughts ruminated on the idea of eating freshly baked bread with thick butter. He remembered the smells of the bakery wafting at him, though at the time, the thought of food repelled him.

The children made their way down Hart Street when Francois noticed Beatrix breathing heavily. They were almost to the alleyway that would short cut them back to Middleton's.

"Beatrix needs to catch her breath," Francois said.

"Stop a moment, Beatrix," Bernadette replied.

"Just one moment. Alright then, I'm fine now." Beatrix shifted Michael, and moved forward. Francois moved at Beatrix' pace.

"I'm indebted to yeh for savin' Michael. But what's to become of yeh now, Beatrix?"

Beatrix kept focused as she struggled with Michael's weight around her neck, but Francois could see his question affected her deeply. She stopped short again and shimmied her left arm from behind Michael, twisting herself just enough to free it from under Michael's armpit without causing him too much discomfort.

Michael's arm still hung around her right shoulder as she managed to bear her weight to the left to hold him up with her right arm tucked around his side. She swung her left hand and reached into her apron pocket, which she first patted, and then scrambled to open.

"What's wrong?" Francois asked.

Slipping her hand inside, she felt the cold metal and sharp flint, alongside the tinder box, breathed a sigh of relief, and swung her arm back around Michael.

"My striker and flint!" she smiled, exposing her front tooth, chipped and brown.

Francois did not understand what she meant by this—striker and flint—but he said nothing.

"You can never go back now, Beatrix! She'll flog you to pulp, or worse, sell you to some horrible creature worse than her!" Bernadette cried.

"For certain, I will not return on my own will. Good riddance. Perhaps it's the other way around, Francois?" Beatrix replied, breathless.

They continued their slow struggle against the uneven cobblestone surface, against Michael's weight bearing down.

"What yeh mean by that, other way 'round?" he asked.

"It's a sign," Bernadette replied.

"Not a sign," Beatrix replied gently, "I'm indebted to you, Francois. You're my saving grace. I'd still be at the shop if you two didn't storm into my world! I'm free, for now anyway!"

"'Tis a sign!" Bernadette repeated.

A wave of calm overtook Francois, though he knew they were still in the eye of the tempest. At least, he no longer felt the weight of Beatrix' masters bearing into him, caged inside the shop.

If we make it to the bakery, perhaps!

But Francois' momentary peace was interrupted by screeching sounds emanating behind him.

"Did you hear that?" Beatrix cried. "Her endless screeching! Will it never leave my head? I'm so tired, but we must move faster!"

Michael began to groan.

"That screeching isn't in your head!" Bernadette cried, "We hear it too!"

Francois pivoted his neck, about-turned, and focused his eyes through the thickening fog, which now seemed impervious to daybreak. They had traveled down Hart Street some distance now, but when he squinted, he was able to distinguish a blurred hefty image, whose earsplitting screams traveling toward them gave away her identity.

"Beatrix!" the ear-splitter called.

"She calls my name! Faster!"

"Who's that down there?" Mrs. Beauchamp's stentorian shrill echoed, and so absorbed in her pursuit she was, she seemed to care little for her neighbors at such an early morning hour. But then, she hesitated, stopped her chase, and just as suddenly, turned back around in the direction of the floral shop.

The morning chill bit through his bones, even against the burned energy he expended from carrying Michael, and the added warmth of Bernadette's shawl tied tight around his neck.

She's still in her nightdress!

He thought perhaps she returned for her coat, and would soon seek Beatrix again once she was more properly suited. Or, worse.

Maybe she's alertin' Mr. Beauchamp?

The sight and sound of Mrs. Beauchamp catapulted everyone out of their exhaustion. Even Michael tried bearing down on his two feet to carry his own weight. But, their renewed energy didn't last. Once again, they could hear Mrs. Beauchamp's high-pitched piping close in on them.

The hawker hunts her prey! The hawker hunts her, pray!

Francois' strange habit of breaking into word play in his most distressed moments didn't soothe him as it usually did. The distraction of Mrs. Beauchamp's screams narrowed in on him, as they all heard another noise at the same time, but in front: clip-clopping horse hooves on cobblestone, which drew closer and nearer.

"Someone's coming up on us! Should we hide in the alley way up ahead?" Bernadette asked.

"No, that one's a dead end," Beatrix replied. "At the next one, we turn. Keep straight for now!"

Francois was the first to see the apparition break through the dense, thick, wet, grey vapor.

"The horses in front of us! Look!" Francois pointed.

Everyone except Michael stared at the horse and cart, no longer obscured by fog. Mrs. Beauchamp's bird calls from behind, and horse hooves clopping in front, they hoped the driver would mind his own business, as Francois' stomach and bowels shredded.

"Yah alright?" called out a familiar Irish brogue. "What's the trouble?"

Beatrix cried out, "Praise, it's him!" Bernadette and Francois turned their eyes to the ground, covert and hidden, hoping the stranger wouldn't take interest, but their heads jolted in unison at Beatrix' relief, as they wondered what could possibly cause her contentment at a time like this.

"Mr. O'Brien?" Beatrix called in disbelief.

The Irishman? Naw, could it be? What chance of that?

Francois didn't know what to make of chance, let alone the Irishman. His instinct and life experience told him not to trust. But, as Beatrix sighed greatly, her expression wore a hint of hope, and he loosened as he stared at the man who had delivered flowers to Beatrix earlier that morning.

Mercy for us? Or are we to be lion's supper?

Mr. O'Brien pulled his cart forward until it was aligned to them. He halted Benny and Matilda and they neighed stubbornly.

"Beatrix, lass, what of this?"

"Who's this, Beatrix?" cried Bernadette.

"Our salvation, Bernadette!"

Francois watched helplessly, that same Sledgeham-sickness wafting over him as he felt the shadow of her master closing in. He turned around and could see Mrs. Beauchamp, still somewhat in the distance, but tottering closer now.

"Jaysus Mary and Holy Saint Joseph! What's on yah? What's this strange sight about me?"

"Mr. O'Brien!" Beatrix nervously cleared her voice, "Can you help us? This boy? Michael…he's badly beaten…She's coming!"

Mr. O'Brien looked up the street through the fog toward a thick visage wobbling slowly forward.

"Aye, that plump fowl, 'tis?"

Mr. O'Brien jumped down from his cart, his eyes fixed on Michael; on blood matted hair, on dried rusty blood stained shirt, on bruised face; he conjectured that the injuries happened some time ago but within the last twenty-four hours.

"Mr. Beauchamp—'tis his art work, Beatrix?" Mr. O'Brien sighed, as his eye measured Mrs. Beauchamp's distance from them.

"No….but if we don't hurry, Mrs. Beauchamp will find me and take me back! Please, help us now, and ask me later!"

"Aye, I've seen the bruises on yer face enough tah know what's in store for yah."

Mr. O'Brien threw off his thick tweed coat, and with the help of Bernadette, put it over Michael's shoulders, as Francois and Beatrix held him up. Then he ran to the back of his cart, shifting around crates to make room, pushing aside a horse blanket and a hay basket. Scrambling against the clock, he lay several potato sacks around haphazardly, then ran to Michael.

"Give 'em to me, and git yer'selves in the cart!"

Francois and Beatrix surrendered Michael over to Mr. O'Brien, who lifted him up as if he were a mere rag doll, torn and tattered. He rested Michael onto his left side in the back of the cart on the heap of potato sacks. Michael corkscrewed into a loop, lifeless.

"Cover 'em quick!" Mr. O'Brien called, jumped to his seat, grabbed the reigns, and clicked his tongue sharply as his horses complied immediately.

On Mr. O'Brien's orders, Francois, Beatrix, and Bernadette ran to the back of the cart but only Beatrix jumped in, her dress caught on the cart's wooden lattice, and tore, as the horses started to pull away, neighing.

"Eh, do as I tell yah, git in the cart!" Mr. O'Brien yelled.

Bernadette hesitated briefly, but then Francois grabbed Bernadette's hand, thrusting her forward. He leapt catlike, not letting go of Bernadette, hoisted her up and inside, then himself. Mr. O'Brien brought the horses to a trot, in the direction of Mrs. Beauchamp. Francois watched in horror as they moved closer toward her.

What's he doin'? Traitor! To the lion's den, is it?

"Well, what are yah waitin' fer? The pope? Now, cover the boy with the blankets and such! And you as well, Beatrix. Tuck yerself away, and warm Michael up. Keep him quiet! We're heading her way!"

Mr. O'Brien's words confused Francois: Head toward her, but keep hidden? He didn't know what to think.

Beatrix heeded Mr. O'Brien, laid down, and spooned Michael, as Francois grabbed an old crumpled quilt that smelled of horse and hay, and quickly placed it on top of Michael and Beatrix, covering them double-fold.

Bernadette continued to cover Beatrix and Michael with leftover potato sacks, her hands shaking.

"Mrs. Beauchamp's a few meters away!" Francois cried.

"Francois, my shawl!" Bernadette pulled it from his shoulders and wrapped it around her head to obscure her face and blonde locks from view.

"As fer yerselves, huddle together, best you can, low. Keep the boy's head…" Mr. O'Brien paused. "What's the lad's name, eh?"

"Michael, Sir," Beatrix said.

"Keep Michael's head steady, 'tis a bumpy ride back to the farm, it is. Now quiet! I'll do the talkin'".

Already settled under the blanket, Beatrix placed her left hand under Michael's head as she curled behind his body, her left arm in terrible discomfort. Bernadette and Francois sat at their feet, each on separate sides, and pressed themselves lower, sinking deeply into the cart, making certain the stacked empty crates on each side didn't fall onto their hidden cargo. Michael's shivering finally ceased underneath the layers of warmth—a tweed coat, several empty potato sacks, a scented quilt, and Beatrix.

By now, they heard the wild screams of Mrs. Beauchamp running like a plump gobbling turkey toward them, but a combination of cold air, fog, excess weight, and lack of exercise, slowed her down considerably.

"Beatrix? You no good for nothin' half-wit! Show yehself!" And then....

"Mr. O'Brien? That you, is it?" Mrs. Beauchamp keeled over, out of breath, as the horse and cart drove closer toward her.

Clicking his tongue louder, the horses cantered, pulling their load.

"You, Mr. O'Brien! Stop that cart! Ain't stealin...stealin me maid, are yeh? Arrested...I'll have yeh arrested, I will...." Mrs. Beauchamp loon-crooned.

Beatrix's heart beat so fast she thought it alone would betray her, as it thumped life into the blanket that hid them. She calmed herself by focusing on Michael's slow breaths, and then, attuned herself to his rhythm. Francois and Bernadette, two frightened figurines, held still.

As he drove his horses steadily along toward Mrs. Beauchamp, Mr. O'Brien removed his cap—a sign of respect to the old hag, though he hated doing so—as Mrs. Beauchamp was now just several feet ahead, on the left side of the street.

"Good morn! Aye, just finished now with me deliveries, an' headin' home!" he chattered, as if he hadn't any cares in this world.

She glared at him, annoyed by his friendly trifles.
"Seen Beatrix, 'ave yeh? Stop cart! Who's that in back?"

Mr. O'Brien ignored her behest and placed his cap on his head.

"Sorry, Madam, can't stop now! Horses'er on route back and nothin' but nothin' stops their feedin'! That's me mac and iníon yah ask 'bout—'tis me children. William, Mary, go on then, stand up and give a greet to Mrs. Beauchamp, the flower lady from up the street. Got a bad back, yah see, and makin' em' earn their keep today, the way it should be, eh?"

Neither Francois nor Bernadette moved, as the cart passed Mrs. Beauchamp, her heavy frame steadfast.

"Go on, then!" Mr. O'Brien said cheerfully.

Wrapping her shawl further around her worried eyes, tucking in loose hair strands, Bernadette straightened just enough for Mrs. Beauchamp to glance her, and nervously cleared her voice.

Stop actin' sheepish! We'll be found out soon enough with that!
Immediate shame took hold of Francois, at his judgment of Bernadette, after all she had done for him and Michael.

"Hello, Madam."

Bernadette spoke first, in a masked voice more ethereal than her own, and this prompted Francois to nod in surprise and approval.

~ 65 ~

"Good morn," he replied.

Then, Bernadette quickly added, "Only saw a glimpse of her this morn, when we delivered flowers to you, but does she have dark-hair? I can't remember. Anyway, I can't say for sure, with the fog and all, but I think I just saw someone fitting such a description only a moment ago, pop out of that nook ahead, and run toward your shop!"

I misjudged! Got it in yeh, you do! Francois grinned.

Bernadette pointed toward the flower shop as Mrs. Beauchamp's eyes scanned ahead in the same direction.

"Ain't see no girl! I see no one!"

"Aye, I saw her, too, just ahead, as God is me witness. Don't see 'er now, though," Mr. O'Brien called from his seat.

Thrown off her scent, disgruntled and ragged, Mrs. Beauchamp waved her hands in the air, and muttered under her breath, "Move on, then, feckless micks!", but not quietly enough to go unheard.

She started back home, trailing in hot pursuit of Beatrix, thinking about the broom bristles she'd use to beat the girl.

Then she screamed, "Beatrixxxxx! I'll find yeh, wretched girl, and when I do!" pounding her fist, waving her imaginary broom into air, gritting her Baba Yaga teeth.

Francois and Bernadette watched with caution, as her hideous scoffs frightened the fog away and called daybreak out of its hiding, until her visage grew smaller and smaller, and finally she was out of sight, not out of mind.

Chapter 6: Finding O'Brien Farm

On Route to O'Brien's farm, Fulham, Saturday April 22nd, 7:45 am

Out of immediate danger, and heads no longer covered up by burlap potato sacks and horse quilts, Beatrix and Michael breathed freely again. Michael laid still on his side, resting his head, as Beatrix sat upward, staring at the back of Mr. O'Brien's tweed cap.

"Mr. O'Brien, what brought you back to Hart Street this morn?"

"Aye lass, by chance, I took Hart to loop around. Delivering me wife's tinctures to her client—a midwife on Bow. Got there early. 'Not before eight,' she told me, so I did all me morning deliveries, and looped around...But in the end, what brought me back? Fortune and fate, it seems. Aye, it'll take some explaining to me wife why her paying customer didn't get her order. But, no matter. We're headed toward Bow Street now, and I'll just drop it off as quickly as I can. Before eight'll have to do. I'll leave it by the door and collect the money next week."

Mr. O'Brien turned down Bow Street and soon halted his horses in front of a grey sandstone building with wrought-iron fencing.

Francois' suspicions rose, as he kept careful watch.

To the lions after all?

He tracked Mr. O'Brien as he sprung down off his driver's seat, bolted up the steps, placed a satchel near the front door, knocked three times, and then turned and sprinted back into the cart. Francois settled himself.

Mercy, then! This time anyway.

"Bernadette, where to? Where's home?" asked Mr. O'Brien.

"Bedford Street, Sir. Middleton's Bakery. My father's shop. Do you know of it?"

"Aye, lass. Seen it, but ne'er been in. Am rarely 'round when shops are actually open. Let's see, Bedford from Bow. Can't go down Hart a'gain, that's fer sure. I'll pass through Tavistock and then loop 'round to Bedford through Maiden Lane."

"That is quite near to our bakery, Sir. Where Maiden Lane meets Bedford, I mean to say."

"I'll drop yah back with yer father, and take the tíre óg to me farm. Mrs. O'Brien'll see to Michael's wounds. Beatrix can't go back there, to that mog and simpleton. We'll figure somethin' out."

Beatrix said nothing, but worried lines in her forehead settled into her alabaster skin, leaving creases. Francois silently absorbed the words, *We'll figure somethin' out,* hating the unknown and unfamiliar, but knowing both conditions beat their current state. Anywhere was a better alternative to Beauchamp or Sledgeham.

Luckily the detour to Middleton's Bakery was on direct route to Mr. O'Brien's farm in Fulham, though everyone in the cart felt the burden of time weighted against hunger, fear, daylight, lifting fog.

Francois looked to the mostly empty streets; at the pockets of damp horse waste, mixed with human sludge, dirt and soot, along the street, everywhere, everywhere; the street sweepers, boys his age and older, with their scrapers, shovels, brooms, and carts, under the watch of a rigid inspector, shoveled, and swept, and scraped the city muck. After a while, his eyes met the horizon of shops around him, and he began to notice candlelight emit from windows, one by one, showing signs of life inside, of day commencing, which stirred in him the panic of being seen.

Finally, Mr. O'Brien pulled the horses to a halt in front of Middleton's bakery. Bernadette hugged Beatrix and Francois.

"Mr. O'Brien, please come back for me. Once father is well again, I'll find a way to return with you to the farm…please promise me, Sir."

Turning to Bernadette, Mr. O'Brien nodded, she jumped off the cart, and felt the sting of feet hitting hard dirt. "Wait!" she cried.

"Time's against us, lass…."

"Just a moment! Please!" Bernadette called as she ran inside.

After two minutes passed, Mr. O'Brien shook his head and sighed, "Can't wait any longer. Tisn't safe. Too close to the Beauchamp's. They'll be out on the streets lookin' for her by now."

Francois' nerves collided against the reference to *her*.

Her. Beatrix. Lookin' for her. Who's lookin' for us?

Mr. O'Brien clicked his tongue, but still pulled Benny and Matilda's reigns, and the horses piaffed before he released.

Just as suddenly, Bernadette ran outside the bakery, cradling in her left arm a basket of freshly sliced baked bread and apple tarts.

"Mr. O'Brien, here she comes!" Beatrix pointed.

Bernadette precariously held a jug in her right hand, which spilled out some contents as she quickened toward them.

"Whoa!" Mr. O'Brien halted the horses. Bernadette held out the basket and jug of cool tea to Mr. O'Brien, who helped himself to one of each, nodded approvingly, then grasped the jug and took a swig.

"Yare a good lass. Pass the basket an' jug to Beatrix."

"Yes Sir, but first, Mr. O'Brien, please, I beg you, don't forget your promise. I must know they are well. I couldn't bear not knowing. It's not just Beatrix. It's Michael, and…and…the boy…Francois."

As Bernadette passed the basket to Beatrix, Francois thought her response odd. *The boy?*

"Lassie, my word's my honor."

Mr. O'Brien clicked and grinned, as neighing horses moved.

"There's a jam jar and spoon in the bottom, for Michael…if he can manage swallowing," Bernadette called out.

Francois stared at the brazen girl whose courage bewitched him, as the distance grew greater between them.

Words to say. Mercy. Angel. Merciful angel of morn.

His words failed him as he called out, "It's because of you."

His moody emerald eyes shifted to absinthe, locking upon her, not realizing how his prophetic words folded into her like an origami twin—paper-thin, layered, easily torn.

"Francois! Your sweet name….It is dear to me!" she cried out.

My name? Francois thought it another odd comment, as he sunk his mouth around an apple tart which had the immediate effect of reawakening his hunger, preoccupying his mind, and lulling him softly, muse-like. He swallowed whole bites of sweet apple chunks, soft and moist, then washed it down with the tea jug Beatrix passed him.

He waved his hand, his last thanks, toward Bernadette, and passed the jug to Beatrix, who wrestled to get some liquid into Michael's mouth without spilling it everywhere.

As the horses carried distance between them, Bernadette studied Francois' diminutive frame and heart-shaped face; he looked to her flawless, like the French porcelain doll her mother had given her on her ninth birthday.

Finally, when the distance was too far, Bernadette stood alone, watching them go, lost in the boy's parting words, as she whispered, "'It's because of you'…but what? What's because of me, mother?" Realizing she'd spoken out loud, she looked around to make sure she was alone, and even so, blushed into silence. What did he mean by this? She thought of her mother in that moment and straightened the green dress and white apron, stitched with cherries, the one her mother had sewn for her so long ago, before her death. Bundling her cold hands in her apron, she ran inside, like a spinning toy, so deep she was, circled in thoughts.

O'Brien's Farm, Fulham, Saturday April 22nd, morning

Benny and Matilda took less than two hours to return from London to Mr. O'Brien's farm in Fulham, some eight miles, more or less, from Middleton's Bakery Shop. They made excellent time considering it was an old cart, they pulled extra body weight, and Mr. O'Brien walked his horses most of the way since it caused Michael too much discomfort to trot. Michael lay in and out of consciousness, moaning while awake, and seemingly lost to this world while asleep, but other than his periodic moaning, the ride had been eerily quiet and not terribly comfortable; no one complained or spoke a word, so muddled down they were by their own complicated circumstances.

Only Mr. O'Brien knew where they were headed but he didn't reveal when or where they were destined to end their journey. Early morning fog finally lifted, and rare rays of April sunshine broke through the sky, blaze-yellowed fingers curling at Francois, as if to say, come here, boy, let's take a look at you.

Francois had never been to the countryside, at least he hadn't remembered so, but the scenery awakened inside him a sense of longing he couldn't quite understand. From the moment the city's charcoaled walls fell away, replaced by patchworks of blue green hues, and unlimited sky, his tenseness dissipated further, and he somehow remembered having been touched by nature, some other time, some other place. But touched.

Stretching blue. Tickling grass. Laughing wind.

He marveled at the distant rolling hills and English Oaks, scattered plentifully along the rutted, rocky road. The fields popped slap-dash with white, blue, and purple wildflowers. They passed farmhouses and country churches, winding paths that whittled into woodland groves, new Victorian estates on lands vastly covered in rapeseed, the flowers bursting forth like tiny yellow canaries singing spring. Francois breathed in the intoxicating sights of the countryside like a child tasting his first sweet, only now realizing that life had such color. Yet, all this beauty contrasted against his thoughts, questions, endless worry.

He piecemealed together facts: Mr. O'Brien's wife made medicines. *The kind to help Michael?* Mr. O'Brien said she could help him. *Would she?* Mr. O'Brien had two children, since he and Bernadette masqueraded as them earlier. *Friends to us or foe?* The Beauchamp's. *Will they come after Beatrix?* Bernadette. *That strange savior.* His thoughts darkened. His letter. *Gone.* Michael. *Please live through this.* Sledgeham....

When Francois finally had enough of his head, he broke silence.

"Mr. O'Brien?" he asked, clearing his voice.

"Aye."

"May I ask a question, sir?"

"Aye, lad. I've questions of me own, yah can imagine!"

"Is yeh wife a nurse, Sir?"

"Not titled. But, she's a healer, she is. Helps women with their babies—bringin' em into this world an' such. An' everythin' else besides!"

Francois wondered silently about the 'everythin' else besides' part.

"Mr. O'Brien? I..."

"Aye, lad. Spit it out...."

"Forgive me, Sir, to ask and all?"

"Aye, get on."

"Will your wife help Michael?"

"Aye."

"Would yeh still help us, if yeh knew Michael and I did somethin' wrong, some people might say against the law?"

"Ah, Jaysus, Mother Mary, what trouble have I taken on?"

Francois bent his head low, wishing his tongue could fish back the words that flapped mid-air out of his mouth.

Beatrix spoke up.

"Sir, their master makes mine seem mild in comparison. They've escaped. No troubles taken on, just troubles relieved."

"And yah done nothin' to bring it on yerself, lad?"

Every dose, been brought on by me.

Francois said nothing.

"No more than I have done so, Sir," Beatrix replied boldly.

"Aye, fer God's sake, I'll chance me arm and hope yah don't cause me too much grief. Well to that, no one knows where the boot pinches on another's foot. I'm sure yer own boots are causing some mighty blisters, eh?"

"I'll be good, Sir," Francois answered, not understanding what had just been said to him.

"I imagine someone, somewhere's lookin' for yah by now." Mr. O'Brien sighed deeply. "Well, we'll find out the facts soon enough. Let's just get the boy well first. Ah. Chance me arm and pray I'm not in over me head, though it swells like an overcooked sausage."

"Mr. O'Brien, weh're strong, well Michael is, and we don't complain much. Work hard for yeh, we will, no compensation necessary, Sir?"

"Well to that, we're in the countryside now. Tis a different law here, outside the belly of the beast. On me farm, if yah work, yah get yer fair pay, though it may be in food and shelter. Ahh, the fresh air'll show yah another way, help yah find yerselves. Give yah time to make a plan. Figure out what yer to do."

Mr. O'Brien turned back and glanced at Beatrix and Francois, who remained quiet, unsure of Mr. O'Brien's meaning and speech. As he pulled on the horses' reigns, they whinnied and resisted, but eventually slowed, snorted and stomped their warn-down horse shoes into the grooved tracks.

"How's the lad?"

Michael's head rested in Beatrix' lap and her hand lay across his forehead. "Burning with fever, I'm afraid," Beatrix said, with dithery eyes. Francois' weighted sigh moored into Beatrix and she reached out to comfort him.

"Stay low. That's me farm, way up yonder 'round the bend. Look ahead there. That's it." Then, Mr. O'Brien added, "Jus' what load'a trouble I carry home, I know not!"

"None, Sir, I promise."

"Well, I need somethin' to tell the wife. Anyone got anythin'?"

"Sir, I'm not sure I understand myself. That's the truth of it. You see, this morning's turn of events happened so fast. One minute I'm cutting stems and next thing I know, little Francois runs into the shop with some boys—who disappear, mind you, as quick as they arrived—begging me to help Michael....then, Francois runs for Bernadette, I'm sewing up Michael's wounds...my heart nearly stops when I hear Mrs. Beauchamp screaming out for me, we run

~ 75 ~

out the door, down the street, and by divine intervention you came and saved us!"

Francois listened to Beatrix ramble, impressed by her clarity.

"Aye, lass, 'tis true. Happened fast, it did. Yare a good girl, Beatrix. Yah've no reason to be nothin' to no one, but yah risked yer own hide an' helped. Things'll unfold as they should, in time. There's a time and a place, neither of which is about us yet."

Conversation momentarily lulled, and Francois wondered how well and how long Mr. O'Brien and Beatrix knew one another, as Mr. O'Brien continued, mainly for his own benefit.

"Alright then, let's all just relax and calm down. Yer tight-lipped, after the night yah had. Understan' that. We'll work it out, in good time. But let me be clear. Not right now, but soon, I'm goin' tah need to know yer secrets. And while I don't expect yah tell me what yah don't know, I do expect yah tell what yah do. Me brood will look after yah, 'til we sort it through. Yah got any news to add to my soliloquy, lad?"

Mr. O'Brien turned to Francois for some sort of confirmation. Francois shook his head, thinking deeply about his response.

Michael'll know what to say and not say.

"Pray Sir, I understand."

Satisfied, Mr. O'Brien turned around, released his reigns and the horses gaited quickly home as wheels creaked, feet splattered mud, cart squeaked, and Michael's drowned moans were heard by all.

"Don't worry," Beatrix whispered lightly, as Francois read her lips, "Mr. O'Brien is good."

"What do yeh know of him?" Francois mouthed.

Her eyes welled tears.

"He's shown concern for me over the years, and great contempt for my masters...."

She quickly buried her hands over her face to hide her eyes.

"What's wrong? Ain't worried about your masters, are yeh?"

"Ha," Beatrix whispered, and dabbed her eyes, "I'm not a crier. But I've been thrown off course. I woke up this morning thinking it an ordinary day, filled with duties, filled with orders and threats. But for the first time, luck has finally turned itself over to me, and I'm a bit unnerved."

Francois touched Beatrix's hand.

"I have the same first. Firsts are promisin'!" Francois felt immediate shame overtake him.

Temper yehself, boy. Yeh're still in the thick of it.

Sledgeham's shadowy presence haunted him, Michael's health remained precarious, and there was still the matter of the letter they desperately sought—this parchment that equally ensnared him to his past and presented his possible future.

Mr. O'Brien's horses turned up the long dirt drive way. Francois stared at the farmhouse ahead—warm eggshell tan, thatched roof, dark wooden beams running parallel down the sides. To the left of the farmhouse stood a red barn with brown trim and a weather vane at the triangular roof top. Stone fencing surrounded the farm property, which felt large and expansive to the eye.

"Aye, here she is, me pride and joy—all two hectares of it!" Mr. O'Brien said as his horses neighed and raced to their feed.

~ 77 ~

Emerging flowers broke through the earth.

"Crocus and daffodils!" Beatrix's mood shifted as she pointed.

Though Francois couldn't distinguish which flower was which, he was taken by the pockets of purple, white, and yellow.

"Look over there! And, I know what glory to expect, though they shan't bloom for a while," Beatrix semi-smiled.

Though Francois didn't know the apple trees from the cherry trees, the Wyche Elms from the Chestnuts and Poplars, he could see differences amongst the bark, shade, and leaf, and calm overtook him as he studied the pregnant pods, bursting forth white star petals and pink tea cups.

Heavy farm smells mixed together—of cows, horses, sheep and chickens, of manure and earth and soil freshly turned. Though he had no name to refer to each flower, shrub, or tree, the sights and smells made him think of his new found freedom outside the walls of Saint Mark's. He had lived most of his life in darkness, but deep and distant memories now emerged, provoking in him a sense that he had seen such things before.

In a past life. In a life pre-Sledgeham.

The horses trotted faster.

"They know what's waitin' fer 'em." Mr. O'Brien called, "Slow down, slow down!"

Michael woke up again, this time wincing loudly in pain. Francois and Beatrix both padded Michael's head from the bumpy ride, and tried to soothe him at the same time.

"We're here now," Beatrix calmed him.

"Won't believe yeh eyes, Michael!" Francois patted him.

Just then a black and white border collie shot in their direction, barking as the horses trotted toward the stone gates even faster now, and Mr. O'Brien harnessed their reins to slow them down, calling to his wife and children even before the horses reached the farmhouse.

"Gertie! William! Mary! All of yah come out and give us a hand. A boy needs tendin' and yah best come quick!"

A tall, slender, regal-looking woman with fiery hair ran outside the front door, wiping off flecks of debris on her skin and smoothing her hands into her apron to dry them. A younger version of the woman followed.

"Where's William?" Mr. O'Brien called, his words competing against the dog's incessant barking.

Mrs. O'Brien shook her head curiously.

"This isn't your usual greeting, Mr. O'Brien. What is it?"

Her eyes turned almost immediately toward the back of the cart, as her gaze locked onto Michael, who was awake, groaning.

Francois found comfort in Mrs. O'Brien's concern, as she too, yelled for William.

"In the barn, da! William's in the barn!" Mary stared in shock, then turned to Francois and Beatrix with the same surprised look.

"William!" screamed Mr. O'Brien, "Drop what yer doin' and come! Aye, Jingles, shut yer trap!"

Francois turned to Jingles, who finally stopped his racket, and instead took to running in circles, chasing his tail.

"Seamus, what on earth is going on here? Who are these children?"

"Jaysus, Gertie, ha empt a clew! I've been askin' meself that since mile one, but by the looks of the boy laying kilt stone dead in the cart there, now is not the time to figure who's who, aye?"

Mr. and Mrs. O'Brien both stared at Michael. At the same time, a tall, fresh-faced young man came running toward them from the green hill side. Francois fixed his eyes on the younger, thinner, spitting image of Mr. O'Brien. *His father's son. Son of the father.*

"Da! Who's this?"

"Carry him inside, William," Mr. O'Brien demanded.

"Do as your father says. Don't ask questions. Just carry him in and place him carefully on our mattress. Mary, get the fire on upstairs, and boil up some water…get some clean rags, too. Mr. O'Brien, go fetch me my medicine bag," Mrs. O'Brien said.

Jingles nipped at Michael's dangling legs as William raised Michael from the cart, then carried him in his arms toward the house.

Francois got up quickly to follow inside.

"Not now, boy," said William to Jingles, who wagged his tail and followed him to the door, but stopped short of entering inside.

William carried Michael up the narrow stairs with ease, even though he had to walk step by step sideways, ducking his head to miss the jutting ceiling beams. As he laid him down, Michael's body sank into the warmth and comfort of the mattress, but still he moaned and cried out about his pounding head.

"Let the Mrs. have a look, Michael. She's a healer, they say." Francois felt embarrassed at his words, not sure why.

Beatrix instinctively followed Mrs. O'Brien upstairs, explaining Michael's injuries—his back shoulder blade and head wounds—and Francois found extreme comfort in their talk of Michael as their ailing patient.

Mrs. O'Brien washed her hands in the basin, calling out orders like a five-star field marshal, as she fiddled in her medicine bag.

Beatrix whispered to Francois, "In all the years he's brought flowers to the shop, I'd never have fancied Mr. O'Brien's life to be this! It seems a strange and marvelous turn of events, doesn't it?"

"Too strange..." Francois began, but he was cut off by Mrs. O'Brien's current command.

"Help me turn him over onto his stomach, William, and take off his shirt and pants."

William stripped Michael, leaving him in his bottom undergarment. Everyone gasped, except Francois.

"A thousand beatings, I'd gladly give 'em back!"

Francois knew Mr. O'Brien referred to Sledgeham, since it was Sledgeham who put those scars there. Francois had seen Michael's scars enough times that they no longer elicited response. They were just a part of him. *His river Thames*, he called it.

Mrs. O'Brien cursed. She shook her head by what she saw— fresh wounds oozing against a canvass scarred over with ridges—a geographical road map that detailed the terrain of this boy's suffering.

Mrs. O'Brien examined Michael's head wounds closely. Michael's puffy, swollen wound below the shoulder blade looked particularly vile where three stitch marks held together a damson marbled circle from which streaked angry red spirals, like a dark sun about to explode.

Mary cried out, covering her mouth, as William comforted her.

"Another day or two untreated, and this infection would fester," Mrs. O'Brien said. "William, fetch me some poppy juice."

William ran downstairs and came back up with a small drinking bottle, which he placed in Mary's hands.

"Beast!" Mrs. O'Brien muttered under her breath, as her eyes took in the stitch marks below Michael's shoulder.

Francois took special notice of her utterance, as he calmed his nervous mind by tossing the word *beast* into the air; it rose and fell, reminding him of a passage his Sunday school teacher often recited to the shut, borded up ears of boys who were tired of the rector's ironic speech; tired of returning home to the very beast itself: *And I stood upon the sand of the sea, and saw a beast rise up out of the sea, having seven heads and ten horns and upon his horns ten crowns....and the dragon gave him his power, and his seat, and great authority.*

Michael lay on his stomach, head turned sideways, moaning, conscious now, as Mrs. O'Brien calmly spoke.

"We must flip him so Mary can administer the poppy juice."

As the three turned Michael onto his back, Mrs. O'Brien added, "Lift him. Go on. Position him to drink."

William propped up Michael from behind, serving as his bedpost, arms inserted under Michael's armpits, each hand resting on one side of Michael's jawbone. Mary tipped the bottle to Michael's lips, pushing it into his mouth, scraping past teeth.

"Mary, make sure he swallows all of it," said Mrs. O'Brien.

Mary poured the bitter fluid down, as William held him, and Michael tried but failed to reject it, as he gagged, and Mary soothed him, there now, there now.

"What is that?" Francois asked nervously.

"Michael will relax. His pain will cease soon," Mrs. O'Brien said, but she did not answer his question.

To the sounds of retching, William kept Michael's mouth shut, until finally, Michael stopped.

"Is it safe? He's on an empty stomach," Francois asked.

"Yes." Mrs. O'Brien said, and then added, "Mr. O'Brien, take the boy downstairs, and get him some nourishment."

"No, please, I won't say another word," Francois pleaded. Mr. O'Brien placed his hand on Francois' shoulder, but he let Francois remain.

Mrs. O'Brien waited—what seemed eternity to Francois—for her tincture to kick in, and then wasted no more time. Once Michael relaxed fully, she cleaned Michael's wounds with soapy water, then, poured her handmade antiseptic solution generously over each cut and puncture.

"Stings! Hurts!" Michael managed to say, "Francois! Dizzy, I'm...."

"He's fadin' out again," Francois said, "but he's mumblin' and slurrin'...what does he say?"

"It's the opium in the poppy juice," Mary said, "He's quite comfortable I assure you."

"I've heard about the power of the poppy seed! Is it true?" asked Beatrix, but no one answered.

Mary dripped the bottle's last drips into Michael's mouth, but his lower face went limp, and it drooled down his chin. Between half-laugh slurs and silence, Michael suddenly opened his full moon eyes, but they rolled back, eclipsed, and shut.

"Michael?" Francois called to him.

They turned him over once more and Mrs. O'Brien applied a thick, smelly ointment onto Michael's head and back sores. As she felt bumps and ridges hidden underneath matted hair, she said, "Mary, scissors."

Mary fetched and fumbled scissors quickly from her mother's bag. Mrs. O'Brien cut thick black locks of curl off his scalp, exposing nasty wounds, and applying ointment to each.

"Snip, snip, snip," Michael mumbled, trying to roll to his side.

"He hears yeh!" Francois worried, as Michael's black locks fell around him, "Why's he actin' so foolish?"

"Michael, lay still," Mary said.

Michael stirred even more.

Mr. O'Brien came over to assist William in securing Michael down, but Francois thought quickly, knowing how Michael responded to force against him under any circumstance.

Poppy juice or not!

He devised his own quick remedy to allay Michael, and lied to keep his brother still. Leaning down to his ear, he whispered, "Michael, I know where Sledgeham hid the letter! I know!"

Michael's body fell limp, and Francois knew he held him at bay.

"Who did this?" Mrs. O'Brien asked, tending again to her patient, who settled against Francois' proclamation, "I know."

"The master…Master Sledgeham," Francois said.

"No, I mean to ask who sewed up this puncture, right here above his shoulder."

"Me, ma'am, as best I could, but I only had boiled water and a fired needle….nothing like you…" Beatrix offered shyly.

"You did well under the circumstances. Mary, look at these stitches! Where did you learn something like this, girl? And what of such instinct to do so? What did you give the boy to calm him?"

"Nothing, ma'am…."

"He took it? Simply laid there? Without numbing the pain?"

"Ma'am," Beatrix nodded.

"Well, as impressive as your instinct and his pain threshold may be, unfortunately, these angry tentacle streaks show sure sign of infection. We'll have to open it up and put in some medicine to fight it. We'll sew him up again, but not quite yet. I want to treat it for a few hours first."

The moment Mrs. O'Brien said, "open it up," Michael squirmed furiously and Francois knew the source behind Michael's writhing.

Needles and pins, needles and pins, when a boy's sewed, his trouble begins.

William and Mr. O'Brien pressed their hands against Michael's legs and left shoulder, but Francois implored them to let go.

"Please, no. He's a natural fighter. Beg yeh, no force. Let me talk to him."

Francois quickly whispered in Michael's ear, "The letter, Michael. Return your thoughts to the letter! That's right. Calm down. The letter, Michael, it's in the outside shed, buried!"

~ 85 ~

This news excited Michael to no end, having the opposite effect Francois sought, exacerbating kicks and flails. Beatrix quickly ran to Michael's side.

"Michael…it's me, Beatrix. Michael…listen to me. Michael…."

"Dark hair girl…" Michael mumbled, repeating her name in slurred rhythm, "Beatrix…Beatrix…Beatrix." He stopped moving again and drifted.

"He's awfully active, mother. Shall we prepare more elixir?"

"No Mary. He's inebriated enough to feel nothing. I'll begin."

Her hands were skilled instruments, cutting thread from laced epidermis, pulling until strand emerged; angry tissue flaring forth warnings as her fingers gently separated thin-sheeted skin, exposing the deep crater of hot blistering, foul-odor ooze inside.

"I didn't know what else to do," Beatrix said, her cheeks reddening, "…It seemed a proper fix at the time."

Francois watched Beatrix stare at Mrs. O'Brien's toiling hands.

"You did well, with little to no resources. You could learn more, so watch." Mrs. O'Brien fixed her stare on Michael's wound.

"You're a kindred spirit, Mrs. O'Brien," Beatrix answered softly. "I believe it to be true."

Mrs. O'Brien ignored Beatrix, but instead, placed her hand inside her medicinal bag, picked up a tiny vile, unscrewed the cap, and ordered Mary to crush the whitish powder in a pestle with half parts boiled water.

It took less than five minutes to prepare the sticky sludge, but during that time, Mrs. O'Brien loosened the dozen or so of

Michael's lash marks by massaging skin slightly apart, often producing fresh blood, but necessary for greatest medicinal effect.

"Ready with the ointment," Mary said, carrying the pestle over.

"Liberally smear over each lash, as I open," Mrs. O'Brien said.

Mary daubed the wounds, and then just as quickly, Mrs. O'Brien pushed Michael's skin together, while she rubbed a thick sticky cream onto the seam of each tear.

Mrs. O'Brien turned her attention back to the puncture wound.

"What caused this wound? A sharp object of some sort?"

"A nail did it, from a picture hangin'," Francois said.

He did not want to relive that moment—the broken face of Jesus, dangling from his brother's back, split halo flapping over, his ripped half-smile still at peace in spite of the turmoil.

"Mary, heat my scraper in the fire and bring it directly to me," Trying to hide her renewed anger, Mrs. O'Brien reached inside a small muslin sack packed loosely with what looked to Francois like dry brown weed clumps.

"William, pull out some crushed peat moss with these pincers. Heat it first, mind you, and make sure not to touch it with your fingers! And, someone bring me some garlic juice."

Francois and Beatrix shared a surprise glance, in part due to the list of natural ingredients Mrs. O'Brien mentioned, but even more so, by the unity with which mother, daughter, and son worked.

Mary handed Mrs. O'Brien a scraper and garlic juice, while William removed the peat moss with heat-sterilized pincers, heated the large clump in the hearth, wrapped it up in a soft linin square, and handed the linin square to Mrs. O'Brien as directed.

Mrs. O'Brien scraped out the pus, like magma surfacing ruptured crust, until she saw raw pink skin underneath. She poured a solution of garlic water into the wound, dabbed it with a clean rag, swabbed the hole with a generous supply of thick ointment, and covered the wound with heated peat moss linin.

"We'll keep it covered an hour, then repeat. That should stop the festering for now. Then, we'll close the wound. Now it's Michael's job to fight and stay strong. Let the boy rest. Come, let's go down."

They bundled Michael, who lay quiet now, eyes closed. He seemed to not exist, to have entered the world of nothingness again.

Francois and Beatrix followed the O'Brien family down the narrow stairs to the kitchen. With the exception of William, who left the farmhouse to prepare the barn, they all sat around the kitchen table, and Beatrix told the O'Brien family everything she knew about Michael and Francois. Francois listened again to the same story Beatrix told Mr. O'Brien in the back of the horse cart.

"I beg you not to contact the constable. They'll be given back to that horrible half-man, and as for me...."

"What of you? To whom do you belong?" Mrs. O'Brien asked. Beatrix fell silent. Francois wondered why she did not easily answer the question, and he suspected Beatrix needed time to think.

"Yes, that presents a problem, I suppose...." Beatrix stalled. Francois' interest peeked.

Everyone belongs to someone, don't they Michael?

"...I suppose I belong to no one," Beatrix finally replied.

"You must belong to someone?" Mrs. O'Brien inquired.

Yes. Everyone belongs to someone.

"Aye, I'll tell yah who—that fat pigeon and cock, that's who. She's a servant to them—a carpet to beat, she is, day and night to those two foul creatures!"

"Are you their servant, Beatrix? Is that true?"

"Well…Yes, ma'am…I…suppose I am," Beatrix nodded, her cheeks flushing to rosy hue. "I…yes. That is what I am."

Beatrix's response momentarily allayed the O'Brien's, and they shifted their attentions to Francois, determined to know more about him and Michael. Their litany of questions deeply exhausted him. The cortisol rush that had coursed his veins since early morning hours took a great toll on his spirit, leaving him disoriented and uncertain of any facts he should admit before he could speak to Michael.

"Where is Saint Mark's Orphanage? How long were you there? What about Michael? Who is Sledgeham? Do you have scars like Michael to show? How did you escape? Who was with you—just Michael? Beatrix mentioned two others. Who are they? Where are they? Was Master Sledgeham aware you escaped? Do you think the master will look for you? Why did you run away? Was it because Michael was being beaten? What caused this particular outbreak of violence? How did you find Beatrix?"

These questions circled in his head, bouncing into and against one another aggressively, relentlessly, until he began to provide short viable answers, one by one, reciting by rote:

"Saint Mark's, in London. Near and between Ludgate and Saint Paul's…Been there since a young tot…less than two, Michael

~ 89 ~

says…Michael was there when I arrived…Sledgeham's our master at Saint Marks…he's a drunkard, liar, and thief….a scar or two, but not like Michael, ain't no one's as bad off as him. We escaped through the front door…Alfred and Farley came with us, but ain't sure what happened to 'em. Boys like me and Michael, they are. Alas, maybe been caught for all's I know…. …Ay, he's aware…Ay, he'll look for us….Don't know what started it, haven't talked to Michael yet…We came upon the flower shop. She looked safe. She took us in…."

Finally, a worn-out Francois bent his head down into his crossed arms on the table top. His exhaustion apparent, Mr. and Mrs. O'Brien gave him a rest, but turned their attentions back to Beatrix once more.

"Beatrix, what are we to do about you? Have you any family, any relatives we might contact? Anyone at all?"

"No, ma'am, none of whom I can speak. But, I am a hard worker. I can start fire quicker than anyone I know. I can wash and clean and…well…do anything you ask. And, I eat very little."

Mr. and Mrs. O'Brien looked sharply at each other, wearing sad expressions.

"It's an issue of the law. Are the Beauchamp's your legal guardians, Beatrix?" asked Mrs. O'Brien, afraid to hear the answer.

"No, no…it's not like that. I've been with them longer than I can remember, and I don't really remember how I came to be there in the first place. They have no legal rights to me….I know I can't go back, ma'am. Please, don't make me go back."

"But, Beatrix, it may not be in our hands," Mrs. O'Brien replied.

"In me hands, that's where I'm putt'n it, Gertie. And, she's not go'en back there. Imagine Mary cast into the hands of that banshee and balor. No, she'll stay here, that's what she'll do."

Mary embraced Beatrix, who held onto Mary like a rosary.

"I promise to be a faithful servant, and work without idleness."

"We'll find you a bed here, and you'll stay…but not as a servant. You've had enough of that in your lifetime. No, we'll put you to use, and you'll earn your keep, but no more nor less than the rest of us." Mrs. O'Brien paused, then said, "As for Michael, the boy can't be more than twelve, thirteen tops! I've treated many ailments in my life time, but this was done by the hands of an animal. I'm not sending these boys back to meet their deaths!"

"Aye, agreed. Then we best lay low and keep our guests and their secrets to ourselves."

"You shan't be disappointed. I'll earn my keep and more," Beatrix offered repeated thanks as Francois turned inward, wondering about his own secrets, and appraising the value of his silence without Michael there to guide him.

Lay low, skilled secret-keeper.

"I'm tired, Sir, may I be done?" asked Francois, "May I sleep?"

"Aye, lad, I'll take yah out to the barn-loft, where William's there now, settin' the hay mats and blankets. Yah've been beat tired, forgive the pun. William'll keep yah company tonight. Michael's sleepin' inside fer now, but he'll move to the barn soon as he's fixed up. Beatrix, you'll be sharin' a bed with Mary."

In the barn-loft, Francois sunk into his hay mat, needle-thin lost, listening to unaccustomed night sounds around him. He replayed each step of this strange day, each fortunate series of events that led them on their journey to this place. *This Haven.*

He thought about the distance he and Michael had come, that they still must go. He thought of Farley and Alfred. *Alfred.* Francois had wanted to go a different direction, but Alfred insisted they took that particular route which in turn led them to the floral shop. *Beatrix.* Who saved them, who sent him to Bernadette. *Bernadette. Other night angel, who speaks my name so dearly!*

He thought about time and place coming together perfectly as coincidence collided them with Mr. O'Brien at exactly the right moment. *Strange coincidences.* What strange coincidences led him so long ago to Saint Marks? He thought about the letter. *The letter, which might have set me free, which leads me back to Sledgeham.* He cast him out quickly, focusing on his conversation with the O'Brien's, hoping he did not reveal too much—forgetting what he did and didn't say. He said a prayer for Michael. He fell asleep.

Chapter 7: Finding Recovery

O'Brien's Farm, mid-May

Michael recuperated slowly over three weeks. Francois visited several times a day, whittling time for Michael by describing life on the farm, the O'Brien's, Bernadette, and Beatrix. Michael tried not to show his curiosity about Beatrix, but found ways to bring her into their conversation. Each visit, Francois watched for signs of Michael's strength returning, and as it did, his own will was restored. The events of the last few weeks began to settle within, and Francois knew with certainty now that Michael would live.

While Michael rested, he spent his early mornings following William and Jingles around the farm, waking at five am to milk a set of Jersey cows named Bee and Bonnet. Then, they tended to the sheep, horses, pigs, chickens, and other livestock, and by the time they finished feeding the animals, filling their troughs and water buckets, and cleaning up messes of all kinds, it neared the noon hour. Faithful jingles followed along, stealing licks from Francois whenever he bent down to do his tasks.

One farm morning, William turned to Francois as they set together mending a portion of dry stone fencing.

"You're proving yourself a formidable worker, Francois. I leave in autumn to the London Mechanic's Institute. Can you believe it? Me? Anyway, Da' could use your help around the farm when I'm away."

Formidible.

He would not give this word away, though he didn't know what it meant.

"I've not heard of a mechanic's institute. But I do like the farm work here."

William laughed. "One man's drink is another man's poison, I suppose. Ah, well, that's good to hear, Francois, that's good."

William spoke of his farm chores as endlessly boring, but the last three weeks brought Francois profound pleasure. His body ached a good kind of pain at the end of the long day, a purposeful kind, and as he took care of the animals, appreciating their predictable ways, he trusted their reciprocal friendship.

As William and Francois went further up the hill to fix another patch of old stone wall, Jingles ran after Francois, just a few feet ahead of him, swirled his body around, dropped a stick, and wagged his tail.

"He wants me to throw the stick."

"Then throw it!" said William.

Francois bent down to pick it up as Jingles watched his every move. In the second that Francois threw it, Jingles bolted through the grassy hill, leapt into the sky, and swept the stick out of mid-air.

"Good boy!" Francois called.

Jingles ran back to Francois, stick in mouth, and tongue panting. Francois knelt down to the sheepdog's level, the dog jumped into his arms, and pushed him down hard. Francois heard hearty laughter, and looked around, but saw no one other than William staring. It was then he realized the sound had come from him. On this day, for the first time, Francois recognized the sound of his own laughter.

This was Michael's first morning waking up in the barn loft, and he liked it out here with Francois and William. He woke up much earlier than usual by the rooster's crow, lay on his back, thinking deeply, and stared at the thick wooden barn beam ceiling.

Francois was also awake, on his own hay mat, staring at Michael, wondering what he was thinking about, and wishing he'd share it. But, for that, Francois also took comfort in Michael's silence, which was a familiar constant since the beginning of time. Michael always only revealed things to him on a need to know basis.

A mixed bag, this need-to-know.

"We should get up now, Michael. William's already out workin' the fields. But, I'd pay a quid for your thoughts, I would."

Michael's lips together, he smiled wide.

"Well you just happen to have one, don't yeh?"

"Michael, tell me what yeh're thinkin' bout," Francois' voice shifted to a serious tone.

"Same things yeh're thinkin', probably."

"'Bout Alfred and Farley?"

"Off and on. But no, not exactly." Michael bit his upper lip, hesitating, holding back.

"Michael, weh're here almost a month now. Yeh're well now, mostly, and I'm thinkin' we've some decisions to make?" Francois was still trying out his newfound approach of saying what he thought, and wasn't sure his point came out the way he wanted.

"That we do," Michael said. "Bloody hell, Francois! What yeh think I'm thinkin' 'bout? The letter! What else?"

"What's ideas yeh got, Michael? I'm seein' things different, maybe, then you be? 'Bout the letter, I mean…"

"How's that?"

"Well, for one thing…don't get upset…maybe we should just forget it. Just settle ourselves here? Just let the past go?"

Michael's cheeks reddened, his brow furrowed, and his large chestnut eyes squinted into half shells.

"That's guff! You ain't any idea how ridiculous yeh are?" Michael turned away and pounded his fist on the ground.

"Michael, there ain't no letter. Or if there is, wherever it is, there's Sledgeham. Ain't nothin' to go back to, the way I see it. Don't even care no more. Letter, no letter, I like this place. Maybe we should focus on bein' useful 'round here, at least for now?"

"Spent my whole life thinkin' 'bout that letter, takin' countless hits for that letter, all for the likes of you, and in a few weeks, willy nilly, yeh just decide it don't matter no more?   Yeh ungrateful.... Just bog off!"

William whistled to Francois from outside the barn, his signature call that he had come to collect his farm-hand. Francois rose up, his shaking hands unsteady, confused by Michael's anger.

So stubborn! So stuck! So single-minded! Sledgeham-minded!

Francois tried to stifle the anger welling up in his chest. He was many things to Michael. Bad luck. Hardship. Misfortune. But ungrateful?

Why couldn't Michael see his good intentions? See the probability in front of them instead of the unlikely possibility they left behind? He would leave it for now. Come back to it when Michael cooled.

He ain't goin' back. His death-wish won't be on me. Past is past. Now, how to convince?

Francois collected himself, and whistled his signature tune back to William. He would work harder than ever today, make himself more noticeable, less dispensable.

That same afternoon, after a steady day of hard work and contemplation over how to persuade Michael, Francois came upon Beatrix tending to Mrs. O'Brien's garden. He reflected on how little she spoke about her past, present, or future, and felt he didn't know her at all, even after all this time together, after all they had been through.

"Hello, Beatrix."

"You startled me!" Beatrix gasped, "You seem to do that well!" Francois liked their private joke and he thought immediately of how he first came upon her in the floral shop—a time that seemed so long ago, another lifetime ago, and yet it hadn't been so long.

"Yeh enjoyin' your work, are yeh?" he asked.

"I don't mind it at all. Quite opposite. I'm busy with house work, of course. But I tell you, how I love my time with Mrs. O'Brien and Mary! They brew up the most unusual things! Out of regular old nature, you'd never think, Francois! Why, just this morning I've made lavender soap and some medicines too!"

"That's lovely, Beatrix."

"How's Michael today? I've not seen him round about yet."

Angry, unyieldin', that's how he is. Maybe even ungrateful!

"Fine. Much better, each day."

"Good! Then, I'm going to ask him to come and gather roots and twigs with me later this afternoon."

"He'd probably do that," Francois replied, suspecting Michael would do whatever Beatrix asked of him. Michael looked at her the way painters studied their subjects.

Just then, Mrs. O'Brien came out of the farmhouse calling to Beatrix in a hurried, rushed manner. She shielded her eyes against the May sunbreak which prevented her from seeing Francois at first.

"Oh, Francois. I visited Michael earlier while you were doing your chores. What a strong constitution that boy has!"

Francois nodded in agreement, knowing too much what Michael was capable of living through. Mrs. O'Brien turned to Beatrix.

"Beatrix, do you think you could stomach a birthing? The first can be quite alarming," Mrs. O'Brien asked.

"I've never birthed a live animal before," responded Beatrix, causing Mrs. O'Brien to laugh heartily.

"Sorry," said Beatrix.

"It's not an animal I'm talking about, love. That's Mr. O'Brien's territory."

Beatrix stood still, excitement overtaking her.

"With you and Mary, ma'am?"

"Beatrix, I've laid awake at night wondering how you, at your tender age and in your circumstances, just plum sewed that boy up …and, under that pressure, too. How did you think to do it?"

"I'm not sure, ma'am, I just did what I thought to be done."

"That's my point, Beatrix. Here you are in front of me, so shy and quiet sometimes I forget you're even here, and yet, you seem to know just what to do when a person needs it."

Francois watched Beatrix's neck and cheeks flush crimson red.

"Yes, ma'am. Thank you."

"Then it's settled. We're paying a visit to Mrs. Thomas in Roehampton. Her baby's coming. Go inside and get your overnight belongings, just in case. You can watch Mary fix up the medicine bag so you know what to collect for a next time."

Mrs. O'Brien turned and went back inside. His chores for the moment completed, Francois followed Beatrix and Mrs. O'Brien into the kitchen. Mrs. O'Brien threw her work apron onto the table, began collecting herbs and rags, and then, just as soon, ran outside calling for William to saddle the horses. Beatrix and Mary met Mrs. O'Brien outside, followed by Francois, as they waited for William to bring the horses around. Mrs. O'Brien whispered to herself as she ran back inside for something she said she'd forgotten. Mary complained that William was taking too long, so she went to help him, and Francois and Beatrix stood alone, both enjoying the unusual warm sun that beat down on them.

"Beatrix, did yeh ever imagine this?" He spoke vaguely, but knew full well she knew what he meant. Beatrix momentarily paused, then spoke with a melancholic tone.

"I used to slice my fingers and hands so, like this, missing my striker just right here and here with my flint shard." Beatrix held out her left hand. Francois noticed tiny scars, a dozen or so, like thin worms on a plate of skin.

"It took me a hundred times, maybe more, to get those first sparks, without drawing blood. But then I did it, and then I did it again, and soon I did it so well, that starting fire was second nature to me. So, I guess, if you really want to know the truth, the answer is yes, I imagined this, the same way I imagined that I would one day create a spark from flint and striker."

"Really? Imagined this, eh?" He gestured his arms outward sweeping them against the backdrop of the farm, barn, and hilly green landscape.

"Well, to be certain," Beatrix replied, "Not this specifically. I couldn't know exactly what form it would take, but yes, I imagined a destiny of some sorts, away from that wretchedness....Didn't you, Francois? Didn't you ever think of the future?"

"A thousand times," he said.

A thousand hers.

"Mrs. O'Brien asked me how I knew to stitch Michael's wound. I didn't want to tell her that I learned by sewing up my own over the years." Beatrix lifted her dress to expose her left shin, halfway covered by brown laced boot. Francois saw a three inch scar, thickly healed, its puckered teeth biting into buttermilk skin.

Beatrix dropped her skirt, which fell loosely to her ankle boot, as she said, "Well, I grant you, this exceeds my hopes."

Mrs. O'Brien came outside again, Mary and William brought them the saddled horses, and Francois watched them ride away, Mrs. O'Brien on one horse, Mary riding the other, with Beatrix' hands clasped around Mary's waist, her braids whipping wind.

Beatrix found her destiny. With all that is good on this earth.

He began to think that he would need to imagine so deeply, so fervently, that he could will his own destiny into existence.

PART TWO

Chapter 8: Finding Solace

Middleton's Bakery Shop, Tuesday May 16th, early morning

One early Tuesday morning before dawn break, Bernadette and her father were up preparing scones, bread, and Yorkshire pudding for the day. Bernadette had spent much of her time during the last month brooding over the morning of the anniversary of her mother's passing. It consumed her daily thoughts and altered her routes. She was terrified to pass anywhere near Hart Street for fear of running into Mrs. Beauchamp. Mr. O'Brien had not kept his promise. She longed to see Beatrix and worried deeply about her safety. She wondered about Michael's recovery. But, her true curiosity lay with the boy—Francois.

The smell of fresh roast beef filled Middleton's Bakery shop. Bernadette poured the roast beef drippings into a heated castor iron skillet and placed it for just a moment into the baker's oven to heat. At the first sign of fat smoking, she took out the skillet, and poured her thick, rested batter over the fat, then placed the skillet back into the baker's oven, savoring the rich golden smell. Among other sweets and savories, her father was to sell roast beef and Yorkshire pudding at the bakery while she sold baked goods at market in Covent Garden. Though Saturday was their most lucrative market day, Tuesdays proved profitable, but this was true of all merchants, and Bernadette thought of the Beauchamp's.

She thought for some time, but, then remembered her pudding, which was golden perfect, so she placed it on the cooling rack, and almost immediately heard horse hooves outside. After the 'Michael morn' as she silently referenced it in her head, she had taken to peering out the hung sash window of the bakery shop every time she heard a horse and cart pass by. But she never saw whom she hoped to see. He had promised her! He had promised to return, but he hadn't kept to it.

Bernadette ran to and held open the marsh-colored curtains with her left hand, peering out the small glass diagonal frames, her nose and her breath imprinting itself, as her fingertips lightly traced zinc came.

She thought her eyes duped her! Could it be? After so many days of waiting for nothing? Bernadette's heart beat excitedly as two horses, one midnight black and the other brown and white-spotted, pulled a horse cart toward the bakery. She immediately recognized the handsome stout man, whose signature cap, worn coat, and rugged smile gave him away. So many weeks she had impatiently waited but now he was here!

Bernadette ran to the bakery front door, swung the heavy oak wood open, and sure enough, Mr. O'Brien's horses, Benny and Matilda, halted to his commands.

"Papa!" Bernadette cried. "Come papa! It's Mr. O'Brien!"

Perplexed, Bernadette's father quickly rubbed his hands against his apron, then took the apron off and placed it on the counter as he hurried to the door to look outside. He did not know a man named Mr. O'Brien, though it was a common enough name in the streets of London these days. He turned the name O'Brien over in his head, coming up blank.

Right outside the shop, James Middleton saw a tall, robust man with a thick head of brownish-red hair tucked under a cap, getting down from a cart pulled by two draught horses. Mr. Middleton stared at the man, who he figured was about half way to meet his maker, give or take, and probably only a few years older than himself, though more wrinkled no doubt due to natural weathering from working day in and day out against the elements.

Mr. O'Brien patted his horses, gesturing to Mr. Middleton, and called, "Maidin Mhaith!"

Bernadette wasn't quite sure if he was talking to his horses or to her and her father as she watched Mr. O'Brien open his bag and feed the horses, who bumped noses impatiently.

"Wait yer turn you big hard chaw, and be a gentleman, would yah?" Mr. O'Brien said to the brown and white spotted horse who pushed the black horse's nose out of the way every time he put something in front of it. He patted their muzzles and loosened their bridles, then straightened his cap and coat, and turned toward the bakery shop.

"Sorry 'bout that. They need nourishment like the rest of us, don't they? Good morn, Sir. Seamus O'Brien's the name." He cheerfully held out his hand for a gentleman's shake, which Mr. Middleton hesitated to take, but then relented.

Mr. Middleton's brows knitted into a deep furrow, and he stammered before saying, "Mr. Middleton...uh, call me James."

"Aye. Grand morn. Tis' pleasure to finally meet yah, Sir." Mr. O'Brien tipped his tweed cap, took it off, brushed his hair from his eyes, and gently added, "Bernadette, Beatrix has been askin' for yah, so 'as the lot back at the farm an' all."

"Come inside, Sir...You can tie your horses to that hitching post over there," said Mr. Middleton, still flustered, as he gestured with his hands for this stranger to follow him in.

"No need, they don't go anywhere without me, that's fer sure." Bernadette noticed Mr. O'Brien's missing upper side tooth which didn't affect his handsome smile.

Mr. O'Brien stepped in through the front door of the bakery shop. "Quare delicious it smells in here!"

"Bernadette, why don't you offer Mr. O'Brien a cuppa and scone, and some of that clotted cream and jam?" Mr. Middleton pointed to the bakery goods ready to be sold.

"Mr. O'Brien, if you please." Mr. Middleton pointed to a table, where both men took a seat.

As Bernadette heated the tea kettle, her hands shook and her head raced. For as many times as she had hoped for Mr. O'Brien's visit, she had never thought about what she might actually say to him or him to her father. Her father's current confusion unsettled her, but she felt it was warranted, since she had not spoken to him about anyone involved or anything to do with the 'Michael morn.'

Bernadette brought refreshments and tea to the table, politely asking Mr. O'Brien if he would like some cream and sugar.

"'Aye, lass, all the fixin's."

Bernadette placed the sugar bowl and a cream holder conveniently next to Mr. O'Brien's left.

"Thanks for receivin' me in such grand manner. I 'spose yer wonderin' bout the happenin's back at the farm? Now it's all good, but it took some handlin', I tell with all honesty."

Mr. O'Brien took a giant bite of the scone in front of him, then sipped his hot tea. "Very lovely, very, very lovely. Yer daughter's surely learned her hospitable manners and kind ways from you, Mr. Middleton."

Bernadette blushed as she filled Mr. O'Brien's plate with another fresh scone since he had eaten most of his first one. In his same confused state, Mr. Middleton paused, cleared his throat, and shifted his eyes between Mr. O'Brien and Bernadette. Bernadette looked away quickly.

"May I ask you, Sir, what is behind the meaning of your visit? I'm afraid I've not had the good fortune of your acquaintance though it seems my daughter is well acquainted with you, and you with her. I do not like this familiarity," Mr. Middleton's uncharacteristic anger erupted.

"Aye, Sir, vexed, yah are. Think I understand....Bernadette, yah haven't told your da, haven't yah?"

Bernadette nodded, her head down toward the ground.

"Sir, my apologies. I thought she'd 'ave told yah...at least something...yah know nothin' at all?"

"Perhaps, Sir, you care to enlighten me, as my daughter has failed to do?"

Bernadette tried to explain, but Mr. Middleton held up his hand to her, his stern eyes slanted sharply at Mr. O'Brien, and she knew silence was her best remedy.

"Well then, I've come to yah about the gravest matter. A great stink, it is! I suppose I ask yah to remain calm as I unfold a most strange event that occurred two fortnights ago, more or less. It involves yer..."

Mr. Middleton stood up quickly, knocking the table and spilling tea.

"Sir! I do not like the sound of this!"

"Father, sit down, please...let me explain...it's not what you think...."

"What I think? I don't know what to think! What should I think?"

Mr. O'Brien stood up immediately, interjecting, "Houl yer horses, man! Give me a chance...let me explain...she's as safe and sound as ever yah knew her, Mr. Middleton. It's not about yer daughter so much as it is about her bravery. She helped a matter, 'tis all. Tis' a thing to be proud of, if yah just let me finish...."

Then, Mr. O'Brien took a breath, and calmly said, "Bernadette, I'm a father, meself, and it's best to be upfront with yer da' when evretins up in a bollox."

"Yes, Sir. I should have...."

Mr. Middleton stared into Mr. O'Brien's eyes before slowly sitting down, taking repeated deep breaths and intermittent sighs to calm himself. He placed his hands behind his head, fixed his stare on the knotted wood floor, and muttered, "Not like me to rile up."

"It only involves yer daughter in the most benevolent way, Sir. She's a saint, yer daughter, and her quick wit helped save a young boy—aye, two young boys-—from the grim reaper himself."

Mr. Middleton's emotions—half defused, half confused— teetered pell-mell against his logic, which was thrown off course.

"I apologize for my display. I admit, I'm totally confounded by all this, and jumped to a terrible conclusion. It's not like me to over-react...to assume such improprieties where Bernadette is concerned, but she's been acting strange lately. She's my daughter and I think you understand perfectly what I mean but I'll speak now for clarity sake. I'm raising a proper English lady, who does not leave my home or converse with boys and men unchaperoned, without my approval. Clearly you have some knowledge I don't possess, and it doesn't suit me well."

"Father, if I may...."

"You may not! Let the man speak," Mr. Middleton rebuffed.

Mr. O'Brien took another sip of tea and cleared his throat.

"Like I was sayin, about a month prior, I was deliverin' florals and farm goods an such to regular customers, as I do every Saturday, break a' dawn. Passin' by the floral shop over on Hart Street—I'd delivered flowers there earlier that morn, but was loopin' round again—and that's when I sees a bunch of children leggin it...."

"See who, Mr. O'Brien?"

"Well, Beatrix, the flower shop girl, Bernadette, an' another boy, whose name I come to find out is Francois…they was all holdin' up another boy and draggin' em down my direction. That'd be Michael, yah see…."

"Francois?" Mr. Middleton's curiosity heightened at mention of the boy's name, and he turned sharply to his daughter, who looked into her father's eyes and the two shared something that would be missed on the world around them—certainly on Mr. O'Brien—but their locked gaze told each other they understood.

"Aye, that's the boy's name—the younger one. Like I said, they was leggin it, strugglin' to carry another boy, Michael, who'd been half-banjaxed; oh, he took a real hidin' by their master's belt, he did. Course, yer lovely daughter was helpin 'em escape their miserable lot, carryin' Michael along-side Beatrix…." Mr. O'Brien paused a moment.

He looked kindly at her, and gently spoke, "Bernadette, yah earned yer wings for helpin' these two unfortunates. Michael'd been hit hard just about every inch of em, and draggin' 'em down the street, was what they did. Could barely make their way, heavy as a sack he was. An' when I checked in on this odd thing I see happenin', next thing I know, I see the boy's bleedin, barely conscious to this world, and it was the right and only thing to do, help this boy. He'd 'a died, if not. He's back at me farm—over in Fulham, with me wife an' children, and Beatrix and Francois."

"Beatrix?" Mr. Middleton asked. "You mean your friend, Beatrix?"

"Yes, papa, Beatrix."

"Why, I recently crossed paths with Mr. Beauchamp off King Street and he carried on like a madman that I might know where Beatrix might be—said she'd run away! He accused me of hiding something. I told him I hadn't seen her around the bakery shop in weeks, but that I would inquire with you. He was persistent! Of course, by the time I arrived home, my mind was somewhere else entirely, and I forgot to mention it."

"When did this happen, father?"

"Right after I recovered from bed rest. Now that I gather, it's around the same time you speak of Mr. O'Brien—about two fortnights ago."

"Oh father! You never mentioned...."

"I don't know how it slipped my mind...I'm sorry, Bernadette."

"You know 'em, then? The Beauchamp's? Oh, he's bad, but can't hold a candle to that savage, aye she is! Never cared for Beatrix, never showed an inch of kindness. Beatrix's better off now, and it'll stay that way," Mr. O'Brien grumbled.

"So you know her then? Beatrix?" Mr. Middleton asked.

"Now I do, but not then I didn't, not well, mind yah. Just from me deliverin' all these years. She was always such a meek one, but a mighty fine lass."

"Mr. O'Brien, you are aware that the Beauchamp's are looking for her—at least they were?" Mr. Middleton asked.

"Aye, sure of it."

"Father, she can't go back! Mrs. Beauchamp will beat her!"

"What about these boys of whom you speak? This Francois, and the other one, Michael?"

"Aye. From what I've gathered, they're runaways from Saint Mark's—tis an orphan home—an' they've run from the hands of a brute who answers to the name of Sledgeham. And, let me tell yah somethin', this boy Michael? Beaten to a pulp, not the first time neither. A common occurrence, these two boys had at this devil's claw. Oh, Michael, hammered he was, such a bad dose of it, he's only now recoverin'. Thank God, above, for me wife, who knows the healin ways."

Mr. O'Brien sighed heavily, then, reached for his second scone and smothered it with freshly clotted cream. Mr. Middleton sat ardent and dumbfounded by Mr. O'Brien's disclosure, and turned to Bernadette.

"Bernadette, what is the meaning of this? Is this true?"

"Father, I....I...." Bernadette stammered. "I didn't want to risk you getting involved. You're all I have!" Bernadette began to cry.

Mr. O'Brien continued, "Not a truer word, though nasty 'tis. Yah can't make a silk purse out of a sow's ears, now can yah? But the Mrs. and me, we're tryin', we are. And, that's why I've come. Two reasons, really. The first is, truth of it, I need another man's help, Sir, to sort this mess out. The divil o' one, he's twisted! I know I'm a stranger. I know yah don't want no trouble at yer doorstep, no scandal on yer daughter, but I ask man to man, for help. God as witness, those boys can't go back. They're safe with Mrs. O'Brien and me kin."

"And Beatrix?" Mr. Middleton interrupted.

"Aye, safe as well. I ask for yer mercy, not to tell her whereabouts. The wife says she has the gift of healin', though the

~ 111 ~

girl doesn't know it yet, on account she's never been treated as nothin' but a stray dog. Now, the second reason's more personal...The other boy, Francois? He's been askin' daily 'bout me promise to get Bernadette to the farm to visit. He says she deserves that much fer what she did. Promise is an honor's debt, I s'pose."

Within Mr. O'Brien's second request, again, Mr. Middleton heard the boy's name that silently stung his chest. He knew Mrs. Beauchamp well enough to draw his own conclusions about Beatrix's safety, but what was this talk about runaways and cruel masters? And what of this coincidence of the child's name? Francois!

"Who is this boy...Francois?"

"François? A young lad, no more than nine, though small wisp of a thing, he is. He's overly preoccupied with yer daughter, worried that Mrs. Beauchamp has found 'er out. He's afraid Bernadette will buckle under pressure, and lead Mrs. Beauchamp to the farm. Strange thoughts for a young lad, eh? They can't go back, Mr. Middleton. That monster Sledgeham, he'd damage these boys beyond repair if given another chance, and I can't allow for this. There's my conundrum."

Mr. Middleton shook his head, ran his hands through his thick hair, raised himself up from the table, and paced to the sink. He stood there, staring at the wall for what felt to Bernadette like eternity, then, washed his hands in a basin, dried them on his apron, which he slipped on, and began slicing his juicy roast against the grain. He plated three thick marbled cuts next to three

Yorkshire pudding squares, and served each plate, one by one, then sat down.

"Mr. O'Brien, whatever goodness my daughter bestowed, I'm sure of it and more. She's her mother's daughter. Now, let's eat. I can't make plans on an empty stomach."

"Go raibh míle maith agat!" Mr. O'Brien said as he sunk what was left of his teeth into tender meat.

"One more thing, Mr. O'Brien."

"Grand, aye, two, three, whatever...."

"You have my word. I shall keep this conversation between us, but I implore you to remember that no harm can or shall come to my daughter. And, before I help these boys, I must see this all for myself. I must come—with Bernadette—to your farm. I shall write to my sister at once. If you can retrieve us, Bernadette and I shall be ready three weeks from today. No sooner than that I'm afraid, and, all contingent upon my sister's willingness to run the bakery while we're away."

"Consider it done, then, sister permittin,'" agreed Mr. O'Brien, "Consider it done."

While Mr. Middleton and Mr. O'Brien solidified plans for their pending trip to O'Brien's farm, Bernadette found her father's quill, ink jar, and a small piece of used parchment from his work desk upstairs. Her father had some written book-keeping notes on one side, but she could tell it was from long ago. She flipped the parchment over to its usable side, knowing better than to waste valuable ink and paper. She whispered her thoughts out loud but did not write them down.

Dear Beatrix, I've longed to see you these past weeks. I haven't seen Mrs. Beauchamp anywhere, but feel her constant presence at every turn. I hope you never return to her, but then I think about never seeing you again, and can't bear it.

Bernadette's thoughts turned to Francois, and her words, like winged maple seeds, spun lightly from her lips. *Francois, who are you?* Her confusion played tricks on her, and thankful she had not wasted a good piece of stationary yet, she whispered no more, but opened the ink jar, dipped her quill, and began to write in tiny cursive against mottled fibrous paper, the ink's blue blood tattooing tanned skin.

Dear Beatrix, It seems I shall see you in a few weeks! You have my support, and father's, too. With luck, we'll help settle your uncertain circumstances. Yours, Bernadette

After drying, she carefully tri-folded the paper, lit a match to candle, dropped melted beeswax on the folded edge, and pressed her mother's letter sealer deeply, kissing ℬ into hot wax. She went downstairs again, and handed the letter to Mr. O'Brien, politely requesting he deliver it to Beatrix. Mr. O'Brien nodded. Plans were underway.

That night, while father tucked her into bed, Bernadette repeated the Lord's Prayer with her head already nestled on her pillow, as Mr. Middleton pulled her blanket cover to her chin, where she liked it. He was about to leave his daughter, when she abruptly spoke.

"Father?"

"What is it?"

"I'm wondering about something...about the boy...."

"Francois, you mean? Yes, that is a curious coincidence. It's gotten under my skin as well. Been pondering, all day, in fact."

"Do you think it is a coincidence, father? Or maybe something more? Maybe a sign of some sort?"

"A sign from the boy, Bernadette? Or someone else?"

"Maybe both? Maybe Francois is trying to tell me something. Or, maybe she is—mama, I mean."

"Bernadette," Mr. Middleton cleared his throat, desiring to say so much but unable to find a beginning point.

"Father, what is it?" Bernadette desperately stared at him.

"Bernadette, I've wanted to tell you something for a very long time. About your mother," he cleared his throat again, "She...before she...well, passed to heaven...she spoke to me...she told me she knew it was her time...that you would be fine...that you...." Mr. Middleton stopped. His composure weakened as his wet eyes stared past her to a distant memory.

"It's time we talk about her, father, after all this silence. I think she sent him to us. It's her way of telling us we must talk of her. Father, I didn't mention this in front of Mr. O'Brien, but this all happened on the anniversary marking mother's death. That's the morning Francois showed up. How can that not be a sign? He came to me—to us—for a reason, father. She sent Francois to remind us."

Mr. Middleton didn't have the heart to tell his daughter that Francois was but a mere coincidence in a befogged and bizarre turn of events. Though, he did register how odd the timing was. To hear such an uncommon name—a French name—that meant so much to him and his daughter, and on the anniversary of his beloved wife's death?

Mr. Middleton cleared his throat, finding it difficult to speak, but coincidence or not, he knew his daughter was right.

"She told me you were a survivor, Bernadette. When she said it, I knew she wasn't going to get better. She said…she said that she would never stop watching over you, she would be your angel, and you would feel her walk with you. But, it was me she worried about. She joked and said she couldn't be in two places at once."

Bernadette had longed to ask her father about her mother's last words so many times, but sorrow stopped her. Now, her unbearable pain—the pain of missing—choked her silent. She closed her eyes, and tears trickled down each side of her face, pooling onto her pillow like two rivers meeting an ocean of grief.

Her father leaned over her, whispering, "It will be alright. We will both survive."

Mr. Middleton only left Bernadette's bedside when he thought she was asleep. She was not asleep, though her eyes closed; she tried to remember her mother's touch, what it felt like on her cheek, her skin. She could not distinctly recall, though she held onto what she could, and brushed her own hand against her arm. But the feeling didn't compare, and the picture was hazy and fading still further. She could see her, and yet she could not see her. *Sometimes I cannot feel you walk with me, mama. Sometimes I forget you.* With these thoughts, Bernadette finally slumbered, deeply locked in her sad dreams.

Chapter 9: Finding Michael Dead or Alive

Middleton's Bakery Shop and Covent Garden, Saturday May 20th

Four days passed since Mr. O'Brien's visit, and Bernadette once again prepared herself for market day. She placed her mother's bonnet onto her head and tied the crimson ribbons into a bow around her chin. Then she packed her two baskets of freshly baked goods, gathering her warm, delicious hot-crossed buns, current scones, and delicately positioned her clotted cream jar at the center of these arrangements.

"I'll have more for you later, if you run out again like last Saturday. I'll walk them over around noon, when the busy rush is upon you," said Mr. Middleton.

Bernadette headed East onto Maiden Lane's cobblestone street, eventually turning left on Henrietta toward open market. Since the 'Michael morn' she didn't dare venture two blocks North, South, East, or West of Hart Street where the Beauchamp's floral shop resided. Beatrix had commonly attended open market for many years, so naturally, Bernadette spent the last month worrying she might run into Mrs. Beauchamp in Beatrix's place. Luckily that hadn't happened, and Bernadette calmed her nerves. Still, at all costs, she avoided any encounters with the Beauchamp's.

As she sold today, Bernadette reflected how there was a time she enjoyed the sights, sounds, and smells of open market, holding her mother's skirt tightly as they passed street peddlers selling ointments that promised to sprout hair growth on the bald, make ingrown toenails disappear, shorten tall people and lengthen short people. She loved watching the merchants display colorful fabrics and European tapestries. But it was the smells of freshly baked goods wafting together that intoxicated Bernadette and drew in crowds. It was her mother's French pastries that the people of London wanted.

Since her mother's death, the joys of Covent marketplace slipped away into a faded memory of her mother's petticoat gently guiding little Bernadette through the market to buy fresh produce and vegetables for Mrs. Middleton's stews, and to sell their own baked goods. The sounds, colors, and smells diminished by the dulling of Bernadette's heart. But sell she did, and now, as she looked down into her basket, she realized that she had no more scones, and only a few other treats left. It was a lucrative morning and she wasn't able to wait for her father's noon hour arrival. Her heavy money pouch clinked and sagged against her skirt. She would walk home, refill the baskets, then return to sell some more.

Her thoughts turned again to her mother, selling, selling, selling, just as she sold now. Market days did this to her, helped her remember with clarity and purpose what so frightfully slipped her mind most other days.

On this day, it was her mother's red bakery smock and brown dress that she remembered; and, her firm grip of basket handle that

Bernadette now held onto so dearly—it was the closest she would come to holding hands with her mother. She heard her voice. *'Scones for zee Gentlemen and ladies, baked fresh.'* But the memory left as quickly as it came, so Bernadette started for home.

Bernadette passed by the market's central building in the square. Attached to the building's pillar, a poster bearing a sketch of a boy caught her eye. There was something familiar about that sketch, pulling her toward it, and as she came closer, Bernadette could not believe the sight. It was a sketch of Michael! Not in perfect likeness, but close enough for her to make out. Of course, when she last saw Michael, he was barely conscious, bloody, and bruised. Perhaps this sketch was more to his true appearance had she met him on better terms.

Surely some other person—all it took was one—would also recognize him, and such recognition could have terrible outcomes for Michael, Francois, and everyone involved, her father included. She read the words underneath Michael's sketch:

WANTED for: KIDNAPPING AND ASSAULT
Michael, orphan boy, age twelve, WANTED for assault and stabbing of Sir Wickem Sledgeham, Director, Saint Mark's Orphanage. WANTED for kidnapping of orphan boy, Francois, age 9. Armed and Dangerous. 2£ reward upon return to London authority.

Almost asphyxiating from fear, she reached to tear the poster down, but stopped herself, realizing how suspicious it would look. She glanced around her, and spotted another poster of Michael on yet another pillar a few feet away from this one. She dizzied, the poster blurred, and she grasped for inner strength, calling upon her mother's last words, and one in particular. Survivor. *To survive.* The action itself flayed against her raw nerves, freshly opened, and tested her resolve, just as it mocked her mother's wish for her.

She ran through the cobblestone streets, her basket hitting against her money purse, clotted cream container falling, cracking against sidewalk.

To calm herself, she began to rethink and revise the topsy-turvy words on the poster:

WANTED for: KIDNAPPING AND ASSAULT
Master Wickem Sledgeham, WANTED for assault and battery of orphans at Saint Mark's Prison for Boys. WANTED for stealing them from a life of human decency! Deranged and dangerous. 1000£ reward, dead or alive.

As her feet pounded uneven stones, ankles twisting, she ran haphazardly, the wind carrying her like a tousled leaf. She held onto one threadbare thought, *No fairness in this life.*

In her hurried state, and unconscious to her surroundings, she sprinted directly toward the lion's lair she had avoided these last few weeks, clunk chunk, right into the backside of a podgy dour woman surrounded by flowers.

Mrs. Beauchamp turned around immediately, pecking her beak forward, as her beady black eyes tore at Bernadette's face.

"Yeh rude gypsie! How dare, bang-thrash me behind? Nearly knock me over? Don't jus' stand there! Look at me, ragamuffin...."

"I...um...um...I...sorry, so sorry...."

Bernadette pulled her mother's weathered satin bonnet toward her forehead, and cast her eyes downward, but not fast enough.

"Wait...is that you, girl? The baker's daughter? What's 'is name, Middleton, eh? Yeah, married to that Frenchie! She died, didn't she? I think I heard that in passin', some time ago. Well, that must have been a shock, but by now I'm sure yeh're past it. I've been meanin' to pay a visit, I 'ave. An', I think yeh know what it's about, don't yeh?" Mrs. Beauchamp's magnified cockney slang struck the girl's head as she choked back her tears.

"My father, he's expecting me, I can't...."

"Don't yeh dare! Such gumption, she's got? Knocks me over, and then don't got the decency to answer me questions? Not that I expect nothin' different from French stock!"

"I..I...." Bernadette stammered as Mrs. Beauchamp's claw fists tethered to Bernadette's shoulders, and she felt the force of fingernails pressing into her, just enough to imprint.

"What's the matter? Cat got yeh tongue? Hidin' somethin' from me? I think yeh are, girl, and it's an offense!" Her sable eyes flattened Bernadette, but Bernadette held fast.

"Now, where's she, eh? Where's Beatrix? I'll serve yeh head on a platter to the law if yeh don't fess up! Answer me now, or I'll scream for a watchman this minute!" Mrs. Beauchamp's fierce voice quivered loudly enough to garner attention from others.

Just then, someone across the street began yelling, "Bernadette! Take your hands off her immediately!" Her father's voice!

Bernadette looked to her left and saw him running swiftly toward her. Mrs. Beauchamp removed her talons from the girl-mouse.

"Mrs. Beauchamp!" Mr. Middleton's steel cut eyes stared down at the withered woman, as Bernadette took refuge in his embrace. *I survived, just like you said I would, mama,* she thought, shaking.

"Let's go home, Bernadette," Mr. Middleton said softly, "But first!" He leaned closer to Mrs. Beauchamp, and in a flat low voice, he said, "Gentleman that I am, I shall say this discretely. Just once, so you had better listen well. You will never lay a hand onto my daughter again. You come to me with any questions you might have, but you will not bother Bernadette with your personal affairs! Now we are understood!"

"I'll have yeh know she's withholdin' information about my...about Beatrix's whereabouts. Information that's my right, it is! Information that'll bring that ill-bred scrubber back to me, where she belongs!"

"I dare say, that's an extreme and imprecise charge against Bernadette. Your accusations are most uncouth and boorish, and I'll have you arrested for slander if you so much as speak such lies again! Good day, Mrs. Beauchamp."

Mr. Middleton took Bernadette's hand and swept her away down the streets, finally returning to Middleton's Bakery Shop where he locked the door behind them, shut the window curtains, and placed a sign in the window shop that read, "Closed."

Bernadette and her father sat at the wooden table with three chairs, as Bernadette had a good cry, then collected herself.

~ 123 ~

"Father, I was running home…that's how I ran into Mrs. Beauchamp…literally barreled into her. I saw a sketch of Michael on a wanted poster pinned to a market hall pillar! There were at least two of them, and most likely many more. And they say horrible things! We need to warn Mr. O'Brien immediately and…."

"What did the posters say, Bernadette?"

"That Michael was wanted for kidnapping Francois, that he stabbed Sledgeham! When Mrs. Beauchamp saw me, she…I hate to admit…but…she…she told the truth! I do know where Beatrix is!"

"Bah, the truth," Mr. Middleton scoffed under his breath, "Who's truth, Bernadette? The truth…the truth…."

Mr. Middleton held his daughter's hand across the wooden table, reflecting on the emptiness of the third chair to his right— how the light in the room, the aura of the bakery shop, and everything about their lives was brighter when his wife was alive, when Bernadette's mother was a glowing flame, a blanket of warmth.

He looked at his admirable daughter, a spitting image of her mother, though he had not yet been able to say this. Her blonde curls fell forth from her mother's bonnet, cascading ringlets of golden light softening her already tame features.

"Beatrix has been a good friend to you through this past year. This I know."

"She has comforted me, father."

"Well, then, a friend we shall both be to Beatrix in her dark hour. Bernadette, bring me my quill and ink, and a sheet of stationary."

Mr. Middleton cleared his voice, "your mother's stationary, with the robin eggs. And make it two sheets. Please."

Bernadette ran upstairs to her mother's inlaid mahogany keepsake chest by the foot of her father's bed. She knelt before it, rubbing her hands along the walnut-wooden trim. After her mother's death, she and her father had stopped uttering her mother's name, had been unable to address her mother's belongings as anything other than, "the hat, the scarf, the kettle pot...the stationary," as if these were just random items left in a corner or on a shelf or by the bed to find and use at their discretion, without a history or memory or person attached.

For Bernadette and James Middleton, any reference to her mother, to his wife, to all that had been stolen from them, unleashed a wave of sadness and despair, guilt and anger. The pain that gnawed at their hearts was too weighted a grief, and perhaps if they didn't speak about the loss, they might surpass the wave coming their way, threatening to sink them both for good.

Opening her mother's chest, she welcomed the memories as she searched inside for her mother's stationary—*her* tan parchment paper with robins in nests etched onto the sides. She found it, gently undid the moss-colored ribbon holding the sheets together. She pulled two pieces from the bundle, retied the ribbon, carefully replaced it, and went to shut the chest.

But something silver caught her eye. Her mother's chain with locket glistened. How she missed playing with this locket that her mother had worn every day!

Bernadette touched the silver, then picked up the locket, and it felt cold, in total contrast to the warm heat it once radiated when it lay around her mother's neck. She opened the locket, and found on one side, a tiny black and white drawing of herself as a toddler, her curly locks shading her face. On the other side, a sketch of another child—a baby boy born, baptized, and buried with the name Francois.

Bernadette placed the silver chain around her neck and closed the chest. She retrieved her father's writing materials from his desk, and brought them, along with her mother's parchment paper, to him. As he looked up to thank her, Mr. Middleton noticed the pendent dangling, falling much lower than it did on his wife. He smiled warmly at Bernadette.

"It's time, isn't it? I'm glad you found it."

Bernadette grasped the necklace, her hand sliding down the chain until it held the locket, warm again.

Mr. Middleton took out his ink quill, and began his first letter.

Dear Patricia,

I hope this greeting finds you, Thomas Sr. and Jr. and Bess, well. B and I continue along as well as can be expected. The bakery is in top form, in spite. We put our labor into it, which helps, I think. I penned a brief letter to you four days ago, which you may have received. I write again, this time more urgently, and in greater depth, with the utmost desire for your assistance and discretion. I cannot say more than this for now except to say that new events have evolved that require expediency on my part. As aforementioned, my request requires at least a fortnight away from the bakery—possibly longer. I respectfully ask that you and Bess come as soon as possible to manage bakery affairs during Bernadette's and my travel away from London. Please explain to Thomas Sr. that I will cover your travel expenses, and that you shall keep all profits, after the bakery's expenses are paid each month. I do realize how bizarre my request sounds, but there is no one closer to me than you, and no one I can trust as deeply. I will wait for your immediate response, as time is of essence.

   Your loving brother,
   James

Mr. Middleton wax-sealed the letter, addressing the envelope to *Mrs. Patricia Whitman, 22 Queen Elizabeth's Walk, Stoke Newington, London.* He dipped his quill in fresh ink, and began his second letter.

   Mr. O'Brien,

   B found wanted posters of M today accusing him of kidnap and assault. To my dismay, Mrs. B confronted her, suspects her involvement, even went as far to challenge her knowledge of a certain someone's whereabouts. Travel arrangements hinge on my private matters, which shall resolve within the next few days. Plan to retrieve B and me in a fortnight, a week earlier than we originally planned.

   James Middleton

Upon addressing the second envelope, Mr. Middleton retrieved his hat and coat on the coat rack by the door, told Bernadette he would be home by half past five, and left to secure a private mail carrier to ensure prompt delivery of the letters at all cost. Bernadette wished she had time to add her own personal note, but her father's haste didn't allow for it. She looked down upon her chest, opened her mother's locket again, and stared at the drawing of the newborn boy, her brother, as she cradled him in her hand, then, shut the locket once more.

Chapter 10: Finding the Lockbox

O'Brien's Farm, Monday May 29th

Though it seemed like a lifetime ago, only several weeks had passed since Michael, Francois, and Beatrix arrived at the farm to begin their new life. They had settled well into daily routines, but they carried the weight of their own worries privately, wherever they went. When Mr. O'Brien first received Mr. Middleton's letter he waivered, debating if he should share the contents, but he decided he must for safety-sake. He called a meeting, and gravely warned that they must all be cautious and remain hidden from outsiders. The news added an oppressive layer to their existing burdens, and each expressed concern over more news Mr. Middleton might bring.

"Keep it quiet round here," Mr. O'Brien demanded, "No more leavin' the farm. Beatrix. People talk."

Mrs. O'Brien's line of work brought the occasional visitor to their farm, sometimes at strange hours in the night, but when this happened, Francois, Michael, and Beatrix made themselves invisible. With years of practice, such discretion was an easy task for them. Mostly, the farm was quiet—a tiny haven tucked away from the madness of the world outside. Francois even half-believed

Mr. and Mrs. O'Brien's comforting words that they'd be alright in the end, but he couldn't help but wonder, *the end of what?*

Mr. Middleton's letter awakened their sleeping demons— Beatrix became sullen and introverted, Francois turned pensive and edgy, but Michael remained unyielding and poker-faced, defying fear, almost challenging it. He spoke to Francois only when it was imperative for him to do so, but in this matter, it had never been different.

As for Beatrix, she was bound at the moment to the confines of the farm, and could no longer accompany Mrs. O'Brien and Mary on their outings, but took solace in hiding herself away, and buried herself in her tasks, still shadowing, still learning the healing arts. She absorbed Mrs. O'Brien's knowledge of the natural world like a sea sponge and awakened to the possibility of how much more there was to know.

Francois and Michael set up a good home for themselves in the barn hayloft, and Francois spent his days absorbed in farm labor, never tiring of it, completing any task willingly, especially if it had anything at all to do with caring for the animals. Jingles stuck to him like maple sap to a tree, following his every move. And, William took pleasure in Francois' enthusiasm, since he disliked farm work but couldn't shake the guilt he felt about leaving his father to run the farm on his own come autumn. With Francois here, he felt calmer about his pending leave.

Michael worked hard, as well, and Mr. O'Brien took note of his strength. Michael kept a protective eye on Francois, and became possessed with Beatrix's charms, but he showed little affection to the O'Brien's regardless of their kindness.

He held his own, but his heart wasn't in it, like Francois. By now, he had gained his energy back, and Mr. O'Brien and William remarked to each other time and again that Michael's horsepower was that of two men.

"When one man's down, the other gets up fer 'em!" Mr. O'Brien joked, as Michael continued to prove his aptitude, his impenetrability to pain, exhaustion, or hunger.

Now that Michael's strength had returned in full, Francois knew his wheels were turning. It's what they did when he was a hundred percent. *Michael's still thinkin' 'bout the letter, he is! Goin' back for a thing that doesn't exist! This farm exists! The O'Brien's exist! Don't he realize by now that I'm not leavin'?*

When the boys found themselves alone, Francois asked Michael incessant questions, hoping desperately to find out his plans, but Michael always responded with the same furtive nonchalance. Ruffling Francois' hair, Michael would say some version of, "That's a stupid question. Look at us, eatin' three square meals a day and livin' like princes. But just don't get too settled. For now, it'll do."

These responses kept Francois in an agitated state, but also deflected the depth of Michael's ferocious appetite for retribution.

Hayloft, 9:00 pm

Michael turned over on his straw mattress and looked up at the rafters overpopulated with bird's nests. His thoughts ruminated on the night of his last beating. As the owls hooted and nocturnal animals sounded their calls, he played out the scene. In his mind, he was far away from this peaceful place, back in Saint Mark's Orphanage, inside Sledgeham's sleeping quarters, kneeling on the floorboards.

He remembered every acute detail. That fateful night had begun like so many other nights, when the whole orphanage slept and Master Sledgeham lay in a drunken stupor slobbering down his soiled shirt. So many years, so many nights, he methodically searched nooks and crannies of each room, leaving no prints or proof he'd been there. Search after search spent in vain—of kitchen cupboards, canisters, book-shelves, chairs, sofas, beds, inside and outside the walls of this fortress—and for what? Even he began to doubt the existence of the parchment letter, began to see it as Sledgeham's cruel joke, intended as much for him as for Francois. Sledgeham's wild goose chase.

On this particular night, Master Sledgeham had taken to the bottle much earlier in the evening. He remembered watching him, listening carefully to the intervals between his belligerent ranting.

He prided himself on his ability to predict Sledgeham's drunken patterns and slovenly behavior: First phase, the mad gibberish, which sometimes lasted fifteen minutes or more; second phase, the interminable, raging rants; third phase, destruction—plates thrown, books hurled, tables overturned; forth phase, the unbearable weighted silence; fifth phase, intoxicated slumber.

He remembered that dreadful feeling of waiting out the fourth phase. It took so long, that waiting weightedness.

Twice before that fated night, he'd ventured into the master's room on two separate occasions, managing both times to escape by the skin of his teeth and empty-handed. But not that fated night! After all these years of slinking around thief-in-the-night, fate intervened earlier in the day, and in that moment, changed everything.

He was late coming downstairs for lunch that day. The other boys had already begun to eat their bread and watery soup without him, which was a stupid thing for him to let happen, since they'd finish his portion, and he'd go hungry for the rest of the day.

Slinking out of his dormitory, he noticed Sledgeham's door ajar—this had never happened before!—and in a matter of seconds, the future reworked itself for him and Francois. He saw Sledgeham sunken on all fours, burrowing on his floor with a lockbox in his hands. But Sledgeham must have heard him, or some noise, because he startled, and hastily stuck the lockbox back into the floor boards. He secretly watched it all!

Sledgeham sprung up quickly to his door, slammed it abrasively, and slurred, "Whad'jeh see? Yeh'll get 'it feh spyin', I'll box yeh ears!"

~ 133 ~

He responded, "No, Sir. Didn't see nothin'," as he flew double time down the stairs, blood pounding in his ears with the mere thought of his future punishment.

All day he wondered what was in that lockbox.

There he was again, watching himself wait patiently for confirmation of Sledgeham's fifth phase, which finally happened. As the master's body lay strewn across the sofa, his face bent sideways, his contorted mouth drooling foul spit, he crept upstairs, careful not to step on certain stair floor boards.

He remembered the sound of creaking door as he slowly stepped into Master Sledgeham's quarters, and how he gagged at the smell of Sledgeham everywhere. He stared at the rug rumpled in a curled heap by Sledgeham's bedpost, then shifted his gaze to the area of floor that the rug had once covered, his eyes fixed on some discolored wooden beams that didn't match the rest. The seams surrounding these wooden beams had slightly larger gaps between each floor piece.

He bent down, touching the wood, moving his fingers over each edge, and seeing that these wood slats weren't nailed together, he applied pressure to the corner of one such piece, and up shot a slat, which he jiggled loose, picked up, and laid next to him. He removed the next slat as well.

To his surprise, below the floor boards was a makeshift secret compartment containing loose shillings, some ivory trinkets, three wallets, and a few other items, presumably stolen. He remembered thinking he should look inside the wallets for money, but decided to stay focused on his true object of desire: the wooden lockbox that Sledgeham had held earlier—rectangular, six inches long, three inches wide. Just the right size for a letter.

Michael remembered how his heart beat through his chest as he reached for the box. Seven years of searching! He suspected Francois' history was locked inside, and he finally found it!

And then, out of nowhere, the sudden sound of footsteps thrashing up the stairs, as he threw the lockbox down inside the hole, his hands shaking, as he tried to place the first wooden board back. Then, the thrashing footsteps at the top of the stairs, and the paralysis that struck his fingers as he grabbed for the second wood plank, in desperate panic to replace it. The shuffling footsteps outside dragged closer, as his forehead broke into sweat and his mouth filled with dry-cotton. His shaking hands finally snapped the wooden pieces together, he jumped up, ran and grabbed the rug to roll out, but then threw it back into a heap where he first saw it, and quickly turned around. But, it was too late. Master Sledgeham slumped against the door frame that held his body upright, watching with delight as he scrambled like an animal cornered.

"Find what yeh're lookin for, boy?"

Sledgeham hyena-screeched and sprung across the room, grabbing him as he curled into the smallest ball he could fit himself into, covering his head. He knew to do that, protect his head.

"What yeh got to say for yehself, eh? Pilferin' like a no good cracksman! I owe yeh a box now, don't I? Promise is a promise...."

That was when Sledgeham reached for his side, where he carried that old leather horse switch.

He tensed as Sledgeham's leather switch cracked down hard on his head, shoulder, neck, legs. Ten fast strikes, Michael remembered counting them, until he couldn't stand to count another, and begged that he'd had enough.

"Please, no more, Sir. I thought yeh called me…I…I came to check on yeh, came to see what yeh called for…" he pleaded.

That's when Sledgeham slunk down onto the ground in front of him, drained from his outburst.

"If I ever catch yeh in my quarters again…."

"No Sir, never…I was checkin' on yeh! Heard yeh call me!"

"If I call yeh, yeh knock at the door, and wait till I tell yeh otherwise…."

"Yes, Sir…."

Sledgeham glared fiercely. "Yeh aren't lyin' to me, eh? What'd yeh do in here? Eh? What'd yeh find?" Sledgeham cracked the whip three more times into his side and back, as he buried his face in his hands and leaned down to his knees, his threshold of pain broken.

"Nothin', Sir, on my life! Please stop, I beg!"

Sledgeham grabbed him by the hair, punched his face, dragged him into the shat-room, threw a bucket and brush at him, and slurred orders for him to start scrubbing it clean.

After a long while, he thought he heard Sledgeham's body sinking outside, against the hallway wall. He heard the metal clank of Sledgeham's flask, and Sledgeham's glugging gulps, then silence. Time passed, how much he didn't know, but he finished scrubbing, and laid his heavy, swirling head down on the floor to rest.

Then, after some rest, he tried to push his aching body upright, but couldn't. Instead, he knocked the cleaning bucket over with a clang. Outside the door, he heard noises. He bit his lip, thinking Sledgeham was coming back for another round. Then, strangely, Francois appeared next to him.

"Michael, get up. He's out!" Francois nudged his back, and he tried to push himself upward.

He caught Francois' terrified expression, as it looked past him toward the doorway, then, turned his face around just enough to see Sledgeham standing there by the door, urinating on the floor. He felt the urine spray his back and legs. He remembered Sledgeham telling him to clean up the mess, threatening to hurt Francois if he didn't. He felt a murderous feeling inside and no longer cared whether he lived through the night, but fight Sledgeham to death, he would.

That's when he picked up the brush, stood, and threw it hard and fast against Sledgeham's head. Then, he picked up the bucket with dirty slop water, lunged at Sledgeham, darting forward, pushing the stunned, drunken man over. He grabbed at the key around Sledgeham's neck, ripping with such force, as he ran for his life, calling for Francois to follow.

Francois' voice called out, pulling Michael from his nightmarish memory back into the barn loft where he now laid dripping in sweat. Thankful for the interruption, he watched Francois climb the ladder upwards, as Jingles barked below.

"There yeh are, Michael!"

"Yeh found me," Michael said, wiping sweat from his forehead. Francois knitted his brows, and jabbed Michael's arm playfully.

"Yeh alright? Right now, looks like yeh've seen a ghost!"

"Would yeh stop askin' me that bloody question every time yeh see me? I'm plain sick of it."

Francois changed the subject, knowing there was no talking to Michael when he was in one of his moods. Instead, he lay down on his hay mat next to Michael's and stared up at the rafters exactly where Michael's eyes fixed.

"William says Molly girl's due any day. Said I can watch 'em deliver her, maybe even help!"

"The sheep, is it?"

"Yes."

"That's good. That's really good, Francois."

"Wouldn't yeh like to watch, too? It'll be something else, at least that's what William says."

"Yeah. I'm interested," Michael paused, pointing his finger upward. "There's lots of nests up there now, probably ten, maybe more."

Francois looked up in wonder. In each corner of the barn ceiling beams, hay and twigs mixed with mud to form wiry, round nests. Francois smiled and listened to the owlets and other newcomers to this world.

"Listen, Francois…This ain't permanent. Ain't like I don't like it here. I do. I'm just sayin', it's not…it's not our final place to be. Do yeh understand?"

"Mr. O'Brien likes my work, thinks I've got a knack for it."

"I don't care what Mr. O'Brien likes or don't like." Michael shook his head abruptly. "I don't mean that…look, Francois…at some point we'll need to move on."

"But, I don't want to go…."

"Ain't sayin' now. I'm just sayin' soon. An' when it happens, there can't be any uncertainty on yeh part. We'll have to be quick and quiet, slip out, like it's just another day."

"Go without me, then!"

"I think yeh'll feel differently when the time comes."

"Ain't gonna feel no different, 'cause I like it here, and Mrs. O'Brien likes me, too. She likes us both, Michael."

"Like I said, yeh'll think about it differently when the time comes. For now, just forget about it. Right? Just pretend we ain't never talked."

Francois paused for a long while, and then said, "I'll forget alright, 'cause I ain't leavin'."

Michael didn't want to get into it with Francois, who was changing out here on the farm, he could see that. He used to go along with everything when they were back at Saint Mark's. Here things were different. Francois kept throwing in his own two cents, and Michael wasn't sure he liked it. But he knew the contents in the lockbox would change Francois' mind. It wasn't in his possession, but it would be soon, if his plan worked.

"Go to sleep now, Francois."

Francois shook his head, frustrated.

"Michael, I never want to leave here!" Francois' eyes flooded.

"We've unfinished business, yeh know that."

"Unfinished business? My business is finished!"

"I'm strong enough now, Francois. Stronger than ever with all the food I've been eatin'. I need to get the letter. Give me a chance to finish off what Sledgeham started all those years ago!"

"Michael, stop that crazy talk!"

"A man can't just go unpunished," Michael uttered.

Michael wasn't sure how it would play itself out, but he would return for the lockbox—if it hadn't been moved by now—and he would bring closure. Then, he and Francois would disappear into the night, his only regret knowing that men go unpunished every day, their damage done.

Chapter 11: Finding the Lost

Middleton's Bakery, Sunday June 4th, 4:17 am

O'Brien's Farm, Sunday June 4th, later in the day

The night before Mr. Middleton and Bernadette were to leave
with Mr. O'Brien to his farm, Bernadette could not sleep. She lay in
bed listening to Aunt Patricia's snoring in the room next to hers,
and wondered how her father was faring with his sister. What time
was it? It couldn't be more than a few hours into Sunday, still black
outside except for the moon's illumination.

Bernadette tossed and rolled quietly, trying to find a
comfortable spot. In the dark night, the moon cast a shadow
through diagonal glass frames directly onto her cousin Bess.
Bernadette traced the outline of Bess's profile with her finger in the
air. She felt thirsty and decided to go down-stairs, hoping the
wooden staircase wouldn't creak too loudly to disturb anyone, her
long cotton night-gown shimmying against the steps. She smelled a
burning fire downstairs, and noticed a candle flickering.

Downstairs, sitting at the kitchen table, elbows resting and head
bent low, she found her father, looking like Job, struggling to
understand what had befallen him.

"Father?"

Mr. Middleton startled.

"Don't know how he does it," Mr. Middleton replied, and Bernadette knew he was referring to Aunt Patricia's husband, who somehow had to make peace with his wife's nighttime snores. But she could see that her father tried to make light, not wanting to let her in on his heavy thoughts.

Mr. Middleton had been up some time now, thinking of the curious coincidence of the boy named Francois. He thought of his own son who shared the same name—his son, stolen by death before he could know his father's love. But he also thought of the other Francois. The other stolen boy. How could he forget that boy, who dissipated into darkness without a trace?

"Aunt Bess? Does her snoring keep you awake?" Mr. Middleton asked, but then nodded, knowing it did.

"When I was a very young boy, and shared a room with her, I used to sleep with earmuffs on, even in summer."

Bernadette giggled. Mr. Middleton gestured for Bernadette to take a seat, while he stood up, went to the hearth, and poured her a cup of hot tea from the heated kettle. He scooped a large spoonful of sugar and mixed it in to her cup. Bernadette took a seat next to her father.

"It's hard to imagine you as a boy," Bernadette softly spoke.

"It's not so hard for me to remember."

"Do you think we'll be alright, father, leaving the bakery and...?"

"We'll be fine. Mr. O'Brien said he'll be here before sunrise. If ever there was a night we needed to be sleeping, now would be it," Mr. Middleton sighed.

~ 142 ~

"And if there ever was a night one couldn't sleep, tonight would be the night," Bernadette replied.

"Irony," Mr. Middleton laughed.

The cold air flushed Bernadette's cheeks, and she shivered. Mr. Middleton retrieved his wife's shawl that draped on the coat rack by the door and wrapped her tightly.

"Your mother, she always had a way of calming me. She was the center, wasn't she? I have a tendency to think too much. I think you got that from me, maybe? But, she would always say to me, 'Nothing's ever as big as it seems.'"

Bernadette didn't say a word, but remembered her mother's warm wisdom which used to blanket her with a sense that nothing could ever harm her. *Irony*, she thought to herself.

"Father, I long to see Beatrix, tell her face to face what happened with Mrs. Beauchamp. But, perhaps just as much if not more, I long to see Francois! He's in my head. This whole thing…it's so strange. I can't help but wonder if maman isn't, maybe…." Bernadette held her locket in her hand.

Mr. Middleton took his daughter's hands into his own.

"It's a rum queer coincidence! That is all. Though I admit, the fancy of it. It's shaken me a bit—made me realize it's time to set down my sorrow, and for both of us to return to the land of the living."

Whatever it was that brought Francois to them, he was clear about one thing: Michael and Francois certainly shook him and his daughter out of their solitude, out of their grief. On that fateful morning, these urchins wandered into their broken world—one boy hanging onto life, defying his pitiful lot, the other sharing the namesake of his firstborn child, born still to this world. *Francois.* Was it not also the name of a boy who went missing so long ago? No, it couldn't be.

Father and daughter managed to get some sleep, both laying their heads down on the table where they slept-sat, their arms crossed like pillows underneath, the burning candle melting away, and the fire burning out on its own. Several hours later, they awakened to the sounds of tapping on the window pane and the image of Mr. O'Brien peering inside the bakery shop, his breath fogging up against glass.

"Get up, Bernadette. It's time to go. Mr. O'Brien's here. Get dressed. I'll grab your belongings by the door. Don't forget your blanket," Mr. Middleton said, gently patting his daughter's back as she slumped over on the table top, slowly awakening, disoriented.

Mr. Middleton let Mr. O'Brien inside, boiled up some hot tea, they visited the outside privy, gathered their food basket, blankets, and belongings, placed into the back of the cart, and climbed onto the front seat next to Mr. O'Brien, which he had comfortably padded to lighten the jerky ride. Mr. Middleton covered his daughter with her blanket, wrapped himself in his own, and then turned back and watched his shop recede into the distance, remembering the day he and his newlywed bride, Francoise, purchased the tiny bakery with every Guinea and Napoleon they had inherited and earned.

Bernadette curled up catlike in her father's arms, seemingly complacent and content; but being neither here nor there, just somewhere in between places, this state of nowhere tossed her about. She shut her eyes against the sound of horse whinnying, as the cart lolloped and her thoughts bounced between the 'Michael morn' and her mother.

June gloom tried to feed their anxiety, but Mr. O'Brien's loquacious staccato of words besotted them as he chattered on about his family.

"Gertie, ahh…more knowledgeable than any doctor, 'tis true…and William, a clever lad, mechanical aptitude, he's got! And Mary, ah, she's a whip-smart sunrise after dull dark."

But in the end, even his pie-eyed words weren't enough against gloom's magnetic pull, which led them back to their melancholy.

Finally, after a long ride, Mr. O'Brien pointed upward towards the gentle rolling hill leading to his farmland.

"Grand, we're here. 'Round da bend an up. Spect' yah'll be met with an Irish welcome, indeed."

Spring burst with Cherry Blossom buds and pink-flowered Dogwoods, Stargazer-white and Tulip Pink Magnolias, which lined the dirt road to the farm house and barn, and assorted flowers dotted the ground everywhere like fairies popping out, newly born.

As the horses went from a trot to a gallop toward their home, Bernadette's pulse quickened, as did her father's.

"Aye, there they all are, awaitin' like yer Lugh, the high king and his daughter!"

Mr. Middleton smiled and waved at the group, who returned his greeting with even greater exuberance. Bernadette gasped when she saw Beatrix, but her eyes swept past her to the littlest one as he stood statue still, his sandy blonde hair tousled around his heart-shaped face which slightly grinned. Michael stood next to Francois. He stood watching with almost no expression, though from time to time waved back. She expected that the girl with long red braids standing next to Beatrix was Mary. A tall and slender woman with a fiery billycock of red hair held the girl's hand, and she knew it was Mrs. O'Brien. Benny and Matilda strained against Mr. O'Brien's grasp of their reigns, but kept increasing their pace. And, finally, the distance between Bernadette and the others was close enough to reach out. The girls spoke in unison.

"Beatrix!"

"Bernadette!"

Bernadette's eyes now took in Michael, who stood tall and strong, and was unrecognizable to the boy she last met. His dark black mop of hair was replaced by a mostly cropped cut, distributed unevenly with shaved mounds in places, and the hair around those places was allowed to slightly grow, like patches of mowed grass around a heathen landscape. Michael's broad shoulders and strong chiseled chin seemed in total contrast to the withered boy she remembered.

Her eyes turned next to Mrs. O'Brien, whose hand grasped tightly in Mary's. Just as Mr. O'Brien had said, they were replicas of each other, much like she and her own mother had been.

"Hello! Hello!" called a voice from the northeast of where they congregated.

Everyone turned, and Bernadette knew instantly that the handsome young man running down the hill toward the others must be William. He was followed by a jovial black and white shepherd dog, barking wildly. William kept running until he reached them, and out of breath, he still managed an O'Brien smile. Instead of greeting the new arrivals, Jingles, the dog, leapt into Francois' arms almost knocking him over and everyone laughed heartily at the sight. Benny and Matilda munched their dried apples, as William joined his father's side, removing their bridles, and they wandered free to their feeding trough.

Francois nervously ran to the cart and extended his hand to Bernadette, helping her off.

"I, hello, I'm Francois."

"I know who you are!" Full of nervous energy, Bernadette grabbed Francois and hugged him.

Mr. Middleton was down on the ground now, for a brief moment taking in the faces around him, but his eyes returned to Francois, who looked so curiously familiar. He understood his daughter's draw to this boy, her curiosity with him, beyond the coincidence of his name. Mr. Middleton forced himself to pull away from Francois, and turned to the others.

"It's a great pleasure to meet you all," he said, as he reached for and shook Michael's hand, noting his firm grasp, the healed wounds on his scalp, and the raw scar over his left eye.

Then turning again to Francois, he reached for a gentleman's handshake, and found himself staring into a startlingly familiar face, indistinguishable from his wife's side of the family. *Could it be? How could it be? No. It could not be*, he thought.

"And, Beatrix, look at you. You're not the same girl I remember. It must be the farm air," Mr. Middleton went for her hand, but she innocently hugged his waist, which surprised him, as he patted her back with fatherly affection.

Mr. Middleton turned to Mrs. O'Brien, "Please call me by my Christian name...James. Thank you, Mrs. O'Brien, for your hospitality."

"You must call me Gertie," she said.

"Gertie," Mr. Middleton smiled.

Mr. Middleton turned to the boys again.

"You must be Michael...And you, Francois," Mr. Middleton tried to hide his astonishment over the boy's striking appearance.

"My daughter speaks highly of you," he added, as Jingles barked, which made everyone laugh again, and Mr. Middleton asked Francois, "Is this your dog?"

"'Tis now, unloyal creature! Used to be mine, until Francois stole his heart away," William said jovially.

"And this here's the lad and lass I spoke of, William and Mary, and that there's Jingles, and aye, he's a traitor 'round here lately, but he'll do!" Mr. O'Brien smiled.

~ 148 ~

Francois knelt down to Jingles, took the stick in his mouth, and threw it into the distance.

"Look at him go!" laughed Bernadette.

"Well, we've all made our introductions," Mr. O'Brien said, matter of fact, "Welcome to our farm, James and Bernadette. Now, let's all go inside and warm ourselves with a hearty meal. We've much to discuss. But, first, we eat brown bread and thank God's grace for this happy reunion."

Mr. Middleton nodded, perplexed and befuddled over this boy, Francois. *To Reunions,* he dared let himself think.

Bernadette hugged Beatrix again, who took her hand and wouldn't let go as they stepped narrowly through the front door into the O'Brien home. Francois noticed Michael staring at Beatrix, with a look in his eyes that wished it was him standing next to her.

Everyone enjoyed Mrs. O'Brien's fine brunch of cottage pie; potato, mushroom, and carrot stew; Irish soda bread; rhubarb crumble; and elderflower cordial to quench thirsts. Bernadette and Mr. Middleton added to the feast some delicious baked sweets they had brought with them.

"Yah'll be stayin' in William's quarters while yer here, James," said Mr. O'Brien, as they all sat around the kitchen table.

"Please...I don't want to disturb or displace William."

"No bother, really. I get to join the boys in the loft. I'm looking forward to it...albeit, the rogue company I'll keep," William teased.

"And, you get to sleep with me and Beatrix," said Mary. "Two next to each other, and one at the foot in the other direction! Like we do when my cousins come to visit. It's very cramped and silly, but fun, indeed!"

Everyone ate and drank until they were past satiation, while they all talked in multiple side conversations—with the regular kind of banter folks partake in under normal circumstances. Finally, after much laughter and excitement, their moods settled comfortably into quiet, and the room whittled down to silence.

"Why don't you all show Bernadette around the farm now, while Mr. Middleton..." Mrs. O'Brien corrected herself, "James and your father and I speak...There's much to talk about."

"Bernadette, it's nothing like where we come from," said Beatrix, with light in her eyes.

"They've got horses and other animals, pigs and chickens, and a rooster!" added Francois.

"And endless work...." William gently mocked.

"Get on wid it! Ah, he's set upon city life since he was a wee lad!" Mr. O'Brien tousled William's hair, head-locked him, and rubbed his knuckles into his son's head.

"Alright, then, let go will yah?" William laughed and mimicked his father's brogue perfectly, and Mr. O'Brien laughed too. He released William, who promptly sped outside, with Mary, Beatrix, Bernadette, Michael, and Francois following suit, shutting the door behind him. Silence only lasted a moment.

"Where to begin?" asked Mr. O'Brien.

"I've many questions," said Mrs. O'Brien, raising her hand to her brow.

Mr. Middleton's demeanor turned serious, and he finally could divulge what he hadn't been able to say in front of Bernadette and the others.

"I beg forgiveness for my frank start, but, I think it begins with this," Mr. Middleton said with solemnity, as he pulled out a folded newspaper clipping from his jacket pocket.

"Michael's first page news in London. I hadn't the heart to tell Bernadette, though you know she saw a wanted poster of him. But that's old news now. Look here, see. The Morning Herald. There are others papers reporting the scandal, as well. Seems Sledgeham's bent on getting his revenge, and authorities are looking for both boys."

Mrs. O'Brien took the newspaper article, read it silently, and threw it toward her husband.

"There you have it...this twisted nonsense!" she cried.

"Don' know why yer surprised, Gertie. I'm Irish. 'Spose that's why I smelt the rat before I saw it. Papers go reportin' what they want, not the truth of it."

"What do you know about the boys...about Francois?" asked Mr. Middleton.

"Neither's kissed the Blarney stone, nor got the gift of gab. Michael doesn't speak much, and seems he doesn't let Francois say much either," offered Mr. O'Brien, "but when Francois gets by himself, he shares a thing or two. Michael's keen to hold onto his anger, though as fer that, what man doesn't?"

"But Francois? He's softer, more malleable, I'd say," Mrs. O'Brien replied, "In spite of his misfortune. Though he depends greatly on Michael."

"Michael's as strong as an ox. Protective as well. Oh, you'd best be careful not to cross Francois in front of Michael, that's a sense I've got," Mr. O'Brien continued, "They were livin' at Saint Mark's Orphanage in London. Don't know any other life—neither of 'em, poor blokes. Michael said he's never known life outside those walls."

"What about Francois? What has he told you?" asked Mr. Middleton, trying to hide his deeper curiosity.

"Not much, truth be told. Michael says Francois was dropped at Saint Mark's when he was but a tyke, age two or so, by a priest. Francois doesn't remember the night at all, except through Michael's retellin' of it."

"And what year was that, might I ask?" Mr. Middleton inquired.

"Year? Well, let's see…." and Mrs. O'Brien began to do the math. "It would have been 1830, or thereabouts. Francois says he's nine, though he doesn't look it, on account of being starved to his very bones his whole miserable life."

Mr. Middleton quickly calculated how old Francois—not his son, but the other child—would be based on the year he was born and the year he disappeared. His temples pulsed as he asked himself again, *Could this be?* Only now the answer was, *it is possible, yes, possible!*

Being a pragmatic man, he didn't dramatize or speculate. But, this? Was this not the year the child went missing? He remembered how doubly grief-stricken Francoise had been for her French cousin, who had named her own firstborn son after their first child, Francois, in memory of him, though he had not lived outside his mother's womb.

Francoise couldn't help but feel responsible, as if the link to her own child's fate somehow transposed itself onto her cousin's son—and he too was taken, lost from this world. The color in Mr. Middleton's cheeks faded, covering him in a white sheath, as if he'd revoked a ghost of the past.

"What was the priest's name?" asked Mr. Middleton.

"That we don't know," replied Mr. O'Brien, "Michael doesn't remember. But he speaks of a letter of some sort—which tells about Francois—his kin, history, whereabouts, that sort'a thing. Said the master's got it, hidin' it away somewhere."

"And what does the letter say?" Mr. Middleton inquired.

"An' that we don't know neither," Mr. O'Brien shook his head.

"And, do the boys know of it?" Mr. Middleton asked.

"It's unclear at this point, what they know and what they don't," Mrs. O'Brien replied.

"Well, we need to find out more, if we plan to help them. But if there's one thing I know, the boys need to get out of England, and they need to go quickly. And one more thing. Beatrix. That's another problem. A much more difficult one, indeed. For there's Bernadette to think about."

"Out of England?" Mrs. O'Brien cried.

"I've got family in Ireland, but no one's headin' in that direction. That'd be out of the fryin' pan, into the fire!" Mr. O'Brien shook his head.

"No, I was thinking more along the lines of France," Mr. Middleton replied.

"France! What would become of a young girl? Beatrix will stay here with me!" Mrs. O'Brien spoke with false bravado, her own words threatening to fail her.

"I know it sounds absurd. But I have a family member in France—on my wife's side. She is wealthy enough to help—at least she once was. I haven't spoken to her in many years. My wife's...." Mr. Middleton stopped himself. *My wife's cousin.*

"Beatrix stays," Mrs. O'Brien avowed.

"I wish it were that easy," offered Mr. Middleton, "You see, there is someone back in London who is particularly interested in her—a Mrs. Beauchamp. Even her husband—and he's a scoundrel if ever there was one—he's been asking, too. Mrs. Beauchamp isn't an easy woman to deal with, and she wholeheartedly persists."

"Don' tell me yah've heard again from that black-hearted louse, have yah?" Mr. O'Brien scowled.

"Unfortunately, Mrs. Beauchamp's a force and won't let go of Beatrix. She nearly attacked Bernadette at market, and....Bernadette doesn't know this, but she's been to see me recently with her husband by her side, insisting I know something about Beatrix' whereabouts. Luckily Bernadette was out running errands when they came to the bakery."

"What did you tell them?" Mrs. O'Brien asked.

"That I know nothing. That I haven't seen Beatrix. I did give them a piece of my mind, though. I told them in no uncertain terms that apart from the fact that they've misused Beatrix for years, they have no authority over her, and no business in what becomes of her." Mr. Middleton's forehead and brows knit in frustration.

"What did they say to that?" asked Mrs. O'Brien.

"I'd like to give them a piece of me, I would!" Mr. O'Brien chimed in.

"Mrs. Beauchamp said she'd see about that. She actually declared that she has rightful claim to the girl! She said that she'll get Beatrix back if it's the last thing she does, and when that happens, she'll give Beatrix a dose for every ounce of aggravation she's caused them. I asked her very curiously why she was so interested in Beatrix. Why couldn't she find another girl to help in the shop? Do you know what she said? 'Beatrix is mine, and I own her, that's why!'"

"The she-divil!" yelled Mr. O'Brien.

"Beatrix stays here," Mrs. O'Brien demanded, "I've grown fond of the girl, and I'll be dammed if I take part in sending her back to indentured servitude. She's safe with us on the farm."

Mr. Middleton repeated his dilemma out loud, though he was buried in his own thoughts.

"Beatrix. Yes. She presents for me a problem." His head shook, overwhelmed by the conversations to be had, and the tasks ahead. "Alas, she comes with Mrs. Beauchamp—can't separate the two, and therein lies our challenge. I fear Beatrix will have to go with the boys," Mr. Middleton quietly added, "Though it will break her heart."

Mrs. O'Brien thought about Beatrix's heart breaking, not knowing that it was Bernadette of whom Mr. Middleton spoke.

Chapter 12: Finding Out Secrets

O'Brien's Farm, Thursday June 8^{tth}

By midnight on that first night Mr. Middleton and Bernadette arrived, Michael and Francois' fates were cast. They were to depart to France with Mr. Middleton, Bernadette, and Beatrix, where they would hopefully reside with Mr. Middleton's deceased wife's cousin. Mr. Middleton had already sent his wife's cousin a letter, and now awaited her response, which he hoped to receive within the next month, if he was lucky.

It was a difficult letter to write. Mr. Middleton fretted he might have said too much or not enough at all. He understood the consequences of his actions under the law—Beatrix' guardianship was unclear, Michael's head was on a platter, and Francois was considered to be a victim of Michael's kidnapping.

Mr. Middleton balanced the consequences for alluding the law against a great moral weight upon him. If he was correct in his suspicions about Francois, this was nothing short of a miracle. But, if he was wrong, God help him. He was about to open Pandora's box that had been sealed many years ago. Old wounds laid to rest would resurrect from the fallout of his poor judgment.

There was also Bernadette to think about, who knew nothing of this secondary layer that complicated the mystery of Francois. To

Bernadette, Francois was a connection to her mother and brother. But if he was right about his growing suspicion, Francois represented a possibility of such cosmic force, it would take a lifetime to make sense of.

He despised his wild imagination for running away with itself, for connecting improbable dots to a past and present, so he simply said the boys would be safe in France, that they could find a new life in the French countryside.

"And your cousin in-law would take them on?" Mrs. O'Brien asked.

"I'm not certain. She is a widow now with no children of her own. At least..." Mr. Middleton cut himself short. "I'm certain she has the space. Her husband was a winemaker, and left her with land. She could probably use the help. As I've mentioned, I haven't spoken to her in a few years. My plan all hinges on her willingness."

"When should we tell the boys?" Mr. O'Brien asked.

"The boys need to be told, but not before plans are solidified. They've had too many disappointments in their lives already. Michael's cold and distant, mistrusting. Is it just me or has my arrival somehow aggravated his mood?"

"Well, that's him in a nutshell, but he's as tense as a bull lately," Mr. O'Brien replied, "Maybe our private talks are settin' him off course. He's sensitive ta 'that, secrets an' all. He's been whisperin' to Francois, but I tell yah, Francois' not havin' it, whatever it is Michael says."

"Perhaps I must speak privately with Michael?" Mr. Middleton wondered.

"To what purpose?" Mrs. O'Brien asked.

"I'm not certain yet. But I don't want to lose the boy entirely. He strikes me as the kind who runs when cornered. I suspect he's feeling cornered right about now. Well, by the by, we'll know in a few weeks about France. But that may be too late. I'll be traveling into London in a few days to solidify plans. I think it's best to talk to Michael before I go. B and I should return within two weeks, I imagine. If the letter from my wife's cousin comes…."

"It'll be waitin' fer yah, unopened," Mr. O'Brien said.

"Mr. Middleton, please reconsider Beatrix. Seamus, you know I could teach her, pass along my trade, give her a living," Mrs. O'Brien persisted.

"This is true, but she can only rid herself of the Beauchamp's for good on French soil," Mr. Middleton replied.

They heard noises, banter, and conversations getting closer.

"Quiet down now, I can hear 'em. Let's leave it on the table. Seems we can't agree on Beatrix, not yet anyway," Mr. O'Brien said, playing peace-keeper.

The three continued complicated discussions, talking in private whispers, late into the night and early in the mornings, when they could find themselves alone. If one or more of the children appeared, they jumped into awkward conversations, which appeared suspicious. And stirred the pot. And bubbled the brew.

After a particularly laborious day of farm work, the boys ate their dinner, then excused themselves to the barn earlier than usual. They lay on their hay mats in the loft and listened to sounds of hungry barn owl babies whimpering for their mother to return. Since William slept here too now, the loft wasn't private anymore. All day, Michael tried to find the time to tell Francois his own hatched plan. William would be coming to bed soon. There was little time to explain. The way he calculated it, he and Francois would be moving on in a fortnight. He breathed in and sighed.

"Need to talk to yeh before William comes."

"I told yeh, ain't open for discussion," Francois said. Francois was in no mood to hear what Michael had to say since it probably had to do with leaving the farm.

"Don't even know what I'm gonna say, now, do yeh?" Michael replied.

"Yeh think I'm daft? Yeh message is clear. Ain't as stupid as yeh think. Know what this is about, I do."

Michael leaned up on one elbow, cushioned by straw, and stared into Francois' pleading eyes.

"Francois, don't be thick. They're makin' plans, if yeh haven't noticed?"

"So?" Francois' brazen response hid the fact that Michael's words caught his attention.

"What if the plans include splittin' us up? Have yeh considered that?" Michael asked.

Francois had never thought of this possibility, and he paused considerably.

~ 160 ~

"I need to tell yeh somethin' that's been weighin' on me for a while now. Finally worked out the details in my head. Got a solid plan worked out, I do," Michael paused. He spoke again, "Francois…Yeh don't want to hear this, but I'm goin' back to Saint Marks."

"Michael! Got a death wish, have yeh?"

"Francois…there's somethin' I haven't told…I should have, but it wasn't the right time…. yeh've been so contented here. Haven't wanted to spoil it."

"Brother, ain't it too late for secrets 'tween us?"

"What I've got to tell takes us back to that night. The night we escaped from Sledgeham. I found somethin' earlier that day. That night I went back to look for it, and, well, Sledgeham found me before I found it."

Francois' frustration melted into curiosity.

"The letter? Is that it?"

"Not exactly," Michael wavered.

"What is so important that you want to go back to the orphanage? This is barmy talk again! Lunacy! Yeh ain't goin back! No Michael! Please! Before it was sport, but now? He'll kill yeh for payback!"

Francois' shoulders slunk downward as his thoughts took him back to the starting point of his nightmares. For a split second, he pictured Sledgeham, and then, felt Saint Mark's Orphanage heave its limestone brick against his body, closing in, burying him alive. He felt a sickening punch in the pit of his stomach and the stench of whiskey numbing his senses.

"It's the thing he took from yeh," Michael whispered.

"What? Ain't makin' sense! Yeh found the letter? Did yeh or didn't yeh?"

"Not the letter, exactly."

"Yeh either found me or not…the letter, I mean to say."

"I found a lockbox, Francois. And, I think that's where he's been hidin' your parchment letter…inside the box! In his room, covered up by his rug! All this time, and it was buried under the floorboards!"

William entered into the barn and started to climb the ladder, calling to them. Francois bit his lip, and drew blood, as he brooded about his life in the orphanage. How he ruminated about that parchment letter every day since he could remember. But, farm life freed him from the burden of that letter and the empty promises it held.

Hard-headed Michael. I'll put an end to his hell, but his death won't be on me.

Realizing he would never find a way to change Michael's mind, he saw himself for what he was—a weighted buoy sinking Michael into a past that didn't matter anymore. Michael would never move forward, at least not without that lockbox—that stupid empty lockbox which only promised one certain outcome—endless infinity.

I'll get your lockbox, if that's what it takes to move on. If not, at least my life for yours.

He counted forward two days to Saturday, Mr. O'Brien's travel day into London, and made a plan of his own.

~ 162 ~

O'Brien's Farm, Saturday June 10th, 4:45 am

Mr. O'Brien departed extra early this morning without the last minute loading details that always seemed to produce a late start. Francois first suggested, and then, eagerly helped him load his cart of soaps, tinctures, and medicines the night before, to shave time. His thick burlap blankets protected his goods from early morning dew and hungry insects, but looked like lumpy piles of scarecrow parts, sans hat and pipe. He placed two wooden crates of flowers into the back, cut yesterday, and kept inside last night for warmth, and thought about how much he dreaded this particular delivery, but had to keep a good front which meant no unusual behavior. Then, he jumped up to his driver's seat, sat down, grabbed the reigns, clicked his tongue twice, and his horses headed down the dirt road that led him away from all that he loved.

He didn't feel the extra weight of Francois, who curled up and slept underneath the burlap, but awoke at once to the movement under him. *Pray God, keep me safe*, Francois calmed himself as he steadied his head under his palms, silently recited his favorite psalm, and stared into the fibrous burlap squares, which looked like weaved worm skeletons.

Same day, 9:30 am

    Oddly, Mr. Middleton had slept in, and when he awoke, the unusual and uncustomary quietude of the house led him to dress quickly and head downstairs. Mrs. O'Brien was in the kitchen mixing tinctures, and unfolded everyone's whereabouts: Mr. O'Brien was well on his way to London by now, if not already there; the three girls were out in the field collecting berries and roots; William and Francois were probably on sheep hill tending to the flock, though she hadn't seen either of them this morning; and Michael was painting the barn, taking advantage of this unusual stretch of dry weather.

    Mr. Middleton grabbed a roll with butter and stepped outside into the grey morning—flecks of light breaking through the cloudy welkin sky—and saw Michael at the barn. He decided the moment was here. He gingerly approached, as the boy painted red.

    "Quite a job?" Mr. Middleton summoned Michael out of his trance as he approached from behind, startling the boy. Michael said nothing, but his shoulders and neck visibly stiffened like dog shackles rising.

    Mrs. O'Brien recently shaved his whole head again, since a few stubborn cuts didn't close and another shave helped her catch early infections trying to set up house under his scalp. She inspected Michael's head daily, running her fingers over the ridges, pretending his head was her crystal ball, and read his fortuitous future—some days she saw gold, and other days, Cornish pies. He came to like it—the reading of his crystal ball head.

Mr. Middleton stared at the scarred terrain of Michael's scalp, mostly healed over, except those few angry ones that he suspected Michael kept picking open. There was zero acknowledgement of Mr. Middleton's presence, and he kept his face forward as he continued painting fresh red strips over peeled patches.

"Mind if I keep you company?" Mr. Middleton searched for some indication that he was welcome, but Michael gave him nothing and Mr. Middleton came closer anyway, afraid he'd lose his courage and botch his attempt to speak.

"Michael...though you might think you've no reason to trust me, I'd like to prove otherwise."

Michael's painting hand stopped, and he dangled his paintbrush by his side, fresh red paint dripping onto the ground, pooling like blood.

"That's why I'm here, to ask you to listen and to trust. For what it's worth, I think I might be able to help him. I think I might...it's a risk...oh Lord, I hope I'm doing the proper thing. I'm certainly mumbling, aren't I? I don't know how to start this conversation! It's about Francois," Mr. Middleton fumbled.

Michael said nothing, but listened intently, shackles still slightly raised, hand striking the barn again with red paint, his back shunning this meddlesome man.

"Michael, I need to ask you some questions pertaining to him."

Mr. Middleton skidded his shoe on the ground where the paint had dripped. He weighed his desire to confide in the boy against the boy's desire to shut him out, but did not lose his nerve, after all.

Michael stopped painting again, and abruptly turned to Mr. Middleton, his chestnut eyes darting sharply.

"I ain't blind. I see yeh good intentions. But, I've seen good intentions before. Yeh can't help me an' yeh can't help Francois."

"How are you so certain of this?"

"How might I know? It's the same story. Good men want to help, but get sidetracked. Good men are unreliable. Besides, we come with a past, yeh know."

Mr. Middleton paused. He hated to make promises that he couldn't keep, especially to the broken-hearted.

"We all do. A past, I mean..." Mr. Middleton reached for the boy's shoulder, and lightly touched it, but by instinct, Michael swung at him, then stopped himself before the situation got worse.

"Michael! Listen to me! I need to tell you something! ...Something so far-fetched...and...implausible! You have to lay down all rationale...it's so preposterous that any adult with half a wit would have me committed to Bethlem for even broaching the subject with someone such as yourself...."

"Such as myself? What kind of self is that, Mr. Middleton?"

"I didn't mean offense, boy, it's just that...well, what I mean is...someone...who...who has had nothing but a life of despair, of such bleakness and horror really—that's the only words that come to mind. To create any hope at all for that someone is a...well, a responsibility on the part of the doer. You're a person whose feelings shouldn't be thrown around lightly, is what I'm trying, dismally, to say. I don't know if what I'm saying makes any sense at all. I don't even know if what I have to say has any truth or validity to it....it's just the timing, the curiosity of it—it's such a bizarre coincidence that haunts me...."

"Don't mean to be rude, but I've got a barn to paint. But, before yeh go, if yeh think I can't handle disappointment, yeh don't know the first thing about me." Michael's words fell away, colorless.

"The thing is...it's not really about you at all, Michael. It's about Francois."

"With due respect, Sir, what yeh got to tell me 'bout Francois that I don't already know?"

Mr. Middleton scanned the farm, and turned toward Sheep Hill, where Francois might be, but all he saw was greenery, stone fencing, dirt paths, and leaved trees.

"Michael, what if I was to tell you a story...a mournful tale from so long ago it doesn't even seem it was ever real?"

Michael stood transfixed by his intensity, as Mr. Middleton seemed to float away to the past, transported to another time and space, his cadence trance-like.

"It begins with a child born still from his mother's womb—in his perfect little form. Oh! And all the grief such loss caused between a man and wife—a grief only reconciled by the birth of a beautiful daughter two years later, who brought her mother and father back to life...But that's not the story I'm to tell you. There is another part of this story that seems to haunt me, Michael...."

Michael's own life experiences had taught him to listen carefully for the sound of secrets unfolding, and Mr. Middleton's words, in their feathery softness, folded into his ears, as he caught hold, and let them in.

"…The story continues two years henceforth, when a close cousin of the wife birthed a baby boy far across the English Channel in France. To honor her dear cousin's profound loss, she named her newborn child the same name as the man and wife's first born son. And she and her own husband lived such a blissful two years loving that child, until a great terror struck them down. The child disappeared with a trusted servant, a British woman who simply sunk into the earth like a rotted bog, swallowing him up with her. As if overnight…he was there, and then he was not. He vanished into thin air…."

Mr. Middleton receded into his darkest thoughts, his eyes cavernous, as he slipped down to the ground, leaning against the barn, dragging a line of fresh red paint onto his back.

Michael dropped his brush, and extended his hand to help the man balance, but then thought better of it, and recoiled; his buckled knees forced him down, as Mr. Middleton's tale pulled him into his own search for things that disappear.

"Mr. Middleton, what's this got to do with Francois?" Michael asked, his defensiveness gone, his blood pumping thick and fast.

Mr. Middleton's voice trembled, "My first born son, his name was Francois. The child that went missing was named after ours."

Michael ate the words, peppered and burning.

"Mr. Middleton, their first names? The people you speak of…the cousin of your wife?"

Mr. Middleton hesitated, then spoke: "Claude…and Violette."

Exasperated, Michael fell over onto the ground in prayer position, beating the ground with his fists, and repeated, "Violette! Violette!"

That dark night, so long ago, when Francois first arrived at the orphanage, flooded Michael with the names Sledgeham had spoken out loud, '*Claude and Violette,*' as hot carmine adrenalin coursed through his body.

"Michael, I'm not sure of this…I don't know if…what I'm saying…it's…."

Just at that moment, Mr. Middleton caught site of an open, charcoal-colored gig carriage pulled by a single horse, heading toward the farm. From his current distance, he couldn't be certain, but it looked like the gig occupied a driver and two passengers. Michael noticed too and froze.

"Who's that heading our direction?" Mr. Middleton asked, catapulting them back into their present condition.

"Ain't sure, Sir."

"Did Mr. or Mrs. O'Brien mention guests today?"

"No, Sir. Should I hide?"

"Wise choice, I'd say. And best go warn Francois. He's with William, other side of Sheep Hill, I think? Maybe they're just passing through…or lost, perhaps?

The carriage rolled like a smoke-grey storm, closer still, making it easier to distinguish the occupants, who wore their Sunday best, buttoned up in pretense and wound tightly. High pink-feathered plumes stuck out of the woman's hat, like sea anemone feeding on air.

"Do my eyes deceive me? Could that be Mrs. Beauchamp, wearing one of her trademark imbecile hats?" Mr. Middleton's rhetorical question begged a response, but met silence.

Closer, closer the gig carriage came, and mere mention of Mrs. Beauchamp made Michael want to run, but, he couldn't pull himself away from Mr. Middleton, whose revelation shook him at his core. The two stood side by side, focusing with pinpoint precision, until there was no uncertainty, and Mr. Middleton cursed as he directed Michael toward the back of the barn, hidden from the road.

"Michael, go! Find Francois! And Beatrix and Bernadette! Did they mention when they'd return this afternoon?"

"No. Before lunch? I think? It's her, ain't it?"

Mrs. Beauchamp's harping voice could be heard in the distance.

"Go before she spies you! Find Francois! Then, warn Beatrix and Bernadette, wherever they are!"

Michael peered around the barn, stealing one last look down the country road that led to O'Brien farm. Emerging from the tree-lined artery, came the wheels that kicked up dust and carried the unmistakable piercing cries of persistence.

Foxlike, he turned and ran from the barn through the dense trees that led to sheep hill from the other side, and round the loop. As the branches scratched his arms and cracked under his feet, he desperately ran against time and luck. His legs couldn't keep up with his frenetic thoughts. Dazed, he repeated the name he had forgotten long ago, as he dared himself to believe in the mysterious possibility of happenchance and fortune.

About the same time that Michael sprinted through the trees in search of Francois, Mr. Middleton tore from behind the barn into Mrs. O'Brien's kitchen, fervently hoping the Beauchamp's hadn't seen him, and thump-smacking his head against the door frame as he entered.

"What's the fuss?" Mrs. O'Brien asked, her bent head jolted, as her fingers finished crushing a bushel of dried St. John's Wort.

Strewn across her kitchen table was an array of mortar and pestles each occupied with freshly crushed leaf, flower, or seed. A rushlight holder burned a splinter of tallow-dipped softwood reed, smelling of fat. One look at Mr. Middleton, and she knew something was wrong.

"The Beauchamp's are here! No one saw me. Where's Bernadette?"

In her disoriented panic, she called for her husband, but stopped herself, realizing his Saturday travel into the city, so she repeated her son's name a few times, strangely, as if her call would somehow summon him from wherever he was. She quickly blew out the flame, as she remembered everyone's place: Michael, painting. Check. William and Francois, tending the animals. Check. The girls? The rapeseed fields!

She blurted out, "The rapeseed fields, about two miles inland past the Thames path! Bloody hell, they'll return any time now! Where's the boys?"

"Michael's gone to warn Francois, wherever he is...."

Mr. Middleton was interrupted by the sound of carriage wheels, horses, and natter chatter, at the front of the farm house.

"What now?" Mrs. O'Brien whispered, as she collected herself, pushing away her loose hair strands, tucking her worry inside her bun, as she paced, her elbow knocking over a biscuit pricker from a nearby shelf.

"I can't go out...If she sees me, we're finished. She'll put two and two together and make four. She knows Beatrix is acquainted with Bernadette, and she'll figure that I have no other reason to be at your farm, if not for Beatrix' sake. I'll hide upstairs!"

As he flew up the narrow steps, he called, "Keep your cards up your sleeve, Mrs. O'Brien, and play a good game!"

Mrs. O'Brien nervously wiped her hands on her work apron, and hurried out the door to head off trouble. Her eyes swallowed the image of a short and rotund pointy-faced woman whose low-necked, damask, pipe-sleeved bodice and heavily pleated petticoat demonstrated a kind of flamboyance that immediately annoyed her.

But it was the lady's pretentious feather-plumed hat, sitting with an heir upon her head, which reminded Mrs. O'Brien of a drawing she had once seen of a strange extinct bird called the Dodo.

This ostentatious woman sat in the open gig beside a tall scraggly man, whose long protruding neck resembled an ostrich but at least he was dressed more appropriately suited to his station in life—notwithstanding their contrasting clothes, they fit each other well.

The carriage driver pulled to a full stop, promptly stepped down from his position, next to the carriage footrest, and stood sentient in front of the Beauchamp's, both of whom fought to step down first, as he extended his hand to Mrs. Beauchamp.

"Hello, may I help you?" Mrs. O'Brien asked with a smile, and her face displayed a perfectly packaged combination of surprise and wonder—which was a normal response to provide to unexpected visitors—though she was all nerves, and felt lightheaded. Then she placed her hand over her heart, felt it skip-jump, and asked her visitors if they were in need of directions to somewhere.

Mrs. Beauchamp nudged her husband, who in turn gave a disgruntled look back. As he cleared his pouched throat, his swelled Adam's apple vibrated, and he croaked while nervously fiddling with a vest button, then spoke.

"Name's Henry Beauchamp. I own the floral shop that's done business with yeh husband these last years."

Mrs. Beauchamp poked his side, "Go on, then. Stop dawdlin'!"

The veins in Mr. Beauchamp's nose expanded to an indigo bulb at the sound of his wife's reprimand.

"Well, then, it's a pleasure to meet you. But I do hope everything is alright and you continue to be contented with my husband's service?"

Mrs. Beauchamp eyed her surroundings, looking for signs of life. She grabbed her husband's sleeve, and said, "She could be anywhere!"

She tried to walk past Mrs. O'Brien, whose palpable shock and outstretched arms halted Mrs. Beauchamp from moving forward.

"Please, if you will, state your business, as I must admit, I'm confused by your visit and baffled by your manners!"

~ 173 ~

Mr. Beauchamp grabbed his wife's arm, and she wrestled free, but remained by his side.

"We's missin' a girl, we are. Beatrix. Gone about two months now. Been makin' rounds, visitin' people who might jus' know somethin', ...Well, yeh're about the last visit on account a' bein' so far out of city bounds."

Mrs. Beauchamp interjected, "This carriage ride cost us a pretty penny!" The driver, who sat now on his high seat, mumbled, as his whispered words '*blabbin' chaffer*' fell like horse plops to the ground.

"Why could you not settle this with Mr. O'Brien in London? He delivered flowers there this morning, did he not?" Mrs. O'Brien's surprise hid her stress.

Mr. Beauchamp's smelly soured breath made Mrs. O'Brien recoil. She detected an illness as his rot-toothed grin smiled and he waived his finger.

"Well, that's just it, see? After the shock of her bein' gone lifted, an' the work started to pile, we thought real hard 'bout it. Took us a while to figure, but it all came together, didn't it?"

Though Mrs. O'Brien had no idea where he was going with his train of thought, he delighted in his quick-witted sleuthing, as his finger tapped his temple and his brown teeth hung like stalactites.

"Who's the last'uh see 'er the mornin' she went missin'? Yeh husband, that's who! Awfully chummy with our Beatrix, 'e was. Before she disappeared, asked time and again 'bout 'er. Never 'preciated it, his meddlin' in our private affairs!"

Mr. Beauchamp's face now matched his bulbous nose, which was one shade away from his wife's damask dress.

"And we got to realiz'n that after all these years pryin', the day she goes missin' he's not concerned? Did his deliveries these last few weeks without askin' 'bout 'er?"

Mrs. Beauchamp chimed in, "That's odd, ain't it?"

"No, I don't think it strange at all," retorted Mrs. O'Brien, "What I do think odd is that you couldn't discuss your business with him at your shop. You've come all the way for nothing, I'm sorry to say."

"Well, that's just it, yeh see," said Mr. Beauchamp, "Last week we did ask 'em, an' he acted as if we was askin' about some cat we lost. A trip to his farm might jog his memory, eh? He delivers, she disappears! Get it?"

They heard faint barking and feet stamping the ground. A young man came running quick-speed down the carpeted hill, out of breath, wild-eyed, fierce, as the Beauchamp's stared, and Mrs. O'Brien sighed great relief William was alone.

"Well, then, if you have questions you can't settle with Mr. O'Brien in London, then you'll have to come back another time. At this very moment, he's there, while you're here! It's best you return from hence you came. Perhaps you'll even meet him on your journey back." Mrs. O'Brien desperately hoped this would not occur, but said it anyway, her tone less friendly now.

"I think not!" Mrs. Beauchamp's high-laced boot stomped indignantly. "We'll remain 'til Mr. O'Brien comes! 'Sides, we wanted to see it for ourselves. Good place to hide, a farm is!"

"Is there a problem, mother?" William asked, eyeing the unsightly couple, and hoping not, as the man looked rough. He

~ 175 ~

needed these horrid people to leave immediately in order to tell his mother that Francois was nowhere to be found.

"William, this is Mr. and Mrs. Beauchamp. They are inquiring after a girl....I'm sorry, her name again?"

"Beatrix!" Mrs. Beauchamp squalled, with accusatory eyes.

"Ah, yes, Beatrix. Have you heard your father speak of such a girl?" Mrs. O'Brien asked William.

"No. I haven't, mum," William replied, "Should I have?"

"You see?" Mrs. O'Brien answered calmly. "There is nothing, no news here for you."

"Maybe, maybe not, but come a long way, we 'ave and wha' a pity it'd be to turn roun' now, don't yeh think?" Mrs. Beauchamp scanned William, as her stress strengthened her cockney accent.

"Strange thing, it is. Yeh don't look like the boy in the back of yeh father's cart. Three times the size, yeh are. Remember that mornin'? What yeh said to me, don't yeh?"

William nervously stared back at Mrs. Beauchamp, nodding his head like a marionette as Mrs. O'Brien watched her son struggle to speak about an event he knew nothing about.

"Madam, I don't expect Mr. O'Brien back till late this evening. This is a working farm, and as such, I have work to complete. I respectfully request you depart. I shall tell my husband you've come, and he shall pay you a visit in London."

"There's no harm in us waitin' a few hours, maybe take a look 'round?" Mr. Beauchamp asked in an overly saccharine tone, as he turned a semi-circle, scaling the farm.

"I hate to be rude. I don't think you understand! Please leave!" Mrs. O'Brien's tone and speech caused her son to tensely posture, and he rolled up his cotton sleeves.

"Oh, no, Mrs. O'Brien, I think it's us yeh don't understand! Let's see if I can explain it. After yeh shoddy hospitality, my suspicion's confirmed. The constable back in London? He'll be interested in hearin' what we've to say 'bout Mr. O'Brien's involvement. This little chat's just made 'em top on the suspect list. Henry, let's go! Our business is done with these mick-lovers!" Mrs. Beauchamp balked.

William lunged forward, as the word *mick* stridulated in his ear. Mrs. O'Brien barely restrained him, and lost her balance against his strength.

"Get off our farm, you angling coves," William shouted.

Just then, the noise of girl laughter emanated from the wooded Thames path that bordered O'Brien's farm. It was the twittering kind of laughter that bounced against briar and bramble.

William and Mrs. O'Brien shared a knowing look—that the girls hadn't been warned and were about to be ambushed. Mrs. O'Brien thought fast and called out.

"Mary! We've guests. Hurry on!" She brusquely turned to the Beauchamp's, her amplified voice purposeful, cautionary.

"Good, then, you'll meet my daughter as well. I'm certain she knows nothing of this missing girl. Ask her, if you wish. Then, you'll be on your way!"

Out of sight, but easily heard, Mrs. O'Brien's message wrapped the girls in panic, as Beatrix's body tremored and Bernadette

~ 177 ~

steadied her. Mary held her finger to her lip, then waved the girls back and away, as she faltered forward.

Mrs. Beauchamp stirred pleasurably as youthful laughter fell hard against sudden silence, furthering her suspicions.

"There's more than one girl…where are they, who's there?" Mrs. Beauchamp's pipes shrilled, "Beatrix? Is that you? Yeh come out this instant or I'll come in!"

She sharp-turned to her husband and thrust him with a push to the origin of the sounds.

"What yeh waitin' for? Go on, take a look!"

Mr. Beauchamp's knobby long legs carried his portly frame hesitantly toward the eerily quiet path. William wrestled free of his mother's hold, and ran to block Mr. Beauchamp from moving further.

"Careful William!"

William grabbed at his coat sleeve, and in return, Mr. Beauchamp grabbed William's shirt, ripping it.

"Let go of him!" screamed Mrs. O'Brien.

Mary heard the commotion and sprinted into sight toward her brother, as Mrs. O'Brien pulled on William. William couldn't reach Mr. Beauchamp's face, but he shot his fist into his gut as the man grunted, grabbed, and twisted William's arm before shoving him to the ground.

"Stop! Stop!" called Mary. "Leave him alone!"

By now, Bernadette and Beatrix took off in the other direction—running steadfast toward rapeseed.

"Get off our farm!" Mrs. O'Brien screamed, her hair as disheveled as her spirit.

"Who's with yeh? There were two of yeh! I heard it! Only crack-pots laugh alone!" shouted Mrs. Beauchamp. "Go, Henry! It's Beatrix, I know it!"

But, Henry Beauchamp was out of breath from his scuffle and did not budge.

"I was singing and laughing to myself! That is what you heard! I tell myself tales and make up imaginary friends—to pass the time...so I'm not so alone...." Mary nervously responded.

Mrs. Beauchamp began walking toward the bushes and no one stopped her, not even Mr. Beauchamp, who stood still. William would strike again if he so much as moved, and he was smart enough to know the consequences if he took it further. Mr. O'Brien was immeasurably stronger, and would tie him into a reef knot first, then anchor him to the bottom of a marsh, if he hurt the boy.

"You heard!" Mrs. O'Brien hollered. "She's by herself! No more inquiries! Send the constable if you will! But pray tell, what special claim have you on a servant girl, such that you own her?"

Mrs. Beauchamp gave her husband an indignant look.

"We've the same claim as yeh have to yours, that's what!"

"To my kin? My family? Is that what you mean? Oh, you really are a demented old bird!" Mrs. O'Brien scoffed.

"Who'd 'yeh think yeh are? Yeh're better than us, eh? Yeh're married to a bog-trotter! She's ours!" Mrs. Beauchamp shrieked.

"Have you no shame? She is your domestic servant, not your possession!" Mrs. O'Brien cried.

"Oh, she's ours, thanks to his indiscretions. Had 'er with a mistress who died when the girl was four. Well, ain't me own blood. But his? Unfortunately, she is. So, yeh see, Mrs. O'Brien, why the constable might be interested after all? Perhaps this changes what yeh husband knows, eh? It'd be wise to think on it. Kidnappin's a serious charge. Yeh got a lot to lose!"

Mrs. Beauchamp's triumphant eyes swept expansively across the farm and toward the house, taking inventory, as she calculated the value of land and life, then straightened her hat, turned into the path, and peered first to the left, then right. She stood for some time, zeroing in on any movement, but not even a leaf stirred. Hesitantly, she returned to her husband's side.

"We'll leave now," Mrs. Beauchamp said to her husband, who'd already had enough himself, and was more than ready to depart.

Hearing her directive, the driver jumped down from his seat, and stood, as the Beauchamp's climbed in. Mrs. Beauchamp struggled without assistance to get her plump behind—tucked underneath her layered petticoat—lifted off the ground.

Stunned by the revelation, Mrs. O'Brien called out to her unwanted guests one last time, as the horse pulled away.

"Did she know she was your daughter, Mr. Beauchamp?"

The driver clicked the reigns again, and his horse neighed further down the lane. Mr. Beauchamp turned back toward Mrs. O'Brien, nodding.

"Why should yeh care? But for that, she knew well. The Mrs. won't let 'er forget where she came from, and how she'll spend the rest 'er life payin' for my mistake. Though I'll say this…"

He stared contemptuously at his wife, "Beatrix' mother, now she was a woman a man could love. Would 'ave been different feh Beatrix an' me, had she lived."

Though the open carriage bumped down the lane, Mrs. Beauchamp's backside remained hawk-still on a high post. She did not turn around, but screeched, "Make no mistake, find 'er I will, and she'll pay double for the trouble she's caused!"

The carriage was now far enough away for William to declare, "Francois' gone! I haven't seen him all day! I thought he was back at the house with mum or Michael! But I just ran into Michael up on Sheep Hill, warning me about the Beauchamp's. He thought Francois was with me!"

Mrs. O'Brien turned to Mary.

"Mary, have you seen Francois today, at all?"

"No, mum!"

The gig carrying the Beauchamp's now dotted like a blight on the horizon's landscape, hardly visible, but enough to damage. Mr. Middleton ran down from his hiding place, a full shade paler, having heard it all from the upstairs window.

Mary was the first to see Michael running down the hill, frantically yelling Francois' name. He reached them, out of breath, keeled over, and balanced on his knees, as he spoke Francois' name again. Michael played his last conversation with Francois over, realizing his grave mistake to tell his plans to retrieve the lockbox. He knew three things about Francois: He went for the lockbox; He would try to fight his battle; he was no match for Sledgeham.

"Mrs. O'Brien! Mr. Middleton! Francois' gone back for it, I know it! To Saint Mark's. To Sledgeham...."

Mrs. O'Brien, whose own body still shook, interrupted Michael's nonsense talk.

"Michael, we've all had a shock. There's a million places he could be. Maybe he's with...."

"No! I know him!" Michael insisted.

"Michael, what makes you think this?" Mr. Middleton interjected.

"There's no time! He's gone back for the lockbox! It was supposed to be my plan! I was gonna sneak into Mr. O'Brien's cart, go back into Saint Mark's, and get what's rightfully ours! Francois begged me not to go. I know he went instead! We've got to stop him. He ain't no match for Sledgeham. He'll kill him!"

"Are you sure about this, Michael?" asked William.

"Where's he going, specifically? What lockbox? Where is this lockbox?" asked Mr. Middleton, addled and confused.

"Saint Mark's Orphanage! Just told yeh! Francois seeks the lockbox! I think he rode in the back of Mr. O'Brien's cart, early this mornin'. We're wastin' time talkin' about it!"

"Did anyone see him at any point today?" asked Mr. Middleton already knowing the answer. He had vanished again, this boy, who seemed to leave people and places without a trace.

"Well I certainly haven't. Mr. O'Brien would have brought him back if he saw him!" cried Mrs. O'Brien, wasting no time, bolting out her commands, "William, your da's got Benny and Matilda. Go saddle up Sadie and Jenny. Are their shoes fit for travel?"

"Yes, mum."

"Francois loves it here…won't leave…it was my plan to go…" said Michael, but Mrs. O'Brien interrupted him half way through.

"Oh, lord! What is happening? No mind. It's the eleventh hour, and we best hurry. Mr. Middleton, you'll ride Sadie, and William will ride Jenny. Mary and I shall find Beatrix and Bernadette while you hunt for Francois! Michael, you will stay here at the farm and wait. This will be the hardest job of all."

"Only I know how to get to Saint Mark's! Only I know how to get around Sledgeham!" Michael insisted.

"Francois could be anywhere. You don't know for certain if he went back. Da' should be on route home by now. But you can't come. You're in danger…." William replied, as Mr. Middleton interjected.

"I can find Saint Mark's, Michael. I know it's near Ludgate. I can ask a constable when I get there. I'm familiar with the city."

Everyone's words failed to calm Michael's increasing agitation.

"Mrs. O'Brien," Mr. Middleton spoke, "Bernadette must be sick with worry and fright."

"She'll be alright, I'll see to it. Find Francois. Bring him home!" Mrs. O'Brien said, turning to Michael. "Promise me you'll stay here, just in case Mr. O'Brien returns earlier than expected."

"Yes, ma'am," said Michael, his eyes hazed and roasted. It was the last thing he would do.

"God speed, gentlemen," Mrs. O'Brien called out behind her, as she and Mary walked hurriedly toward the bushy path loop that turned toward the Thames in either direction, discussing strategy to find Beatrix and Bernadette. Mother and daughter waved a last goodbye, then disappeared into the wooded path the girls had named Ladybird Lane, for all the orange and red beetles they found to inhabit there among the stinging nettle.

William finished saddling Jenny, then began Sadie, while Mr. Middleton packed their leather bags and water vessels. While they were distracted, Michael hopped onto Jenny, and she neighed loudly in protest. Mr. Middleton looked up and saw Michael.

"Mrs. O'Brien wants you here, son. London is too dangerous for you right now."

"I'm comin', Sir. Yeh don't know yeh way."

"She'll have my neck in a noose! You must wait here."

"In case da' comes home?" William added, trying to convince.

"I'm the only one here who knows every inch of the hell-hole. Don't yeh understand? He can't manage Sledgeham on his own. Please stop triflin' 'bout it! He could be there by now! Ain't lettin' yeh leave without me!"

Mr. Middleton reconciled that Michael wouldn't yield, and sighed. "You're a stubborn one, Michael! Alright then. William's a horse man. He'll ride her in. Go ahead, move back behind the cantle at the rear jockey and make room for him. Just hold on tight and prey for your rump. I'll deal with Mrs. O'Brien later. Don't look forward to that, I can say with all honesty."

As William's left foot grabbed the saddle stirrup, he grinned wickedly, appreciating Mr. Middleton's keen understanding of his mother's temper, and was certain they'd both have to answer to her. At least Michael would get off scot-free, since she held him to different standards.

Michael pushed himself further against the cantle, gripping the rear-housing for support, as William grabbed the horn of the saddle and sat.

It would be a long, uncomfortable ride for Michael, but his anger fueled him and tempered his discomfort. With no stops, they'd make it in half the time it would take for a heavy two horse cart-load. His thoughts turned to Sledgeham.

It's yeh day of reckoning, Michael ruminated, not entirely sure whether he spoke to Sledgeham, Francois, himself, or some combination.

PART THREE

Chapter 13:   Finding Saint Mark's

London, same day, mid-morning

Mr. O'Brien made good time, though for Francois, the cart ride back into London seemed abysmal and long-drawn-out. They had left early this morning, before the roosters crowed, and Francois had to adjust his eyes to daybreak after being covered so long in burlap. He had wondered so many times along the way where they were and how long to go, and had no idea that Mr. O'Brien had already traveled from Fulham to Old Brompton Road, through Sloane Square to The King's Road, through Piccadilly to Coventry, with a left on Priness and a right on Lisle, to Newport through Castle, eventually to Saint Martin's, and finally to where Long Acre intersected with Drury Lane.

Before the road curved right onto Drury, Mr. O'Brien called out to his horses to slow down and pulled his reigns back tightly, as they whinnied. For the first time that morning, Francois felt the sensation of the cart slow down significantly, and knew it was time to make a run for it; quickly lifting the burlap sacks, he peered into the morning gloom, unfamiliar with his whereabouts. He would stick to his plan, regardless of his unknown location, and exit unnoticed. The moment was upon him, and he was relieved this excruciating trip was over. His head throbbed from lying so still in the same position, in shaded burlap brownness, longing to breathe fresh air, as the rough terrain jolted his neck the last few hours.

Mr. O'Brien suspected nothing as Francois quietly rolled to the cart's edge, like a circus illusionist, twisting his body over and off with the slightest inaudible thud to the ground.

Though there were a few people wandering about, no one paid any attention to him as he bolted behind and to the right side of the street, then ducked down an alley on his immediate left, careful not to make eye contact with some loud men and women exiting a tavern in the brick alley he found himself walking through.

Emerging from the other side of a twisted street back onto Drury Lane, Francois didn't recognize his exact location, but at least he knew he was in London. Hungry and thirsty, he walked, searching desperately for a place to rest and orient himself. Feeling the fool, he hadn't thought about food or drink in his plan, so he filled himself instead with a barrage of curses. He looked north, south, east and west, hoping for a sign of towering Saint Paul's Cathedral, but his landmark was nowhere.

He looked for some street urchins close to his age to ask for directions, but he didn't see any, and his empty stomach rumbled loudly, as he continued past gin shops speckled in between merchandise shops that sold hats, clothing, shoes, books, and butchered meats. Other than a few drinking taverns, all remained closed. Considerably further down from where he had exited Mr.

O'Brien's cart, he took notice that more people speckled Drury Lane, and he watched a few women and girls carrying baskets, and a man setting up a newspaper stand by a gaslight lamp, as well as a vendor here and there in his shop getting ready for the day. Down the road, he saw a dandy, dressed in a high collared stiff shirt and jacket with long tails, and top hat, escorting two ladies with fancy bonnets and long frilly dresses that cascaded out from their waistlines. He wasn't sure if London was waking up or going to sleep, but figured it was a bit of both.

He passed a pub called *The Queen* and found a wooden bench to rest on, trying to summon his courage to go inside and ask for scraps, but lost his resolve and after a while, resumed his disoriented walking. He noticed some street sweepers ahead, piling up horse manure. They looked his age, so he walked to them.

"Excuse me. Yeh got some grub or bub to spare?"

"Yeh askin' us, Pikey? Yeh see any belly-timber on us? As if we'd share our whacks wid'jah!" said the yellow straw-haired boy. The other two boys pummeled Francois with lashings of profanity, so he ran fast and straight, past more establishments, until finally out of breath, he leaned against a brick wall between two shops, and slunk directly on the ground in his own lost circle. For a long time. He sat. Hopeless.

Wanting to cry, he didn't, but just stared ahead, his eyes blurring into swirly browns of shop timber, dirt ground, and waste. Suddenly, a door swung open to his immediate right, and a well-to-do boy appeared—his periwinkle blue knee-length belted tunic and white trousers revealing his wealth. The boy stared down at Francois for some time, then asked, "Want a sip of my lemonade?"

Just like that, he asked.

Reservedly, Francois nodded, suspect of this strange boy's offer, but desperately wishing his current thirst away. The boy sat next to him, handed the drink over, and Francois gulped-it-gone. The boy stared in disbelief.

"What? I said a sip!"

"I'm sorry. I couldn't stop. What was that? Never drank nothin' so good before."

"Got it in there." The boy raised and knitted his eyebrows as if this drink, as well as the sweet shop he pointed to behind them, should be common knowledge.

"Mr. Smith opens the shop early for us, any time of day my father pleases!"

The sign read, *Smith's Sweet Shoppe, EST* 1810, and Francois looked into the window display as his stomach mocked him.

"Was that you growling?" the boy laughed.

"Not me."

"Here...Turkish Delights," said the boy, who stood up, gathered up his tunic, reached into his pant pocket, sat back down, and poured a handful of strange nuggets into Francois' open hand.

"Thank you!" Francois' eyes ballooned, as he popped two into his mouth. As he crunched into the nuts and hard gel, he thought he'd faint! He stuffed in another, cracked down, saliva flowed, and candy cemented teeth.

"You're very hungry, too! You don't look like a street beggar, though. What's your name?" the boy asked.

"Francois."

"Francois? Not English, that's certain. French?" the boy's eyebrows shifted upward in slight curious contempt.

Then the boy changed the subject entirely, "Want me to get some more for you? My father's rich and buys me whatever I desire. I can get some honey sticks if you prefer."

"I'm terribly thirsty. Got any more of that drink? Ain't got no money on me...."

"I'll see what I can do." The boy grabbed the empty tin from Francois' grasp and ran into Smith's Sweet shop. Soon afterwards, he came out carrying another lemonade and handed it to Francois.

"Drink it quickly because father's paying now. He doesn't like giving to beggars. I'm not saying you're a beggar, but it's just that...."

"I'll drink it," Francois agreed, drinking so fast he burped.

The boy laughed again.

"You're funny! I've got a barm cake from breakfast in my pocket. A bit smashed. Want it?"

Francois nodded yes. As the boy handed it to him, Francois asked, "Yeh know of Saint Paul's Cathedral? Or if not, then, Saint Martin, Ludgate? Am I close? To either, that is?"

"Of course I know Saint Paul's! Who doesn't? But not the other," replied the boy who picked sticky white sugar mortar out of his teeth with his finger. Francois' heart quickened at the same moment the shop door opened.

Out stepped a man whose head seemed to balance on his stiff white collar, which protruded from a black cravat that fancifully folded around his neck, as his woolen frock coat, trimmed in dark velvet arrogance, swaggered out the door. He carried two large boxes in one hand, and his cane, which held his top hat, in his other.

Managing to keep his top hat steady, he tapped his son's shoulder with the cane's brass ferrule, and eyed Francois disapprovingly.

"Come along, son. Let's get to the festivities before your mother chastens me for being late again."

The man's toffee eyes street-swept over Francois. "Come now."

"But father!"

The man took a deep breath, exhaled, and turned to his boy, "Don't tell your mother, this is our secret," as he handed the sweet shop boxes momentarily to his son, popped his cane into air, caught his hat, and placed it on his head.

Kneeling down to Francois, he handed him a shilling. Francois hadn't asked for the money, and shook his head no, but the man barked, "Oh, don't be foolish, boy, get yourself fed. Now come, Samuel, I won't say it again."

Samuel got up immediately, shrugged his shoulders, turned around, and followed his father away, leaving the empty lemonade tin on the shop window frame.

Francois stared at father and son as they crossed the street to the other side. Suddenly, to Francois' surprise, the boy turned around and called out, "Follow us. To the Strand. Turn left at the Strand, and keep going. That'll take you there!"

Samuel's father swung his cane around smoothly against Samuel's backside, and the boy turned forward immediately. His father chastened him with words Francois couldn't hear, but they begot the boy to his recite his ABC's: abide, behave, and comply.

Francois quickly rose and pursued from a solid six meters behind for good measure. Every few blocks, Samuel snuck his head around, cabbage-crimped his face, and produced on his follower a slight smile.

They came to a bustling intersection, and Samuel turned around for the last time, stretched his arm left, pointed his finger east, and shouted "Strand!"

His father quickly pulled him by his ear, then let go as they crossed the large intersection, and Francois waved silently to Samuel's back. His *thank you* fell like litter to the ground, and was soon trampled on by the boot of a man passing by.

Finally, after walking an incline for some time, against a crowded traffic of people, who seemed to pop out of building cracks, Francois began to recognize his surroundings. A pending sense of doom set in. Without a concrete plan, without any idea of what awaited him, his belly churned and throat burned, so he turned his focus toward his purpose—the lockbox.

The Strand soon became Fleet Street and it didn't take Francois long to see the mountainous bell tower of Saint Paul's Cathedral in the distance. He passed by Ludgate Hill, by his old church which he despised, not for what it represented so much as for what it denied him.

Finally he came to Ave Maria Lane as a sick wave overtook him and he peered down the street that would lead him back to Sledgeham. He decided he would walk still further and take a rest at Saint Paul's Cathedral steps, as he needed time to think. What would give him the courage to turn back to Ave Maria Lane, he didn't know.

Francois sat upon the grand west steps of Saint Paul's cathedral, weighted by the image of Apostle Paul's conversion above him, shunned by Queen Anne's back posterior which seemed to condemn him. He always hated this place, these steps, the endless pigeons, though he never understood why it bothered him so.

His stern, prim Sunday school teacher would often stop here with the boys on their walk to and from Saint Mark's Orphanage to their church, Saint Martin-Ludgate, so the boys could *"discover God's power on this earth."* But instead, Francois always thought about Sledgeham's power over him and the boys of Saint Mark's.

He felt the shilling in his pocket and was relieved to have taken the money after all. *For later, my reward for the lockbox.* His stomach was fit to be filled, but it would have to wait. Wobble-kneed, he stood up, stepped down cathedral steps, and felt the shilling in his pocket, reminding his sickly stomach of the barm cake in his opposite pocket, now a pocket of crumbs.

Mashing smashed barm cake into paste, hand to hungry mouth, he tried to swallow, but choked on the dryness, and instead ingested a mouthful of fear and frailty. On the farm, he had finally cleansed his diet of these noxious ingredients. But now, so close to Saint Mark's, old residual toxins circulated like burst boils.

He focused on the lockbox, as his unsteady gait took him closer to Amen Corner, but it was impossible to separate the lockbox from thoughts of Sledgeham. He tried to convince himself that Michael was right this time—that he would find the parchment letter inside the lockbox, revealing to him his past, perhaps unlocking his future. His old desires for the letter that had dissolved at the farm, possessed him again, refueling his longing purpose.

There it was, Amen Corner. A fresh sickly wave of demons feasted on his heart, weakening his resolve, but he kept moving forward. Soon now, he would be at Amen Court, where the walls of Saint Mark's Orphanage stood, waiting to devour him. He breathed deeper now, but couldn't breathe deeply enough. His palms sweat profusely. His mind raced.

Witless fool.

A fresh wave of self-hatred flooded him. So close to the lion's lair, he understood Michael's disgust with him. How could he have forgotten the letter's importance?

No good nothin' fool. Not even a mother could love.

The foul street air encased him, threatening to strangle, as he turned left at Amen Court and walked hesitantly toward hell's gate. He took refuge in the dark, cold alley directly across the street from Saint Mark's. Tucked safely inside the alley crevice, he stared across at the stone structure, sullied with soot, dirt, and broken lives.

The cast iron gate in front proudly displayed a lion and unicorn welded onto two shields, and he mused how such a shelter could appear to an unsuspecting passerby an actual place of refuge against the hardships of life. He contemplated how things weren't what they seemed, how that gate locked out the world from bearing witness to the horror of life—the horror that awaited him now. From the safety of the shadow of the alley, Francois felt a cold darkness overtake him as he scrutinized any signs of movement in the courtyard behind the gate, any signs of life at all.

What's my great plan now? He wished Michael was there. *What would he do?* Francois thought deeply. Michael would wait and watch and strike when the time was right.

How long he had been there, Francois could not say, but he was now leaning against the alley wall from sheer exhaustion and a bone coldness he couldn't shake. He listened to the rumbling of his stomach, but his dry mouth couldn't even swallow his saliva. It felt like hours just standing there, waiting. His fingers felt numb, his head swarmed, and he tried to remember Michael's recollection: The lockbox could be found under the rug and floorboards in Sledgeham's quarters.

Yes, that's all! Imbecile! What was I thinkin'?

Signs of Life! Francois barely saw the slice of thick wooden door swing open. He heard the clanging of something thrown outside, and then the haunting, tongue-lashing rant of his master. That raspy, oily, liquid voice iced him over, even at such a distance! The power to paralyze his prey! His stomach responded first as he ran deeper into the alley, vomiting thin, clear bile, as the walls of the alley narrowed and crushed.

Find it, find you, he whispered, wiping his mouth with his sleeve. *Find it, find you!*

Returning to the edge of the shadowed alley, he looked past the iron gates, into the courtyard, toward the wooden door which was slightly ajar. Again, he heard Sledgeham's diatribe, casting anger into dead air. He felt sudden warmth against his legs, and doused with shame, realized he wet himself. Then came the yelping of some poor boy inside the courtyard—which boy, Francois couldn't decipher. He watched a pail fly mid-air, then heard it clank hard against the pavement.

And was unprepared for what he saw next: A boy limping toward the pail, bending to pick it up.

Spare me this.

Was that Alfred, a thinned cadaver of his former self, dragging his left leg behind him like a tree log?

Alfred! Who did this to yeh?

But he already knew. He hoped his eyes played tricks, but then realized it didn't matter. Even if it wasn't Alfred, it was *still* someone else, paying the price of being born.

The boy struggled forward, his leg dragging along, ball and chain, toward the cast iron gate. Francois got a better look. His heart sank.

Found and punished for his crime.

Alfred carried a bucket and rags in his right hand. He reached the cast iron gate, placed the bucket on the floor, took the rag, and began to clean. For only a moment, he gripped both hands around the locked bars, leaned his face forward, and stared out.

Francois understood the longing in that boy's eyes. Alfred had tasted the fruits on the other side of that gate. Life inside the orphanage was now an even crueler fate.

His heartbreak, a color palate of burnt rage, torment, and mettle, subdued him; he knew what it must have taken for Alfred's leg to drag like that, and it was his fault.

Francois breathed deeply and darted angularly across the street, running with all his might, to the left side of the stone fortress, away from the view of the gated courtyard.

Alfred's eyes flashed, his mouth circled, and he rapid-fire-swung his neck back to make certain he was alone.

Francois scaled the building toward the gate, careful to stay out of view.

"Alfred! It's me! Over here, to the left!"

The bucket clanged against gate.

"Francois! Can't believe it! …Where's Michael?"

Even his voice sounded different, like chopped up meekness.

Alfred kept checking behind him, his hands shaking as he pretended to clean the iron gates with his rag.

"He's not here. Where's Sledgeham?"

"Francois! Go! He'll hurt you. Made a stump out 'a me, can barely put weight down on it. And this here doesn't move no more. 'Crushed the bone…."

Alfred nursed his crippled thumb, as his voice fell away.

"Alfred, I've come for somethin', and I'll take yeh with me, too!"

"Farley's still out there somewhere," whispered Alfred, "But I'm finished, Francois. If you was smart, yeh'd do what Farley did, and go before it ain't too late."

"Alfred, I'll get yeh out. But I've got to get in first. There's somethin' I need inside."

"Worth this?" Alfred pointed to his leg, though he realized Francois couldn't see, and Francois realized he didn't have to.

"Worth that!"

"Ain't gonna let yeh in."

"Alfred, I'll get yeh out! But yeh've got to get me in first."

"What's worth it to yeh? Death? And, where's Michael?"

"Michael's comin'. At least, probably. I'm sure he knows where I am by now. Anyway, first, I need to get a lockbox," Francois paused, "Second, you."

"Me? What yeh plan to do, carry me? An' what's the grand plan for gettin' out again? He's gonna kill Michael if he shows up, and beat you so yeh're not even recognizable. Yeh'll beg for death by the time he's through!"

"Not this time. Got a trick up my sleeve, comin' at him. Please Alfred! Yeh've got to get me in."

"Things don't come at 'em! He comes at things, remember? Besides…It's just that…I don't think I could take another…."

Francois heard Alfred stifling his tears and reproached himself for causing this.

"Not to worry about it then. I'm sorry, Alfred, for what I brought upon yeh sorry lot. I'll try and find a way in an' out, for both of us. Ain't leavin' yeh behind. Good bye for now, Alfred."

Francois began to walk away, wet-eyed.

"Wait! Don't go, Francois." Alfred paused. "I know where he keeps another key to this gate!"

Francois' ears peaked to the sound of his mate, who was his old self again, even if for a fleeting moment.

"Can yeh unlock the gate for me, Alfred? Without him suspectin' anything?"

"I heard him say he's visitin' the parish vicar later today. Important church people comin' any day now. Pending visit's got Sledgeham rabid. He's been tellin' us what to say, how to act, for days. We're frothed with his threats, we are."

"When does he leave?"

"Soon. Maybe an hour or two?"

The thick wooden door opened, and the boys bronzed into corniced gargoyles.

"Yeh talkin' to yehself, yeh bleedin blight? I'll box yeh ears, if yeh don't shut yeh trap. Now finish cleanin' til it shines! Got a show to put on in a few days for the hands that feed us, we do! Get on wid'it!"

"Yes, Sir! Shiny bright, Sir!" Alfred cried, his rag frantic and alive, eating iron.

At the sound of Sledgeham's threat, Francois carried the wind under his feet as he flew past Amen Court, turned onto Warwick Lane, and ducked into *The Oxford Arms* coaching inn. Deep inside the inn's timber quad entrails, Francois sought refuge in an open door leading to a small dingy storage cellar.

In the darkest, dampest corner, he curled into a ball and rocked to his stifled cries.

What've I done to yeh, Alfred? Revenge on Sledgeham for what he's done!

Rage boiled forth as he thought of Alfred and Michael, and every suffering they withstood because of him. His blood filled with retribution and his retribution materialized into a plan. But it was now more complicated. Alfred. He couldn't be left behind. Francois rocked back and forth, repeating his plan, and waited out the eternal hour alone.

Chapter 14: Finding Lost Souls

Saint Mark's Orphanage, Amen Court, afternoon

His demons kept his company in the dark alley, as he waited. He lost track of time, and had no way of knowing if it was too soon to return, but the rat scurrying over his foot helped his decision. He peered into the inn's empty courtyard and sprinted out to the street, retracing his steps toward the insurmountable task ahead. Warwick Lane. Amen Court. Saint Mark's Orphanage. *Hell's Gate.*

Francois peeked into the courtyard through the metal bars, and unexpectedly saw the front door slightly ajar. *A sign from Alfred?* Francois pushed on the gate handle expecting it to be locked, but it too was open. *Alfred unlocked it! Sledgeham's out!*

His feet fought against his crippling memories as he pushed the gate open and walked inside the courtyard. As the gate snapped shut behind, he smelled faint hints of Sledgeham, and dry-heaved, then wiped his mouth with his sleeve. Eyes closed, he hesitated, chewing the inside of his lip, but then, advanced to the front door, listening for sounds inside. Nothing but silence, as he fit through the open door with the slightest shoulder nudge.

The fetid stench inside the small dark foyer sickened his stomach as he viewed the sitting room where Sledgeham's drunken rages always seemed to commence. The room was empty, but he could hear boy's voices trailing from the hallway leading to the kitchen. He heard rowdy laughter and clanking of pots—another sure sign Sledgeham was away.

The narrow dark stairway leading upstairs to Sledgeham's bedchamber beckoned him, but also chastened, scolding his impudence to dare enter. As he ascended the creaking, laughing stairs, his stomach echoed in mimicry, reminding him of his smallness.

Midway up the staircase, he gazed at the faded rectangular spot on the wall that once held the Jesus picture. He retched, this time producing bitter liquid bile, and tried swallowing, but his throat was too dry and the juice too rancid, so he spit out onto his sleeve what he could. With each step up, shadows choked his throat, breathed down his neck, swept over him. Finally, despite his mental obstacles, he made it to the top of the stairway and put his ear to Sledgeham's closed bedroom door.

Suddenly, someone grabbed him from behind, covering his mouth, and every bit of him cowered, as he turned about quickly to face his monster, arms swinging, the floor below him falling away.

"Shush! It's me, Francois!" Alfred whispered, releasing his hand.

"Yeh scamp! How'd yeh sneak up like that?" Francois hurled over, resting hands on knees, then braced himself against the wall. "How long's he been gone?"

"Half hour, I think? Been waitin' for yeh! Never thought yeh'd come back! Hurry it up, now! Get the thing yeh need, what's it called?" Alfred paused. "I'll come too, if yeh meant what yeh said earlier?"

"What about the other boys? Where are they?"

"Don't mind. Yeh're wasting time! Just go!"

"I'll be quick!" Francois whispered, as he turned the door knob to the master's chamber and opened.

The regular fetid Sledgeham scent that haunted the halls and seeped into the crevices of Saint Mark's, wafted in such concentrated form toward Francois and Alfred, they gagged in unison. Francois covered his nose with his soiled sleeve, walked to the rug, knelt before it, rolled it back, and saw the discolored lining of wooden planks in the floor. Alfred stared from the door frame, watching guard, and murmuring, "Can't believe it, can't believe!"

Hands shaking, head swelling, Francois lifted the first plank, then the second, placing them gently onto the ground next to him. There it lay, lifeless but for all the life it might contain inside! A weathered walnut wooden box with two metal hooks on each side, and an ornate brass keyhole in the center.

The lockbox! Found it, Michael!

One question remained: Did it hold the object of their obsessive desire? He grabbed the lockbox, stuck it under his shirt, secured it with the rope around his waist, and half-smiled.

He replaced the first wooden plank, then the second.

Suddenly, Alfred screamed agonizing cries, "Ouch, stop, please! Run Francois, run!"

Then, the clanging of Alfred hurled across the hall.

The tortured cry, "Can't get up! Go, Francois!"

~ 203 ~

Frozen solid by the lurker outside the door, Francois bent his head down to the ground. He let out a deep howl.

Then this is how it ends. Then, this is how it ends. Then this is how, it ends. Three times, the punctuated sentences struck, and the irony of his situation snapped him in half. His immediate fears melted away into a mad cachinnation of strange and aberrant laughter.

Terror, anger, and acceptance pitifully converged like arches refracting and dispersing into one another against light. For the first time in this dark place, Francois understood the sad truth of his existence and the futility of his quest.

In spite of being only nine years of age, or perhaps because of it, he shifted his focus solely onto what he needed to do. The belligerence of clarity overtook him.

If nothing else, an end to Sledgeham. If nothing, else an end.

Francois sat and waited but a few seconds. The beast would surely come to him, and predictably, it appeared, blocking the door. Still, Francois remained on the ground next to the floor hole, cradling the lockbox under his shirt, his eyes as wild as the beast.

"Happy to see me? A nice surprise, eh?" The words rolled out of Francois, brazen-faced, crisp around the edges.

"Came back, did yeh? Surprised? Ain't surprised, foolish boy. Knew yeh'd come back. Know what yeh want, what yeh always wanted. It's in there, alright. I kept it right there waitin' all these years, and yeh finally found it. Where's Michael? Yeh come alone? Now that's hard teh believe. What? Michael finally tire of yeh, just like yeh mammy?"

"Lookin' for Michael? Maybe he's in the closet over there?" Francois' audacity confused Sledgeham, who'd never heard the boy mutter more than a few drippy apologetic words. Keeping watchful eye on Francois, but playing the boy's bluff, he tramped to the closet, swung the door open, and in vicious vituperation, he struck a moth-eaten suit, knocking boxes, odds and ends around.

Francois' hand slipped into his left pant pocket, he felt a jagged edge poke his finger, and cupped his fingers around the object, as Sledgeham shut the closet door.

"Had me goin' there. Think it's funny? Play me the fool, eh?" Sledgeham's wrinkled face spit. Francois spoke to delay the inevitable ending he knew was coming.

"I thought yeh was meetin' the church elders?"

"Ahh! That what yeh thought? That what Alfred told yeh? Well, had to put it off, on account of yeh cripple friend over there, who seemed teh think I wouldn't notice an unlocked gate? He knows to keep it locked. Why'd he leave it open, I asked myself? And yeh know what came to mind? Michael, that's who! Figured he'd finally come back for the box. Knew he'd seen it that day! Knew he'd be back for it. Just a matter of time. Timin's everythin'. But relyin' on Alfred? Shame on yeh! Alfred's a thick head. Haven't yeh learnt by now that relyin' on a knuckle head's a piss poor way to go?"

"Get out of my way, so I can take leave," Francois demanded.

"Get outta yeh way? Is that what yeh think I'll do? Found some grit an' backbone out there wherever yeh've been hidin', didn't yeh?" Sledgeham simpered. "Better make yehself comfortable. Yeh'll be stayin' put til Michael shows his mug."

"Michael ain't here. Ain't comin' neither!"

Sledgeham stood over him now.

"Michael's comin,' that much I know. Wherever yeh are, that boy's sure to follow. Like the nursery rhyme, the little lamb, this time headed for slaughter."

Sledgeham leaned over Francois and shot a swift hard kick into his right side, and his rib cracked against the lockbox that cut, sliced, and buttered him.

The kick sobered Francois' bold talk, which fell away to slow boiling recognition of his life ending. Alfred was right. He would never find a way out of Saint Mark's. He would die with the lockbox tucked against him, letter inside, and all the knowledge it contained still a mystery. But this was enough for him. He knew now that Michael was right. The letter was locked away all these years inside this box. And it must have contained powerful information to provoke Sledgeham like it did.

Michael told the truth about the night he arrived at Saint Mark's, as limited as his information was. He was wrongly taken, wrongly kept. This box containing the letter was proof enough that he did have family somewhere on this earth, that for whatever disastrous reason, life fell apart to land him here. Yes, this would have to be enough.

"Yeh're right, Michael's here," Francois winced; it hurt to breathe and speak. He tightened his grasp around the sharp object in his left hand.

~ 206 ~

"Come out of yeh hidin' place, milk-livered mutt," Sledgeham yelled to the air.

By now, the other boys in the orphanage filled the hall outside.

"Come out! I'll sniff yeh out!"

Sledgeham raged, as he ransacked his room like a marauding pillager; searching under the bed, inside the tall wardrobe, everywhere, everywhere, looting in vain.

The lockbox welded itself, hard and unforgiving, to Francois' cracked rib; nonetheless, he held it tightly as Sledgeham dragged him by his hair to the closet, and he released a howling cry.

Swinging the closet door open, Sledgeham reached deep inside this time, further ruffling his belongings, pushing more boxes aside, wafting his closet stench, as his fist slammed against empty closet door frame, and his animal squeal reverberated.

He tow-pulled Francois out of his bedroom toward the boys' sleeping quarters. A three year old boy cried out, and an older boy named Peter, scooped him up while holding another child by his hand, as they scuttled down the stairs.

Alfred still lay crumpled on the ground where Sledgeham had thrown him, his bad leg twisted. Pulling Francois by his hair, Sledgeham stepped on Alfred as he made his way to the dormitory room. Against Alfred's shriek cry, Francois' hatred erupted as he watched Sledgeham reach for his horse switch, but it wasn't there.

Sledgeham's oily voice called, "Fee, Fi, Fo, Fum…I smell a rat named Michael, and I'll gut him, for pleasure."

Still, stale, speechless silence.

"Think yeh can hide from me? I'm no fool!"

In his madness, Sledgeham dropped Francois, who scrabbled down the stairs, as Sledgeham tore through the dormitory, rifling and rummaging soiled cots and tattered blankets. Still, he found no signs of Michael, and ran out of the boys' quarters into the shat room, then out again, calling now for both Michael and Francois, who he realized had slipped through his fingers, which cooked him doubly mad.

Francois disappeared behind the stairway below, as he watched Sledgeham traipse back and forth. Francois made himself visible, taunting his beast.

"I'm here, mongrel," Francois yelled upstairs, his hand cupped around a sharp flint piece turning in his fingers.

Sledgeham darted down the stairs, missed two steps at the bottom, and fell, but rose immediately, shouting violently.

Déjà vu. Francois remembered the same scene playing itself out the night of their escape. *Final act ends different this time!*

Francois' taunts heightened as he turned the corner leading to the kitchen, and Sledgeham pursued, confused for a slight moment, as the front door stood ajar, and the front gate appeared open.

Francois worried the open door would throw Sledgeham off his hunt, and thought quickly: *Michael!* Mere mention of Michael would seduce and ambush. His plan depended on it.

Plan: *Sledgeham's final curtain call, seven years too late.*

Not part of his plan: On his way down the stairs, Francois had seen Peter usher the two youngest residents out of the unlocked door, out the unlocked gate. Good for them, Godspeed, but Alfred remained upstairs and he wasn't going anywhere without him.

"This way Michael, over here! Hide!" Francois baited from the kitchen.

Francois' needling hook lured Sledgeham down the hallway into the kitchen, where the last of the two orphan boys, Radbourne and Bobby, huddled together in front of the kitchen table.

"Step away, Ragtag and Bobtail," Sledgeham grimaced, "less yeh want a piece of it?"

They understood there was no point to blocking Sledgeham, and fell away, pieces of a broken fan, exposing Francois, who held something behind his back, as a rope dragged by his side.

"Front door's unlocked! Go!" Francois yelled to the boys as they scattered away.

"The letter's mine, an' yeh're mine. Hand over the box!" Sledgeham slurred.

Francois stared back at his master and shook his head.

"Give up the box, if yeh want to die quick. Can make it slow too—that yeh wish?"

"Come an' get it."

"Gone mad, queer mad, have yeh?"

"Yeh've no idea!" Ain't givin' up the box feh sure."

"Yeh don't think so? S'pose that kick wasn't enough of a reminder who's in charge?"

"Yeh ain't in charge no more. I'm gone from here," Francois' smiting smile struck Sledgeham. "See? That's me, over there, runnin' out the door, away from here. I'm already gone, and yeh can't find me."

"Lunatic! Such a pity yeh are."

"Yeh're just seein' my ghost, 'tis all, but he's not a pity."

Francois smiled slightly, though his eyes remained empty.

"What yeh blabberin', crazy Frenchie?"

"Gonna watch yeh kill me. Seen it all a thousand times before in my mind. Been the same nightmare for as long as I can remember. And, now weh're here. It's happenin'. But ain't as afraid as I'd expected. Yeh're right 'bout Michael. He'll be here soon. Maybe he's here now. Gonna have to give it yeh best today, master, 'cause we won't stop comin' at yeh til weh're dead. An' then, there's yeh other problem to consider 'cause long after weh're dead, weh'll still be visitin'—in yeh sleep, yeh wakin' hours. We'll be the death of yeh, me and Michael. Come what may, yeh end here today, with us."

Sledgeham stared puzzle-faced, as the boy's ghastly rat-a-tat prattle scratched his nerves. He had never head the boy speak more than two or three words at a time but this loquacious rattling jeered and jibed at him.

"Yeh speakin' riddles, but this'll even yeh mind out some!"

He jumped toward Francois, grabbed his shirt, and threw his arm back to swing.

With great force, Francois swung his left arm out from behind, and jabbed the master in his lower abdomen, sticking the razor-sharp flint arrow deep into the master's hungry flesh, which swallowed whole.

"For Alfred," Francois whispered.

Against Sledeham's cries, Francois' thoughts flashed to Beatrix, who had given him this two inch shard of flint rock, upon his request, just yesterday. She gladly gave several more pieces and even offered to teach him her fire skill. He had other purposes for it, he told her, and she shrugged her shoulders.

How well he had done for himself, fashioning his own fire from flint, rock, and fist; carried into London in pocket and sleeve, his fire burned deep!

Francois pulled his hand away, flint shard stuck inside his master, his fingers bloody, but he felt no pain.

Sledgeham bellowed, grabbed Francois' neck with one hand, and choked hard, as Francois gasped, shimmied his right arm sleeve, and felt another flint blade fall into his hand, and then into his fingers, which rolled the pointed side out. Unable to breathe, he panicked, and swung his fist around, repeatedly striking Sledgeham's face and neck.

For Michael, Francois gasped, though his words croaked thin.

The master screamed, released Francois' neck, and wiped his raw, open cheek. They fell to the ground, Francois wrestled free, and crawled away from Sledgeham toward the kitchen door that lead to the high brick walled backyard and privy. But Sledgeham overpowered him, grabbing his legs, pulling him closer. With what little strength he possessed, Francois kicked and fought but it was no use, he couldn't break free. Instead, he curled his flint fist toward Sledgeham's side, and pushed against tough flesh until the flint was gone. Spent, his muscles gave way, his fight was over.

He had done his job. He found the lockbox. He ended Sledgeham's reign. Even managed to set most of the boys free. Now he was ready to be consumed. He was not afraid to die.

Francois' body fell limp as Sledgeham pulled him inward, and gave him one last blow.

The blow had knocked him out, for how long he wasn't sure, but the screams rushing in from the front door, hallway, and kitchen, traveled to where he and Sledgeham lay in a heap, the commotion awakening him. Then, came trampled footsteps, yells, tables and furniture pushed aside.

He looked up, and saw Michael, who had come for him, and he thought one last time of Sledgeham.

Just a matter of time. Timin's everythin'.

There was Mr. Middleton, and the other orphan boys all hovering around, staring in wonderment as master Sledgeham writhed on the floor. Sledgeham saw them, too. His charred cheeks flushed white as Michael ran to him and stepped forcefully on the hand that held his brother's leg.

"I hate you! I hate you!" Michael cried, kicking at Sledgeham, but Mr. Middleton grabbed Michael and restrained him. Michael collapsed into Mr. Middleton, heaving, and they both sank.

Sledgeham reached his weakened arm up and grabbed at Michael's back. Mr. Middleton grabbed Sledgeham's arm, bent it around and twisted it upward.

"You want a fight? I've brought you a fair one, the first fair fight of your life," Mr. Middleton screamed with no restraint in his voice. He pushed the arm further to its breaking point until Sledgeham first pleaded for mercy, then simply faded away into oblivion, the pain too great to handle.

"Leave him," said a man's voice. A constable walked in with two other officers behind, one carrying Alfred in his arms. Trailing behind the officers were the other orphans of Saint Marks, including Peter, who had earlier run out the orphanage doors to retrieve the law.

"Is this the subject who inflicted your injury?" the constable asked Alfred.

"Yes Sir, the one Sir."

"And the same subject who has terrorized the others?"

"Yes, Sir," Alfred nodded, as the other orphans corroborated Alfred's story.

"Very well, then, pick him up. He's going for a little ride."

An officer walked to Sledgeham and tapped his left foot to the lifeless body. Again, harder this time, hitting the exact spot where Francois' flint invaded. Sledgeham stirred, then cried.

"I'll kill yeh now, bastard...."

Before Sledgeham could finish, the officer's boot pressed into his back, causing him to heave and wheeze.

The officer leaned over him.

"Going to kill me are you? A direct threat against an officer? Shall we talk of your plan over at Horsemonger Lane?"

Sledgeham turned his head up toward the officers standing over him, confused by their presence.

"Horsemonger Lane? Not me! Take the boy there! He's the one yeh want! I've been stabbed by 'em!"

"Save it for your trial. Your worn act tires me," the constable replied.

The constable threw down a set of thin iron hand cuffs and motioned to an officer to shackle Sledgeham's hands. The other officer handed Alfred to Mr. Middleton and helped pull Sledgeham to his feet. Sledgeham barely reached their chins. This detail seemed to resonate with Francois—how small Sledgeham looked when measured against other men.

The boys of Saint Mark's Orphanage and Mr. Middleton, who carried Alfred, followed the officers out, as they dragged Sledgeham away.

Michael and Francois remained alone and quiet for a moment.

"Look under the table," Francois broke silence, his coral lips streaked blue.

Michael looked beneath, gasped, scrambled, and knocked his head, as he pulled out the lockbox. He buried his face in his left hand, held onto the lockbox with his right, and hid his elation.

"Is it in there? The letter? I've spent my life tryin' to find that letter! But yeh've found it, Francois! It's yours for keeps!"

Michael handed the lockbox to Francois, who put it down and took Michael's hands. Their eyes locked and Francois' throat tightened but his sounds still escaped.

"On the farm I said some things. An' I doubted. Then, worse. Tried to forget what yeh done for me all these years. If not for yeh troubles, it'd all be lost. Never would've known there was anythin' to look for. Never would've known there was anythin' to find. I'm sorry. For the burden I've been."

"Burden? Stupid, yeh are. Don't yeh know what yeh've been to me? Don't yeh know why I never turned into a savage like him?

Yeh kept me human all these years, Francois. Yeh gave me purpose." Michael's brown eyes softened.

Francois and Michael sat under the wooden table slab together, Michael picked up the lockbox, placed it into Francois' lap, and they listened to the others return back inside.

"What if it ain't in here, Michael?"

"The letter doesn't matter anymore. Glad yeh're sittin' down. There's somethin' I've been holdin' back."

Hallway footsteps neared the kitchen and both boys turned around abruptly. Standing in the doorway, Mr. Middleton wore a used face as his hands rubbed the silent *k* off his *k*nackered cheeks.

"There's something I've been holding back, as well, but it's time to tell you, Francois—at least just enough to not disappoint or raise your hopes too high."

And, there began the unveiling of pieces of a missing boy.

Chapter 15: Finding Justice

Middleton's Bakery, June 12th-26th

Old Bailey Court-house, London

The days ahead were busy for all the boys of Saint Mark's, especially Francois and Michael—filled with testimony to and inquiry by the law. They spent their days in the justice hall of Old Bailey talking to solicitors—different questions, same questions. Francois and Michael spoke nothing of the lockbox and in turn no one asked them about it, because it didn't exist.

Last Saturday, when Mr. Middleton came upon Francois and Michael in the kitchen of Saint Mark's orphanage, so much and just enough was said between them. Mr. Middleton took the lockbox from Francois, promising to safely hide it away. At first Francois refused to hand the lockbox over, but Michael convinced him that the law might confiscate it during their investigation. Who knew if or when the lockbox or its contents would be returned at the end of this uncertain process? Mr. Middleton swore to protect the lockbox and its contents, at all cost, and because Michael trusted, Francois felt the sworn words to be true.

The boys were to stay with him at the bakery shop. Mr. Middleton had received permission from the courts to house them each night during Sledgeham's investigation and trial, but each day they were expected to return to the justice hall for further examination.

The lockbox resided untouched on Mr. Middleton's desk, yet still, Francois couldn't open it regardless of Michael's persistence. The tick-tock of Sledgeham's adage rang his head every hour on the hour: *Timin's everythin'*.

Not yet, Francois knew. *But when?*

Francois and Michael returned to Mr. Middleton's bakery on Tuesday evening, exhausted from a particularly grueling day of testimony. When they walked into Mr. Middleton's shop, they were surprise-greeted by Bernadette and Mr. and Mrs. O'Brien, who had also been called upon the courts. Bernadette jumped up from the table, ran to the boys, and hugged them both. As usual, Francois embraced her and Michael recoiled.

"How good it is to see you! We've only just arrived. We testify tomorrow morning. Michael, come let me have a look at you," Mrs. O'Brien reached out.

Michael stiffened and wrestled free from her quick embrace.

"Did yah see the papers? Eh? *The Standard*! *The Herald*! *The Town*!" Mr. O'Brien enthusiastically spread out three different newspapers.

"I caught a glimpse," Mr. Middleton nodded approvingly.

"Papers say Sledgeham's bein' kept pre-trial at Newgate prison, next to Old Bailey. Real dirty place rumor has it—infested. Aye, not enough justice fer 'em if I had me way," Mr. O'Brien snarled.

"Listen, it's being reported that his hands and body profusely shook in court this morning—probably delirium tremors," Mrs. O'Brien added, as she read The Herald newspaper.

Francois thought of broken flint shards embedded under skin.

"The papers all say they'll bring about a fast trial for 'em. Public outcry demands it—social justice, they're sayin'. Your story's spreadin' almost as fast as the Great Fire of 1666! Tis good news fer yah both, havin' the public by yer side. That'll ensure those political mites think twice before lettin' him off easy."

"Where's Beatrix?" Michael interrupted, redirecting conversation.

The O'Brien's looked tensely at each other, then to Mr. Middleton and Bernadette.

"Best not mention her, boys. Best keep her far away from yer business and the law. Plans are in the works, thanks to Mr. Middleton."

Mr. O'Brien's reply hinted of lament laced with acceptance, and Mr. Middleton edged in to help explain.

"The Beauchamp's could surface any time soon, especially with my name in the papers, and my association with this scandal. They know something, not sure what, but if they start to inquire with the law and the law asks me about it, I'm not sure...." Mr. Middleton's voice trailed.

"Father? What aren't you sure about?" Bernadette asked.

"It would complicate things for us," Mrs. O'Brien interjected.

How much more complicated can complicated get? Francois mused.

"What father? What complication?" Bernadette asked impatiently.

Complicated like flin-tin-skin?

Mr. Middleton settled his half-baked eyes on his daughter, as he cleared his throat, and straightened his vest.

"Bernadette, when you're betwixt and between the law and truth, you don't always have a plan. You can't predict what you'll be asked. You don't know how you'll respond. Under the law, with the help of a barrister's tongue, the good deeds of man can be twisted into a devil's staff, whilst the devil himself walks free."

Mr. Middleton's words pierced Francois, but it was his perfectly curved vocal inflection, delivering perfectly carved truth, that deeply satisfied. In return, he offered Mr. Middleton a token of his appreciation by purposefully shifting the subject of Bernadette's worry to the words of his own legal advocate.

"Yesterday, my solicitor told me the trial shall be set for Friday. He said he's delivered enough convictin' evidence to my barrister to take to the court judge. Said the assigned judge sides keenly to social reform issues like mine, whatever that means."

"Finally some justice for you, around the corner," Mrs. O'Brien spoke. "For all of you, Beatrix included."

What about Beatrix? Francois turned to Michael, who wondered the same.

Bernadette ran to the table, and began passing out cider mugs.

"To new beginnings then?" Bernadette asked.

Francois, Mr. Middleton, and Michael caught private glances at one another, but shifted their eyes away, guilty with kept-secrets.

Old Bailey Courthouse, London, Friday June 19th

On Friday June 19th, Francois, Michael, Alfred, the O'Brien's, Mr. Middleton, Bernadette, three of the other six orphan boys, a constable and two officers all testified at Sledgeham's trial. Beatrix remained in hiding, far away from London and the Beauchamp's.

It took the jurors at Old Bailey Courthouse two hours of testimony and thirty minutes of deliberation to convict Sledgeham of assault, attempted murder, and perversion of justice—all non-capital offenses, but the combined sentences ensured that Sledgeham would not see light of day outside Horsemonger prison's walls for the duration of his life.

As the courtroom emptied, it was impossible to miss the hollering cheers outside, faint and distant at first, then louder, as someone from the inner court proceeding ran out and shouted the verdict to the large crowd assembled on the streets. Francois and Michael stood together under large court pillars as two bailiffs led Sledgeham toward them, toward the arch door, from the central court.

"Hear that?" Michael snickered. "Where've they been the last seven years?"

"No where, that's where. Came for the show. Like a good endin', don't they, Michael? Can't blame 'em."

Francois led Michael outside the narrow arch door, a few meters ahead of the guards, who were still inside, dragging Sledgeham as he maundered toward his fate. As they stepped into daylight, Francois' eyes swept curiously over the angry, ranting mob. Michael's wolf eyes followed the scent of wounded meat and mumbled curses as he watched Sledgeham dragging.

Francois stared at the crowd of onlookers.

Why'd yeh come?

The bailiffs dragged Sledgeham through the arch, poking him with their truncheons down the steep step, outside, to the dirt ground. Sledgeham's grey, blotchy skin matched the building's masonry blocks, shedding first hint that septicemia took hold to soon fade him into oblivion. Flint shard justice served with a twist.

Francois hit Michael's arm to get his attention, and pointed past the hungry crowd to the prison cart that was to deposit Sledgeham in Horsemonger Lane. The people chanted, calling for Sledgeham's head, screaming vulgarities. Francois focused on their faces, on their moving mouth pieces, but it brought him no solace, as he heard Sledgeham's rants in their own cries.

The court bailiffs handed Sledgeham over to two prison guards, their lustful eyes eager to possess broken things.

Michael's scrutinized stare locked on Sledgeham, while Francois swept his eyes over the horn-mad mob. He was surprised by the unexpected turnout. Wanting to remember each single face, to recall each singular detail of this day at some later point in time, he started with the front row semi-circle of spectators. Dock workers, merchants, mill-hands, mothers, children, laborers, butchers, bakers, candlestick makers…a blurred smear of sweet, salty, bitter, sour human face.

But then, he saw the one familiar face that could not blend with the others. He gasped and whispered to Michael but Michael would not turn away from Sledgeham.

Farley!

It was him: thick, bold-faced, unapologetic, and free. Farley caught sight of Francois' stare, as he had been watching Francois and Michael for some time now. Knowing he'd been spotted, he tipped his cap to Francois, but held up his finger to his lips and motioned for Francois to remain quiet. Francois nodded back.

"Michael, It's Farley! He's out there!"

Michael turned abruptly, sweeping the crowd, and found Farley, who in turn nodded, raised his hand, and saluted Michael. Michael and Francois hid their half-smiles as they watched Farley's eyes shift to Sledgeham, and they followed suit.

The guards led Sledgeham's frail form past the throng of people, who pelted rotten fruits, vegetables, and stones, until finally Sledgeham, flanked on each side, stood but three feet away from Farley.

Michael kept his eyes on Sledgeham, but Francois turned his attentions back to Farley, who held up a brick in his hand, pointing at the convicted criminal. Francois watched intently as Farley's arm rose to possess good aim. But his face looked hesitant, in contrast to the readiness of his body to release. Now Sledgeham was just past him.

Take yeh aim. Take yeh shot!

Francois watched Farley pull his arm back swiftly to catapult the brick forward, aiming precisely at the back of Sledgeham's head. But, in the seconds he had to release, he didn't throw the brick, after all. Instead, he thundered foul words into the air, and threw the brick down in front of where he stood, as Francois watched it crack. Farley grabbed his head with his hands, and muttered under his breath. Then he looked up at Francois and Michael, and his lips uttered, *forgive me.* Sound not seen or heard.

A laborer standing next to Farley saw the brick fall, picked up the larger of the two pieces, and without hesitation, hurled it against the base of Sledgeham's leg, where it cracked with a thump into the back crevice of his knee, tripping the brittle man.

Farley turned against the roar of laughter, and headed away, never looking back to say goodbye.

Good luck Farley.

Francois watched Farley disappear behind a corner, and his gaze turned back to Sledgeham, just in time to watch legs and arms shackled into chains, body placed into cart, and shell lead away.

Good.

The thought left Francois unsatisfied, incomplete.

*Heading to O'Brien's Farm, Friday June 26*th*, afternoon*

A few days following Sledgeham's trial—and Michael's exoneration—the court magistrate granted permission for Francois and Michael to take leave with the O'Brien's, and to remain in their custody while their futures were decided by the courts. Mr. Middleton and Bernadette had already said their goodbyes—they left to O'Brien's farm the day of Sledgeham's conviction—straight from the courthouse, and off to take care of Beatrix—to get her to safety once and for all—though the *how, what, when* details remained a mystery for the boys, and the boys remained at Middleton's Bakery under Aunt Patricia's care, until now.

Today, Francois and Michael would join the O'Brien family back at the farm. Francois' heavy head finally had a chance to rest after an intense few last weeks, but he couldn't quiet his mind.

Mr. Middleton's story of the missing boy had too many holes, too many vagaries and impossibilities. And why did he keep the name of the missing boy's mother, his wife's cousin, so secret?

Tryin' to spare me what?

Did he tell Michael her name?

Would he keep it from me, if he knew?

Francois looked at the soft scenery as he sat in Mr. O'Brien's cart, which held him and Michael together for the second time, while Mrs. O'Brien shared a seat next to her husband. He remembered the morning he first rode in this cart, unsure whether Michael would live or die. But they made it out after all. Sledgeham could never hurt them or anyone else again. Michael had always told him they would find a way out of Saint Mark's. They found a way out and they found a way back in. They found the lockbox. Had they found the letter?

What stops me?

Francois shifted the lockbox in his hands, and moved closer to Michael, who sat at the cart's edge, bent over the side, watching the wheel turn against the wet dirt road.

"I heard the O'Brien's talk last night," Michael said low, still facing the ground.

"What'd they say?"

"Lots. There was more talk about Mr. Middleton and Bernadette's departure to France. Can't believe Mr. Middleton went without us. Ain't never thought to ask if we'd be comin'. Jus' assumed...."

"Did they mention Beatrix?"

"Yea," Michael's body hung out of the cart.

"She alright? When they comin' back?"

"Better off, she is, but who can say? Don't know if the Beauchamp's stopped their search, but can't blame her for wantin' to get away, no matter. Anyway, don't know if they'll ever be back, at least with Beatrix." Michael spit at the road.

"Mr. Middleton and Bernadette? Oh, they'll return," Francois said assuredly.

Yes, he knew that much. But for him, the real question was what news they'd bring, if any. He wasn't sure of anything, but the last few months had taught him that anything was possible.

"How far is France anyway?" Michael asked.

"Prrh! No idea but yeh have to cross the channel so I think it's far."

The light misty rain fell harder now, and Mrs. O'Brien called for the boys to cover up, but Michael kept leaning over the side, watching the wheels turn, the ground spin. Francois covered himself with a sack, then threw one to Michael, who let it fall.

"Yeh gotta prepare for whatever happens," Michael said.

"Yeh mean about what Mr. Middleton told us? About his suspicions?"

"Yeah, that and…" Michael hesitated, "everythin' else that could come of it. Or not."

The fields rain-blurred past Francois like revolving pictures in a spinning drum. His own thoughts spun. The last time he and Michael rode in this cart together, he was sure they'd be found out and Michael was half dead. He ran his finger over the brass keyhole of the wooden lockbox, cold to touch.

Francois' thoughts turned again for the hundredth thousandth millionth time to Mr. Middleton's story. To the tragedy of the boy. To the mystery of the boy. To the possibility of the boy: *Francois. Could he be me?*

His thoughts turned to France.

Who's to return with Mr. Middleton? Someone? Or no one at all?

O'Brien's Farm, late evening

Benny and Matilda had barely halted before Francois jumped out to greet Jingles, who barked and wagged his tail in circles, endlessly harassing, vying for attention. The rain ceased, but clouds darkened, and Francois, followed by Michael, went to sit under his favorite magnolia tree, and shifted close to the tree trunk—its thick leaves and pink bloomed teacups having just collected a downpour of rain, also protected the ground underneath from wetness. Jingles curled up next to Francois, resting his head in his lap, his wet nose pushing the lockbox out of way.

William ran outside to greet them, followed by Mary, enthusiastically waving a letter in her hand. She ran to her parents first, and spoke rapidly as they nodded with approval, and then called out to Francois, whom she ran to, and handed him the letter. He gave a puzzled stare. Michael tensed. William called Mary back to where they stood, but she ignored her brother and spoke.

"It's from Mr. Middleton to you. He wrote it, prompted by the letter he received. Let me be clear…The day before the trial, a letter arrived from France for Mr. Middleton. When he returned here the next day, he opened it immediately, and turned ghost white. I asked him what was wrong, but he didn't say. He told Bernadette and Beatrix to pack their belongings immediately. Out of nowhere he said they were to leave to Calais the next morning! He folded the letter into his jacket pocket, then, borrowed mother's quill, and wrote something to you, Francois. He asked me to give it to you upon your return."

Mary exhaled and then kneeled down to Francois' side, her dress hem soiled from damp earth. Mr. and Mrs. O'Brien, and William, soon joined them under the tree.

"Whose name was posted as a return address on the letter that Mr. Middleton received from France?" Michael asked.

"Just initials. VGD? It was postmarked from Calais, France, addressed to Mr. Middleton, but our farm address."

"Go on, what's it say?" Michael's impatience annoyed Francois.

"Don't want to read it right now, Michael. Here, take it."

"Privacy? Is what you need?" Mrs. O'Brien asked, knowingly.

Francois cast his eyes away from her, fixing instead on a portion of broken stone post fence in the distance, and then, the Jersey cows nearby grinding grass with their teeth. But he shook his head, then replied, "Just Michael. I'm sorry ma'am."

"Think nothing of it, dear boy!" Mrs. O'Brien gathered her brood, shooing them toward the house, calling out, "We're right over here if you need us."

Michael opened the letter, read it over silently, cleared his voice, and read aloud:

Dear Francois,

By the time you read this letter, Bernadette and I will have taken leave with Beatrix by our side, with hope that we can get Beatrix to safety, far away from here. She was sorry she could not say good-bye.

Though I have no idea how this strange adventure will end, I anticipate I might have something for you upon our return to England. At least I desire such an outcome.

If you haven't done so yet, it is time to open the lockbox. I think I know why you have hesitated, and perhaps it is because of what I told you back in London. For that, I apologize. Confusion was not my intention. Nothing can hurt you anymore, Francois. The demon of your past is slain.

Perhaps the letter can provide contentment for you until I return with more news. If not, at least it might appease after wondering for so many years. No matter what, you have a home now, a place you never need depart, if you so choose.

With fatherly affection, James

Francois' lack of expression contradicted the apprehension he felt by Mr. Middleton's note. He thought about the unopened lockbox, about the possible letter waiting inside. The sky darkened again and played a minor chord as thunder sang.

"Open it, Francois. It's time!" Michael insisted.

"There's some things I can't put out from my mind that's stoppin' me," stammered Francois.

He glanced quickly back to Michael, whose patience was spent.

"Might sound crazy, 'cause for years back at Saint Mark's, would've done anythin' to know. But now, ain't certain. This must sound strange."

"Give it to me if yeh don't want to open it, but I do!" blurted Michael, frustrated. He pulled at the lockbox in Francois' hands. No fight. It fell half way into damp dirt.

"Wait Michael!" blurted Francois, grabbing it. "What if what I find inside takes me away? From the O'Brien's? All of this? You?"

Francois heard Mary and William say something, but they were too far away. Then Mr. and Mrs. O'Brien spoke loudly.

Mr. O'Brien called out first, "Yer alright, Francois. Whatever's inside, it'll be fine, son."

"Do you need me, Francois? To help?" asked Mrs. O'Brien.

Francois shook his head no, and Michael grunted, as he passed Francois the picklock he had faithfully carried in his pocket since the day of the lockbox discovery.

Michael shouted, "He'll be fine on his own. Anyway, I'm here."

Michael nudged Francois, who nodded again, exhaled deeply, steadied his hands, and opened the keyhole. Simple jiggling. A few twists. Opened.

Amongst some coins, a watch, jewelry, and other plundered trinkets, Francois pulled out a tattered, thin parchment paper rolled into a scroll, yellowed and cracked around the edges.

He unrolled it: Vertically torn. Liquor stained. Smeared, smudged print. Faint smell of past.

First he just stared through the shapes, through the squiggled curves and lines. Then, silently he read, his eyes absorbing each word, each broken sentence, like golden droplets—and that is what they were: The hieroglyphics of him.

Francois passed the letter to Michael, and then leaned into Jingles, who faithfully remained by his side, licking his hand.

"Take it, then," Francois said.

The O'Brien's ran over, the anticipation too much for them to contain their composure; Francois didn't mind. Hadn't they deserved a piece of this moment, as well?

Mrs. O'Brien lifted the heavy fabric of her dress as she knelt down and placed her arm around Francois, who melted into her. Mary took to his other side, while William and Mr. O'Brien stayed next to Michael.

"It's ripped in half, that scum!" cried Mr. O'Brien, looking over Michael's shoulder.

"But, there's somethin' here…somethin' important! Listen!" Michael read the tarnished letter aloud:

ober 1830

son of Claude
gne France. Please
ken without consent.
to return him. Madame he
een cared for deeply. I am sorry.

"Son of Claude, your father's name! And France! Confirmed! Your father's name!" Mrs. O'Brien's joy spilled.

Michael and Francois glanced knowingly at each other.

"I'd kill 'em with bare hands if he wasn't already a dyin' man," Mr. O'Brien couldn't move past the act behind the tear: Sledgeham's final sick pleasure.

"This here's the part that matters most! The person who was last with Francois!" Michael read the sentence aloud, "'I am sorry.'"

"Is the letter signed, Michael? Who's sorry?" asked Mrs. O'Brien, but Francois figured he knew what Michael meant—the part that mattered most—the 'I am sorry' for what happened part.

Ain't acceptin' apologies at this time....

"Not the 'sorry' part. Listen carefully!"

Michael, read the whole letter out loud a second time:

"'Ken without consent.' 'To return him,' 'Madame he een cared for deeply,' 'I am sorry'...Francois, it's just as Mr. Middleton said! This proves it's you! Taken....Taken without consent!"

Francois' thoughts jumbled as evidence and proof set in.

I could be him.

"What proves what? Whad'jah mean by that, lad? What did Mr. Middleton say?" asked Mr. O'Brien.

"Michael, please hand me the letter," said Mrs. O'Brien. Michael did as she requested.

Mrs. O'Brien deciphered the next broken words, "Something. 'g.n.e, France'. 'Please'...Something, something. Then, like you say, Michael. 'Taken without consent'. Something. 'to return him'. Then, 'Madame he'. Something. 'een cared for deeply'." Mrs. O'Brien began to sound *een* with every consonant she could think of. Then she said, "Been! Been cared for deeply! Has been? Maybe, 'has been cared for deeply'?"

"Francois, whoever penned this letter hoped for yeh safe return! Jus' like I remember, that dreadful night! The priest's insistence! Whoever wrote it, they wanted yeh home!"

"Michael's right! Makes sense, it does," Mr. O'Brien agreed. "But yah haven't answered my question, lad. What did Mr. Middleton know about bein' taken without consent?"

"Don't think weh'll ever know who wrote it," Francois sighed. "Sledgeham ripped it in half—right where the signature would be. Besides, France is probably filled with a lot of Claudes."

Claude. My father's name. But I've known this for forever.

"Jaysus, Mary, Joseph, we'll get a French map! But find it we will!" Mr. O'Brien cried.

"G.N.E. Weh've got those letters to work with! Weh'll eliminate each city one by one!" Michael grinned.

"What if it ain't a city?" asked Francois.

"...villages, towns, whatever!" laughed Michael.

"Aye, yer a pair of quare witty lads, I've the feelin' yah'll figure a solution," laughed Mr. O'Brien, "O m'anam, what a wonder, 'tis been, these weeks!"

"Besides, we don't really have to...." Michael added, flustered, cheeks reddened.

"What do you mean, 'we don't really have to?' Have to what?" asked Mrs. O'Brien.

"Don't yeh know? Nothin? I thought he'd a mentioned?" Michael asked, genuinely surprised.

"Know what, Michael? Who'd have mentioned what?" asked Mr. and Mrs. O'Brien.

Michael paused, settling himself, selecting thoughts carefully, formulating his speech exactly as he wanted, and only then spoke.

"What a strange day, 'twas! First, Mr. Middleton tellin' me what he did. Then, the Beauchamp's showin' up unannounced. Then findin' out Francois went back to Saint Marks. Then, Sledgeham...arrested. All in a day? What a day! A day of reckonin', 'twas indeed!" Michael's hearty laugh and emotional display took everyone by surprise.

"What are yah sayin' lad?"

Francois thought again about Mr. Middleton's private conversation with him and Michael on the day they found the lockbox.

"Mr. Middleton didn't tell yeh nothin'," Michael repeated.

"Tell us what, lad?" Mr. O'Brien beseeched.

"What do we need to know, Michael?" Mrs. O'Brien begged.

Francois could see Michael's guard rise against the familiar wall that controlled the words he kept or gave away.

"He told me his wife's cousin lives in a place called Boo-lonyah or somethin' like that," Michael answered. "Don't hear a GNE in it, but that was long ago. Maybe she's moved?"

"What does his wife's cousin have to do with this letter? What was long ago? Who has moved?" Mrs. O'Brien stumbled over her questions, as her confusion fell upon Mr. O'Brien, who seemed as hugger-muggered as his wife.

"Forget it. Not makin' sense. I'm speakin' gibberish, that's all. Yeh can imagine why! Mr. and Mrs. O'Brien, could yeh find us a map of France any time soon?"

His preposterous request (as if one could just pop over to the local shop and pick up a map of France—this would take time—but it was Mr. O'Brien's suggestion after all) served as decoy to change the course of conversation.

Mr. and Mrs. O'Brien eyed each other suspiciously, with parental expressions that told them something was not right, that Michael was withholding information.

"Michael, all we know is that Mr. Middleton and Bernadette have taken Beatrix to France, to a cousin's, whose name or location he wouldn't share, thinking it best we knew as little as possible, just in case the law gets involved—if it comes to that. He said his wife's cousin may be able to take Beatrix in, or if not, know of a safe place for her to go. What else do you know about this, Michael? Has Mr. Middleton revealed to you something we should know? There simply cannot be surprises for us, especially in light of the fact that...well, what we are doing...for Beatrix' sake...it isn't exactly legal if the Beauchamp's speak the truth!" Mrs. O'Brien persisted.

"Speak the truth 'bout what?" Michael asked.

Mrs. O'Brien and Mr. O'Brien looked at one another and Mrs. O'Brien's lips pursed as she fiercely shook her head.

"We've your best interest for now—that we've proven—as for Beatrix, please don't ask. Time will tell," Mrs. O'Brien said. "But, I shall ask you again, Michael. I expect you tell us."

"No, ma'am, ain't nothin' else I know."

What else yeh hidin' from me, Michael? What else yeh know 'bout the story of the missin' boy?

"'Am'nt sure yah understand our troubles, lad?"

"I understand, Mr. O'Brien. But what about Beatrix? What truth? What yeh mean?"

Francois stirred in discomfort—too many secrets from all sides.

"Leave it, Michael," Francois replied, "We understand."

The rain pelted harder now, and Mrs. O'Brien told everyone they'd best get inside. She rolled up the scroll, handed it to Michael, and he put it inside the lockbox to protect against further damage.

"Francois, I'll find yah a map, and we'll dig out yer roots, and I'll take yah there meself!"

Francois read Michael's voluminous look, the size of a book: a thick book, a book of history, a book of being left behind. —and his eyes softened.

"Not without Michael," Francois said.

"That goes without saying," agreed Mr. O'Brien.

Mrs. O'Brien's thoughts preoccupied her as she recited a slew of French words, meaningless to her company, but gratifying to her.

"Michael, do you mean Boulogne? Is that what Mr. Middleton told you? Because the last three letters are G.N.E. They're just French G.N.E. sounds," Mrs. O'Brien said.

"Yes! That's it!" Michael cried.

"What does Francois' parchment have to do with Mr. Middleton's letter? Or his visit to his wife's cousin?" Mrs. O'Brien asked again.

"I'm sorry, ma'am," replied Michael. "It doesn't. I'm just...."

"I think we're bit overwhelmed, Mrs. O'Brien. Please don't think me ungrateful, but I'd like some time alone with Michael, if it's alright?" Francois quickly defended.

The pelting rain subsided, and a hazy, thin light broke through the choleric clouds, painting pink into the sky.

"We're all drenched! We'll catch cold! Go inside the barn, then, hurry up. We'll leave you two boys alone there to talk ...whatever it is you need to do, but my questions still stand, and I expect answers later. Come join us for hot tea when you're ready."

Mr. O'Brien put his arm around his wife, a quick calm effect, as his wife's hands pulled her shawl tightly, and one by one, the O'Brien family turned away from Francois and Michael, and hurried inside.

As Mr. O'Brien walked away with his back turned, his enthusiasm carried the wind, "A map. We'll find yah lads a map!"

Francois and Michael jogged into the barn, the lockbox in Francois' arms, the contents inside the lockbox hitting against wood and each other—trapped, stolen artifacts once belonging to someone else, some other life, brought together because.

Jingles ran inside as Michael held the barn door open for Francois. Inside, it was warm and dry, but smelled of damp hay and animals. They climbed the loft ladder to their hay mats, and Michael fell onto his straw, laughing, laughing. Francois threw him the lockbox and then dived onto his own mat, laughing as well, and rolled over to his back, then sat up straight.

The pursuance of this letter had caused them each a personal, private grief, but they shared between them a larger collective grief, an unbreakable bond, that came full circle, redressed through the finding and opening of the lockbox.

"Give it here!" Francois said. Michael opened the lockbox, handed him the letter, and then began to thumb through trinkets.

Francois focused on the small, perfect handwriting, and wondered who wrote it, what she looked like, where she was now. Or was it a he? Whoever, he wondered if this person could ever know the depravity she or he caused him by leaving him behind.

"Well, son of Claude," Michael said, licking satisfaction from his lips, "The letter affirms it for me."

"Hmmm, Claude. My father. Yeh remembered it right."

"That's true. But more! What Mr. Middleton told me! Don't yeh see the connection?"

The boy, missing. I am. I am the missing boy. Francois played these words in his head until they fell together in the right order.

They sat together silently for some time, and Francois appreciated this familiar silence between them. He was a thousand miles away, wherever France was, wherever this place with a G.N.E resided; this place he once must have known.

"I'm startin' to think it's true. Yeh think Mr. Middleton'll find her? My mother? He never told me her name."

"I noticed that."

"What? You mean he told yeh? Yeh know her name?" Francois bolted up and grabbed Michael. "Kept it from me? Yeh'd do that?"

"He made me promise not to say. He wanted to wait to tell yeh, in case...yeh know, in case it didn't pan out. But this letter, it's proof!"

"Michael, tell me, please!"

Michael held back, but only seconds before blurting out.

"Violette! You are Francois, son of Claude and Violette."

Nothing could prepare him for the sound of her name.

Violette.

"Yeh alright, Francois?"

Francois' eyes stared into nothingness, but his lips slightly moved, and he repeated, 'Violette.'

"All these years ain't been feh nothin'! It's been hard, it has, keepin' her name these past weeks. Yeh don't know many times I almost told. But the letter speaks! Everythin' Mr. Middleton said! Don't need a map, Francois! We already know where yeh came from and where yeh'll return!"

"Violette?" Francois whispered.

"Francois, there's somethin' else. Mr. Middleton made me promise! I swore to him I wouldn't. But that was before we opened the lockbox. Can't keep it in no more. The night after Sledgeham's arrest, me an' Mr. Middleton talked, after yeh fell asleep. He told me the missin' boy's last name. Are you ready for this? Dubois. Francois Dubois."

Francois stared at Michael—stunned into silence, a total loss of words.

Francois Dubois. Son of Claude and Violette.

Chapter 16: Finding Dubois

O'Brien's Farm, Monday July 31st

For Francois both disharmony and reconciliation came at night, when he lay awake in the barn loft thinking about all that had been lost and all that had been found in his life. In his fragile state, he turned the words of the parchment letter over again in his mind, hating whoever it was that wrote it. Whoever wrote it was the source of his unraveling. But then the written words overtook him, and he took small solace in one single idea: cared for.

I was cared for, didn't it say this much?

The hatred he felt toward this letter writer sapped him of his energy and transported him to his painful past, so he focused on his name. On the name of her.

He spent his days and nights thinking about them: *Claude and Violette.* He had no tangible feeling or memory associated with his father. All these years he had known his father's name, but still, the name *Claude* was nothing more than six letters strung together, hanging solemnly. Now, he knew his name for certain, and yet, still, six letters strung.

But his mother, she was always different. Even without a name, she had always been. She wasn't so much a distinct face—though once in a great while even that visage took shape in his mind—but she was a distinct feeling. She was a sound, a touch, a smell, a color. *Violette.*

Michael rolled over on his hay mat and looked at Francois.

"It's been over a month and nothin'," Michael whispered.

"Thought yeh was sleepin'," Francois whispered back.

"No one's heard a thing. Nothin'. No news. But I've been doing a lot of thinkin' lately, Francois."

"'Bout what?"

"Everythin'! Sledgeham. Farley. Alfred. All of 'em boys. What's become of 'em. What'll become of us. Been thinkin' of you, mostly, Francois Dubois."

Francois felt keenly aware that the last month couldn't have been more different for him and Michael. Lost pieces of him fused together, and even if this was all he would ever know about himself, it was enough. He never realized how a surname could provide a person such solace inside. He was now Francois Dubois. Michael remained Michael.

"The same thing. That's to become of us," Francois replied.

"Huh? That don't even make sense. Francois, was it a mistake to tell yeh name, an' yeh mother's? What if…? I don't want yeh to be disappointed if…."

"What, we plannin' on goin' back to Saint Mark's? Yeah, that'd disappoint."

"No jokes. Mr. Middleton might come back with bad news. Or....He said he'd send word—but so far nothin'," Michael sighed, frustrated and tired.

"Startin' with the negative?" Francois grinned.

"Negative—a reliable friend, he is. Anyway, yeh should prepare for the worst of it."

"Ever considered that maybe yeh're the one needin' to prepare? Sorry. It's true though." Francois asked.

Michael sat up and laughed.

"Yeh're not the same no more. Now, yeh got somethin' to say? Yeh just go ahead and say it! Takes some gettin' used to...."

"Nothin' and no one's ever the same, Michael. Just a sum total of our days, we are. But new days can certainly turn winds, eh?"

"Just the wind, tossin' 'bout the whippin' boys! A sum of our days, eh? We ain't had such a great sum total, the way I count."

"But, yeh can see that's changin'."

"Yeh think so?"

"Know so! Michael, Mr. O'Brien told me that whatever happens, weh've got a place here on the farm."

"Stay on the farm," Michael repeated, tilling the words.

"So, what yeh think?"

"Wouldn't yeh return to everythin' that was taken from yeh? I mean, if ...." Michael stopped mid-sentence.

"Answer the question! What yeh think? About stayin' here?"

"Wasn't my plan. But it's possible. I'll think about it."

Francois sprung up quickly, smiling. *Willin' to think about stayin'. Now that's a change, ain't it!*

Michael quickly added, "But, let's just weigh all options first. Been thinkin' 'bout France lately. Can't get France off my mind."

Can't get Beatrix off yeh mind. It's her yeh can't stop thinkin' 'bout.

"Weigh our options!" Francois smirked at the phrase he'd never heard before, while balancing his own scale precariously.

O'Brien's Farm, Monday August 8th

It was Mrs. Beauchamp's hat that gave the second surprise visit away. As Francois stood at the tip of Sheep Hill, Jingles by his side, he watched the distant horizon as the open Phaeton carriage rolled at furious speed; but it was the hat that held his attention. Even from this distance, he could make out the feathers protruding straight up, slightly bent by the wind.

Immediately, he ran down the hill as he called to William, who was tending to the sheep herd on the lower side that led to the forest bush. Stumbling, he landed on his knees, but rolled forward and up again, unstoppable.

"Warn your mum and dad! The Beauchamp's are comin'!" Francois skidded down the dry, patchy green-brown grass, skinned knees and fresh dots of blood staining ever so lightly through his pants. William nodded, dropped his bucket, and ran home, Francois trailing closely behind.

~ 243 ~

William ran into the house, and Francois took off for the barn, calling to Michael. He found him up in the barn loft studying the map of France that Mr. O'Brien had brought home from a Charing Cross bookshop just yesterday. Michael had already penned large circles around the places ending with GNE, but he inked a tiny single star next to Boulogne.

"Michael, the Beauchamp's!"

Michael sprang up, tucked the map under his hay mattress, whipped down the loft ladder, and ran out the barn door with Francois. By now, they saw the Phaeton clearly, winding around the country road, not very far away from O'Brien's turn path. At the same time, Mr. and Mrs. O'Brien and William came running from inside their home and saw their unwanted visitors approach. Mary was still out in the fields somewhere, picking fresh figs for pies she planned to make later in the day.

"It's the Beauchamp's, mum, you can spot her hat from here!" William said.

"Nerve, they got, showin' up here. I'll give Beauchamp a piece a' this fer any trouble!" Mr. O'Brien swung his right fist upward and punched it into his left hand.

"Enough of that talk, Seamus! No violence today. It looks like there's someone else with them?" Mrs. O'Brien squinted her eyes. Behind the driver, sitting next to Mr. and Mrs. Beauchamp, was a man in uniformed blue coat with a middle strip of round shiny buttons up to his neck, and a black top hat.

"They brought the constable! They said they would!" William cried. Mrs. O'Brien whisked her fallen hairs from her eyes, sighed, assumed her role of general, and beckoned orders that came with her command post.

"Michael and Francois, you're safe. We've got legal rights— court papers to prove it. But the Beauchamp's can't know more than they must, so don't speak more than you should. And, no one knows a thing about a girl named Beatrix! Do you all understand?"

"But what if the constable asks us?" William asked.

"Just calm yourself. We don't know who's with them. Besides, constable or not, we know nothing and that's that," Mrs. O'Brien insisted, adding, "Seamus, no funny business with Mr. Beauchamp. We've got more important matters to focus on. Give the performance of your lives."

"Aye, though it'll be hard not to give 'em a dose or two," Mr. O'Brien spat, pounding his fist again.

Mrs. Beauchamp was close enough to see them congregating in front of the home; she pointed, her yawps carried by the wind, to where they stood.

"Where's Mary?" Mr. O'Brien asked.

"God help us, may she not return until they're gone. I'm not looking for a bad repeat like last time," Mrs. O'Brien said.

"Should I go look for her, warn her?" William asked.

"Aye, good idea," said Mr. O'Brien.

"Not yet," said Mrs. O'Brien, "Stay right where you are. They're watching us. It will look suspicious if you leave now. Besides, I might need you here to remind Mr. Beauchamp of his manners. He best tread carefully, especially with the law present."

The Phaeton's wheels spun fast up the path, now less than nine meters away. Mrs. O'Brien's lips whispered out her last command.

"We know nothing of Beatrix."

The carriage, with its driver and three passengers, now slowed along the tree-lined path, littered with summer's fallen flower petals, brown-edged and wilted. Mrs. Beauchamp's plumaged hat took shape: an undiscovered jungle bird nested upon her head.

Mr. Beauchamp's worn, unsettled look contrasted the officer next to him; he remained unaffected by the ill-mannered company he kept.

Both parties fixed stares at the other, as the driver halted his drays, hopped off his position, stood by the open door, and waited for his passengers to step down.

Mrs. Beauchamp knitted her brow, glanced at her husband, and directed him to help her up and out. Instead, Mr. Beauchamp stood himself, descended the open carriage door, turned to the officer, and said, "After you, Sir," which he concluded with a deep bow. The officer stepped down and the two men left Mrs. Beauchamp sitting alone.

"Well, I've never!" Mrs. Beauchamp struggled to lift herself off the seat, but held onto the extended hand of the driver, who helped her out of the carriage to stand on her two unsteady feet as she straightened her tilting hat.

Mr. O'Brien reached forward to the officer with an outstretched hand, and gave a firm handshake. He managed to produce his O'Brien smile as he greeted Mr. Beauchamp with a less enthusiastic, but friendly, nonetheless, nod.

Francois watched Mr. O'Brien curiously.

His performance has begun, as will my own.

"'Tis a surprise, Mr. and Mrs. Beauchamp, a second visit?" He turned to the constable. "Good day, Sir. This here's Mrs. O'Brien, an' me son, William—and the boys, of course, Francois and Michael."

"Mr. O'Brien," nodded Mr. Beauchamp.

Mrs. Beauchamp nudged her husband repeatedly, which only served to annoy him and he passed her a frustrated glare, then muttered, "Yeh're a pick axe, yeh are!" Though his comment vexed her, she let the insult slide.

"As I was goin' to say, before bein' rudely interrupted," said Mr. Beauchamp, eyeing his wife, "To the point, Mr. O'Brien, this ain't a social call, so drop yeh pleasantries. Don' want no trouble, like last time, 'specially with the boy."

Mr. Beauchamp glared at William, whose father's presence gave him courage, and whose eyes offered the same dirty glance.

"This time we've brought the constable, so yeh might consider tellin' a different version than last time."

"Don't let yer tongue cut yer throat, Mr. Beauchamp. A little pleasantness goes a long way. Tis the first I've personally greeted yah at me farm, and I greet as I wish. As fer the last visit, wasn't here, so I can't say what went on. "

"Hard time believin' Mrs. O'Brien didn't tell of the scuffle, or the lies she told!" Mrs. Beauchamp said, then added, "Yeh hidin' Beatrix an' we've come to get 'er!"

Mr. O'Brien's cheeks reddened, his eyes narrowed, and he felt the pang of his wife's character assassination rise in his chest. It took all he had to find enough restraint to address the constable calmly, his wife's honor having just been maligned.

"Officer, amn't sure what horse hoops they've told, but I don't know why they think I know somethin' cause I don't. Don't know nothin' bout the shop girl bein' gone. They keep at me with their guff, harassin' my family, talkin' gibberish. Last visit, Mr. Beauchamp had the gumption to lay his lug hand on me boy!"

Mr. O'Brien stopped mid-sentence, his red hot face glowing, and pointed directly at Mr. Beauchamp.

"Next time, yah'll deal with me, and deal with me yah will!" Mr. O'Brien's voice shook into Francois' bones as Mrs. O'Brien put her hand on her husband's shoulder. She met the constable's eyes.

"Mr. Beauchamp physically accosted William that day. Mr. O'Brien wasn't home."

Mrs. O'Brien stared into Mr. Beauchamp, ready to tongue-dual.

"Did he mention that to you? We've witnesses to it, and though I haven't pursued this with the law, I want no more trouble from them! Do I make myself clear, Mr. Beauchamp? Officer, we know nothing of the girl Beatrice."

"Beatrix!" Mrs. Beauchamp interrupted, offended by Mrs. O'Brien's slight. "Name's Beatrix, with an x! But yeh know that, don't yeh?"

The constable cleared his voice and spoke.

"Mr. and Mrs. Beauchamp say the girl's their daughter—this Beatrix—though they can't seem to provide any facts to support their claim."

The officer ran an accusatory eye over the Beauchamp's, and proceeded, "Mrs. Beauchamp says you're the last to see her the morning of her disappearance, Mr. O'Brien."

Mr. O'Brien shook his indignant head, and his indignant finger.

"That morn', I carried their purchased flowers into their shop. That's it! Said me goodbyes and left. Never conversed with the girl outside of how's the weather, and such. But, I will say, it's odd, them callin' her *daughter*. She called 'em her masters. That's right! Her masters! Never once did she ever call them by any other name. She was their servant, and I'm bettin' a free servant at that. That's their interest in the girl. Free labor!"

Mrs. Beauchamp's thick petticoat shuffled, as she stamped her laced boot into ground.

"Yeh haven't no right, turnin' the finger to us! She's ours alright, a fact I prefer to hide, if yeh must know!"

Mrs. O'Brien could take no more, and blurted out.

"Officer, what proof have you of their claim? A Church of England record or the child's local parish?"

The blotchy spots in Mrs. Beauchamp's skin brightened as she unleashed a dagger stare at Mrs. O'Brien, and everyone expected her to release a cannon ball next. Instead, she lowered her voice, her whole face pursed into a wrinkled bunion, and her jagged bottom row of teeth strained, as each word pushed singularly through the open spaces between her rotted teeth-gate.

"What...int'rest... is it...to yeh? Meddlin'...in our...family business?"

"I could ask you the same question!" Mrs. O'Brien retorted.

Mr. O'Brien placed his hand on his wife's back.

"Aye, have yah children of yer own, Officer?"

"Yes, two sons and two daughters," the officer replied, "What has that to do with anything?"

"Well...I suppose it has everythin' to do. Fancy them callin' yah *master* this, *master* that? Odd, ain't it?"

The officer rolled his thumb and pointer finger over his shiny uniform button, while his other thumb and pointer finger occupied his moustache, curling the tip just so, and his brows converged together. "Yes, it is odd. Why would you have your daughter refer to you as master?"

Mr. Beauchamp went to speak but was cut off by his wife, who gave him a swift gut kick with her elbow.

"Embarrassed of 'er, that's why! If yeh must know, she's a product of his scandalous affair, threatening to ruin my fine reputation! She's what I got outta it! A constant reminder, that's what!"

Mr. Beauchamp's propensity to turn purple when incensed always began with his nose, which sprouted dark potato roots, and spread underneath his baggy eyes.

"Yeh heartless crone, I've just about had it with yeh!" spit Mr. Beauchamp. "Yeh're the only scandal I know of, and I'm sick of yeh wretched complaints. I'm not embarrassed of 'er, I'm embarrassed of you! Don't even see why yeh want 'er back! Yeh treated 'er like

~ 250 ~

a servant day and night, beat 'er like she was an old' rug. I knew one day she'd run away from the likes of yeh, and God help 'er, I hope she never returns!"

The constable stopped twisting facial hair. Francois' mouth opened full-mooned. Michael's poker face pokered. Mrs. O'Brien's red strands of hair stood on end. William's knuckles whitened. Mr. O'Brien said, "Tis often a person's mouth breaks their nose."

Mrs. Beauchamp's screams scratched at her husband.

"Treacherous leech…. yeh never helped the girl, not a stitch!"

Francois focused on the word: *Stitch*. He thought of Beatrix's scarred hand, as the Beauchamp's went at each other like two fighting dogs, and the Constable stood complacent, hedging his bet on the female.

It was Mr. O'Brien's intervention that stopped them; he jumped between them, with his hands apart, resisting against the pushing of Mr. Beauchamp's chest.

"Please, Mr. Beauchamp. Let's stop this arguin' between and amongst ourselves. I understand why yah want to find her—daughter or not. I know nothin' of Beatrix's whereabouts, and would help if I could. I swear on me life, on that of me kin, none of us here knows nothin'".

Then, he extended his hand to the weary purple potato-faced man, who at first hesitated to take it.

"Don't shake it," Mrs. Beauchamp screeched, "if yeh know what's good for yeh!"

Mr. Beauchamp's potato eyes narrowed, his potato lips puckered, and his whole face shriveled.

"I'll shake yeh hand, and even apologize for all these accusations, that's what I'll do! And, Mrs. O'Brien, I'm sorry, I am, that things got carried away last time."

"How dare yeh!" Mrs. Beauchamp caterwauled, her hat feathers swaying in her own wind, as she waved her finger between her husband and Mr. O'Brien. "Our business with yeh's done—flowers included!" Her velvet skirt swished away toward the Phaeton, as she called the driver to assist her onto it.

"I'll say it's done when it's done, an' it ain't done!" Mr. Beauchamp yelled at her, but the words bounced off her silent back.

That is when the faint noise of Mary's singing drifted from the hedge.

Beatrix's song! Francois' heart dropped, and everyone fell still, especially Mrs. Beauchamp, who knew the forbidden song well.

And as she came hither, out from the bending of the path, Beatrix's melody and lyrics riding the still August air, Mary appeared from the overgrown brush singing, *"The sharp flint strikes against the rod, Burns within, the fire of God. Stare he down, upon my chest, He'll watch and wait, then take a breath!"*

Flustered at the sight of them all staring dead-eyed and spell-bound at her, Mary stopped singing in her tracks, shocked, throat-dry, as Mrs. Beauchamp, turned around, and ran toward her.

"That song! It's Beatrix' song!" Mrs. Beauchamp clamored.

Beatrix's song, timin's everythin'. Francois' head pounded with Sledgeham's words, *Timin's everythin'*, as he remembered Beatrix's lyrics and melody:

As the flames they burn with blue,
I pray the dreams I wish come true,
The sharp flint strikes against the rod,
Burns within, the fire of God.
Stare he down, upon my chest,
He'll watch and wait, then take a breath,
And burn the house, from which I came,
Ash to ash, those lives he'll claim.
The fire burning at my feet
shall speed my path to victory.
He'll guide me to his hearth and home,
And spare me life that's all alone.

How many times Beatrix sang this song for them, Francois couldn't recall. And what had she told them?

It was her song of solace, even though Mrs. Beauchamp prohibited it.

She taught it to Francois, Michael, William, and Mary over the last few months; Bernadette already knew it—the result of their years of friendship together. Out on the farm, Mary, Beatrix, and Bernadette often vocalized in rounds as they walked ladybird lane together, baskets swinging by their sides, gathering nuts and berries and herbs.

The constable sighed at Mrs. Beauchamp's new accusation; he knew her type well, was exhausted by her sense of entitlement and overgrown imagination; furthermore, he had no reason not to believe the O'Brien's. While he dreaded his return ride back in the same carriage, he wanted to get over with it as quickly as possible.

"Right then, deeply sorry to have bothered you on this matter, Mr. and Mrs. O'Brien. It's clear you and your family know nothing of Beatrix's disappearance. Please forgive me for our intrusion."

"It's Beatrix's song! Did yeh hear nothin' I just said? How would this girl know Beatrix's song? Ask her, why don' yeh?" Mrs. Beauchamp insisted. "I demand that yeh ask the girl where she learned Beatrix's song!"

"I don't take orders, Mrs. Beauchamp, I give them!" replied the frustrated constable, who could no longer hide his disgust with the Beauchamp's wild goose chase, their uncouth manners, and Mr. Beauchamp's new revelations about Beatrix, which he should have heard about before this trip out here. Nonetheless, he turned to Mary, mostly because he didn't want to hear about it from Mrs. Beauchamp the whole ride home.

"Young lady, that song you were just singing? Might I ask where you learned it?"

Mary froze and turned to her mother, but her mother just stared back at her helplessly, vexation looking desperate upon her face. Francois watched Mary struggle to act; he'd only always seen her tell the truth as she saw it in the literal sense, and suspected she hadn't had much practice telling any versions otherwise.

Protect the truth and tell the lie. For Beatrix's sake. Francois willed.

Mr. O'Brien took Mary's hand and spoke.

"Tell the truth, Mary. Yer me daughter, and in this house, we tell the truth. Tell the Constable what yah know."

Mary nodded to her father, and breathed deeply, as tears welled up in her eyes, and she stuttered.

~ 254 ~

"The truth is…the truth is….that I don't know where I heard the song, it's been with me as long as I can remember."

Hail Mary, Hail Mary, Hail Mary!

"Then why do you cry?" the Constable inquired.

"I'm scared," Mary said.

"Of what?"

"Of her," said Mary, pointing to Mrs. Beauchamp.

The perturbed constable thought of his own daughters, who would have petrified under Mrs. Beauchamp's glare. He directed his question to Mr. Beauchamp now.

"Is this a song Beatrix commonly sang, Mr. Beauchamp?"

Mr. Beauchamp's eyes brewed as they stared with vengeance into his wife. Francois knew that look well.

"No, can't say it is," Mr. Beauchamp said slowly with a wry expression. "Don't remember ever hearin' it."

Mrs. Beauchamp viciously screamed, "Liar, liar, liar! You're all lyin'…"

The constable quickly interrupted, "It's time we depart. I offer my deepest apologies for Mrs. Beauchamp's unruly display, Mr. and Mrs. O'Brien, and won't trouble you any further!"

Turning to the Beauchamp's, the constable ordered, "My inquiry with the O'Brien's is finished. You've wasted my time with your despicable behavior, you've withheld evidence from me, and your stories conflict. Perhaps an interrogation upon our return to London is in order, Mr. and Mrs. Beauchamp! That you can expect. Now, get in the carriage."

The driver waited by the open door, the officer stepped in first, sat down comfortably, and the Beauchamp's began their fierce argument once again, as they clambered over, and stepped inside the Phaeton.

Mrs. Beauchamp glanced back to Mr. O'Brien, squawking, "He may be done, but I'm not, yeh paddy!"

Mr. Beauchamp promptly covered his wife's mouth with his hand as the carriage pulled away, with their voices in uproar and Mrs. Beauchamp's body flailing for release, as feathers flew, then descended in a dance to the mottled ground, followed by the hat, as the carriage rolled over it without stopping, finally disappeared down the path, and Mary broke the silence.

"I'm going to hell for that, aren't I?" Mary replied sullenly, her words not a question, but a statement.

"No, Mary. Hell just left, but you're still here," Mrs. O'Brien's lips slightly relaxed into a smile, and she hugged her daughter.

"Mary, yah've just saved me skin in one blow, and Beatrix's too," Mr. O'Brien replied.

"I lied."

"Naw. Yah saw the big truth behind it all. And, yah fibbed a bit to get there!"

"Now, Beatrix is free. No one will find her, thanks to Mary! Thanks to all of yeh." Michael's words tasted bittersweet as he thought of Beatrix.

"Aye, no one will find her, because no one with any clout is lookin' further, that's certain."

"No, no one will find her. She's in France now."

Francois watched in wonder as the O'Brien family took joy in Beatrix's escape.

These people seemed to see the shades of gray in everything — except for their devotion to one another; glowing devotion, like the embers Beatrix so easily blew into being with flint and striker.

Some people don't want to be found and some do. Which one am I? Francois saw the good and bad in both options. He even glimpsed gray.

Chapter 17: Francois Found

O'Brien's Farm, Saturday, mid-September, afternoon

Autumn descended as weary crimson-colored leaves dropped into piles around the farm, grassy fields turned golden-hued, and summer's green metamorphosed into a mixture of burned orange and red. As usual, on this Saturday, Mr. O'Brien traveled into London to do his usual business, but he planned to also check in on William at the Mechanic's Institute; Mrs. O'Brien and Mary concocted tinctures in the kitchen; Francois and Michael lingered all morning outside, taking turns jumping into piles of crispy leaves as Jingles leapt beside them. Now, the boys sauntered inside to find some food to fill their empty stomachs. As they dipped their buttered bread into leftover vegetable soup, the sudden knock on the door startled them all.

"Mother, are we expecting guests?" Mary asked.

"It could be Mr. Jones. His wife must be in labor. I'll get our bag, you answer the door."

Mary opened the wooden front door to find a young man in tattered blue coat, red collar, and beaver hat with a small parcel in his hands.

"I've a package to deliver to Mr. Francois Dubois," he said, but as Mary reached for the package, he pulled it away, saying, "Two shillings, three-pence, please. Extra charge for delivery."

Mary's mother appeared with a medicine bag in hand. Francois came to the door at once. He stared pensively at a small parcel, and then the young man in uniform.

"Two shillings, three penny bit! That's absurd! For a small parcel that fits in my palm?" Mrs. O'Brien knitted her brow at the mail carrier's package, locking her eyes on the sender: Mr. James Middleton.

"Mr. Davies, at yeh service, an' a half crown'll do nicely!" Even his hand, held palm up, had a cheery disposition, and it was hard to take offense at his highway robbery, as his price seemed to increase every time he spoke. "Look, ma'am, yeh either want the package or yeh don't. It came on a ship from France that left over a month ago, arrived in town a week an' some days ago, an's been sittin' on the desk of postmaster James until he sent me today to collect yeh charge. We don't normally handle overseas packages an' we don't normally do door deliveries, so count yehself lucky that I've come." His crooked yellow teeth peered through his youthful grin, which slightly turned up at one corner.

At that cost, Mrs. O'Brien would have turned the mail carrier away, package in hand, had it not been for the sender; had it not been for the circumstance. No doubt, Mr. Middleton paid steeply on his end to send it, and she was to pay dear, as well.

"Francois!" Mrs. O'Brien cried, dropping her bag and reaching into her apron pocket, as she fingered around for money to pay the mail carrier, which she found, but came up short, and handed him the change.

"Will this do?" she asked.

Francois felt his pocket, and pulled out the coin that Samuel's father had given him; he had carried it around since that day, attributing to it a good luck of sorts. Now, he was glad that he hadn't spent it and thankful to contribute. He handed the shilling to Mrs. O'Brien, who puzzled over where the money must have come from.

She, in turn, handed Francois' fortune to the carrier, who departed with a sprite step, and even kicked up his black patent heels, as his satchel thumped against his hip, relieved to have received payment, and computing his portion of compensation.

Mrs. O'Brien handed Francois the package, but not without Mary peering over her to see who the sender might be.

"Your property, Sir, addressed to you, Mr. Dubois."

"It's from Mr. Middleton! Sent from France! Addressed to Francois Dubois! Finally, we've some news from abroad!" Mary exclaimed gleefully.

Michael leaped forward and bounded to Francois' side, but his unintended jolt caused Francois to drop the package to the floor. Michael steadied Francois, but also reached for the package, and not letting go, opened the front door with his free hand, and Francois called for him to wait, as he bolted outside.

Jingles barked and jumped at Francois as he leapt out the door behind Michael. Mary sprang to follow them, but Mrs. O'Brien jumped in with a quick reproach, followed by a lecture about the need for privacy, and Mary got the point without further restraint.

The chilled autumn wind, riding a particularly strong maritime air mass, playfully taunted deciduous trees, grabbing at their leaves, further undressing them, until they were almost bare now. Michael fell backward into a pile of fallen leaves, and as he landed into their crisp cracked hardness, he threw autumn up again to the sky. The light leaves didn't go far, scratching his face as they fell back, and he called to Francois, "Open it!" as the parcel lay by his side.

Francois joined Michael on the pile, turned the parcel over in his hands, as it popped like corn, and leaves crunched under his weight.

He read the address, *Mr. Francois Dubois*. And he took great pleasure in the movement of his tongue as it rung inside the roof of his mouth, *de*, slightly vibrating his throat, and his lips met, then parted, as the sound *bois* rolled. He turned quietly to Michael, and whispered, "Dubois," into Michael's ear, as if it were a secret meant only for them. Michael repeated, "Dubois."

"This is how yeh spell my name. First time I've seen it written. D.U.B.O.I.S."

"Well, go ahead. I'm on pins and needles," Michael directed.

Francois shook his head, passing the parcel to Michael, who began furiously tearing at paper, to which Francois kept repeating, "Not so rough, careful." There was a letter inside, along with a white cloth handkerchief folded around a small box.

"Another letter," Francois sighed, "Read it out loud to me." Michael kept the letter but handed Francois the small box, then the handkerchief, which had completely fallen off the box, and Francois grasped onto both items tightly.

Michael cleared his throat, looked at the signature, and sighed, "It's from Mr. Middleton, but you know that." Annoyed by Michael's expectation for someone else, Francois felt the sharp bite of Michael's displeasure.

Who does he expect? Asn't he learnt by now to expect somethin' in between everythin' an' nothin' at all?

Michael began to read:

Dear Francois,

We think of you daily and hope you have remained in good spirit and safety since our departure. By the time you read this letter, we will be sailing on our way home to you. Francois, my boy, you must prepare yourself for the unimaginable. Brace yourself for all that is to come. It is with fatherly affection that I speak these words.

You must know that you are loved deeply and always have been. Please prepare yourself to hear the bitter truth of sorrow and misfortune that struck you and yours. But, you must also know that you are rising out of the ashes of evil and into the light of all that is good—should you be able to make peace with your past, accept present disappointments, and revel in the miracle of your future. We shall see you soon, in a few weeks. Please tell the O'Brien's we are on route. Homeward bound.

Fondly,
James Middleton

As Francois dissected Mr. Middleton's sentences, Michael interrupted, "Wait, there's another letter here! Oh, from

~ 262 ~

Bernadette." Francois' face flushed, and his pulse pounded into his ears, frustrated with Michael's continued disappointment; but then he realized it was his own letdown, and shame flooded him for his judgment.

Did I expect nothin' or everythin'? Can't I settle for somethin' in between?

Francois shut his eyes for a moment.

Accept present disappointments. The bitter truth of sorrow and misfortune. These words tumbled in his head, over and over, rocks churning in fast water, smoothing out and settling against muddy river bottom. He stared out past Michael, past the farm, past the country horizon, staring into the nothingness of grey.

What'd I hope for? Who'd I hoped to find? Ain't the name Violette enough? Ain't Dubois enough? Yea, it'll have to be.

Michael started to read Bernadette's letter aloud:

Dearest Francois,

Father asked me not to say too much, for complicated reasons. We have so much to share with you, but it must happen in person. One thing I can say is that Beatrix is well, safe, and shall be in greatest of hands. What a joy and comfort this is to know though I miss her already. Please share this news.

On this journey, I have thought so much about what you have gone through—life in the orphanage, with no one but Michael to care for you—what a blessing he has been to you, and I know will always be.

This trip has been good for me. I have spent the last months thinking about my mama, and the sadness I feel each day. Perhaps it would be easier had I never had a chance to remember her. I do not tell my father, because it will make him sad to know this. I know you will keep my secrets, just as I will keep yours. I sometimes pretend it

~ 263 ~

is all a bad dream, and that she is still alive but that we just can't seem to find each other—that we will be reunited soon. She's lost, that's all.

In seeking your parents, I've come to realize and accept that she isn't coming back to me. I'm finding ways to get on, but some days are harder than others. I take comfort that you might understand my grief. I take refuge in your friendship.

Bernadette

Francois did not cry, though he wanted to. He knew he had much to be thankful for, just like Mr. Middleton inferred. Somewhere inside of himself he knew: What was not written in these letters was the thing that said it all. Mr. Middleton and Bernadette were sailing home. He must prepare himself for the unimaginable. He was loved. He is loved now—by whom? Michael? The O'Brien's? Perhaps Mr. Middleton and Bernadette? Francois suppressed his rage at feeling patronized, as if he didn't recognize just who Michael was to him, as if he needed his good fortune explained! But nowhere in either letter was there mention of the people he most desired to know about: Claude, a man who was nothing but a phantom ghost; Violette, his mother for whom he deeply longed.

In his stillness, he pictured calm grey again. Only then, in that calm space could he summon Violette to him. His mother, once nameless, was now Violette. He remembered how he used to call upon her in the orphanage at night. How she would sit at the edge of his mattress, tucking his sheets just so, and sing him to sleep. Stillness. She came to him in his stillness. It was his special trick. He told no one about it, not even Michael—how he could resurrect her from the recesses of his mind, conjuring her back to him through the witchcraft of his own desire, in the stillness of the night, as he lay on his cot in Saint Mark's while the other boys slept and Michael snuck out into the halls searching.

Lost in her calm yellow warmth, Francois reached inward, back and back and back to the memory of her, to the obscure picture of her face, though it was hazy and unclear. He heard a voice calling him forward, disrupting his stillness.

"Francois? Yeh alright?" asked Michael.

"No. But I will be," Francois replied, jarred out of his trance.

"It's gonna work out, Francois. The worst is over. It's the not knowin' that does me in."

"They ain't comin' back for me. My parents, I mean. Do yeh ever think I'll know what happened to 'em?"

"Want to know what I think? 'Cause I won't lie to yeh."

Francois nodded, "Yes."

"Don't think so. Mr. Middleton would have said. But, it sounds like he's found out somethin', to fill in the gaps."

Francois rubbed the cloth handkerchief between his finger and hand, and looked at the small box.

"What yeh think's inside? Go ahead," Michael encouraged.

Francois placed the handkerchief in his lap and opened the box cover. Inside lay a man's thick gold ring, and inscribed on the oval face: *Claude Dubois, 1801-1831.*

"My father's ring. 1831. He died a year after I went missin'." Francois wiped his moist eyes, but still he did not cry. He placed the ring on his pointer finger, but it swung around, threatening to slip off. He picked up the handkerchief that lay on his lap, to wipe his eyes which began to fill, and turned the handkerchief over, but something caught his eye. On the back side, stitched in lavender-colored thread, was the name *Violette*. He held the handkerchief to his nose. It faintly smelled of her.

Her smell!

He felt deeply contented, even if her scent on this handkerchief was all he would ever have of her. Though it wasn't all he had. Her name. He had her name.

O'Brien's Farm, early October

The shock of Mr. and Mrs. O'Brien's surprise a few days ago still hadn't worn off. Last Saturday, Mr. O'Brien's return cart from London was loaded with none other than Alfred, his leg muscles healed well, but his crushed ankle bone, calcified and sickle-shaped. Mr. and Mrs. O'Brien had decided long ago that Alfred was to visit Michael and Francois indefinitely, but it wasn't an easy surprise to keep. Alfred would have arrived sooner; Saint Bart's discharged him a fortnight ago to Aunt Patricia after his three and a half month convalescence there, and he was finally strong enough to handle the choppy cart ride to the farm. He looked well-nourished again, minus his twisted ankle and dangling thumb. In fact, Francois had never seen him so fat and pleased.

Alfred had been at the farm over a week now, and his presence greatly softened Francois' recent blow—the knowledge of his father's death, the untold loss of his mother. Alfred's friendship and conversation soothed lingering demons; with Michael and Alfred by his side, Francois found it easier to lay down any false hope of reunions, and to embrace his good fortune.

But, all the same, Francois couldn't understand what took Mr. Middleton and Bernadette so long to return. Yes, Alfred's presence quelled some of his need to reconcile his past with his present, but he greatly desired the information Mr. Middleton and Bernadette had found in France—whatever it might be; perhaps it would fill the gnawing hole inside the pit of his stomach, growing larger.

Yeh've waited this long for answers. Patience, boy!

While Alfred became a diversion from the web of waiting he seemed caught in, Francois' desire to complete his pre-Saint Mark's history grew stronger each day. He prepared himself to accept whatever.

Accept whatever. Except whatever.

The days kept moving forward. While the genuine pleasure of Alfred's presence didn't diminish, the initial shock of his arrival eventually wore off, leaving the boys to once again obsessively speculate Mr. Middleton and Bernadette's arrival date. Now, Alfred joined Francois and Michael in biding their time and guessing the week, day, hour, minute of their return.

With William gone, Francois and Michael filled their days with double-duty farm chores; this helped whittle time away, while Alfred oriented himself to his new life.

On this particular day, Mr. O'Brien had gone to do some bidding on farm equipment, and the boys and Mary were loafing in front of the barn, when it happened. Alfred was the first to notice.

"Look to the road! Over there! There's a carriage coming," Alfred trumpeted, proud he was the first to call it.

"That looks like Bernadette! And, Mr. Middleton!" Mary cried.

"And, someone else! Beatrix?" Michael's tone heartened for a moment, then dissolved; everyone zeroed in, and though the female next to Mr. Middleton was still too far away in the distance to clearly delineate her facial features, Michael self-corrected his statement before anyone disclaimed his hope.

"No. Not her. It's a woman," Michael said, crestfallen.

Francois' doughty-green eyes fixed as best he could upon the woman by Mr. Middleton's side but his emotion clouded his focus; his heart thwacked and his heart thumped and his heart trounced.

Mary nodded, "Mother's inside. I'll retrieve her," and she ran to get Mrs. O'Brien. Closer the carriage came.

"But...my eyes playin' tricks?" Michael whispered, hypnotized by the woman, "I know who! It's her, ain't it?"

Mrs. O'Brien was outside within seconds, standing next to Francois as she waved down the carriage, so close now, that she covered her mouth with her hand, trying to contain small squeaks of delight, as she saw who was inside.

Francois remained transfixed on the stranger next to Mr. Middleton, as he squinted against light, against the futility of his clouded sight, and shaded out the sun's blare with hand cupped over his brow.

"It's them! Mr. Middleton and Bernadette!" Mary cried.

"I do believe so!" Mrs. O'Brien smiled and fixed upon the unfamiliar guest next to Mr. Middleton; a refined lady, well-attired in what appeared from the distance to be a mustard colored cloak with a foliage of leaves delicately embroidered, blending her into autumn.

"Mrs. O'Brien, who's the lady by their side?" Francois' chest tightened, and he was afraid to ask, so terrified of the catastrophic casualty of failed expectation and utter disappointment that might come with her answer.

"I don't know. I simply don't know," Mrs. O'Brien said. "But she's a fine sight, isn't she? She outshines the sun."

Mrs. O'Brien placed her hand over her eyes, as she strained against the sun's rays, then pulled Francois into her side, and wrapped his shoulders into the folds of her modest day dress, as her shawl fell slightly draped over her side.

Though he usually took comfort in her motherly ways, Francois resisted Mrs. O'Brien's affections this time and pulled slightly away from her until she sensed his discomfort. She stared at the lady, as they all did, and let go of her embrace of Francois, in spite of her desire to hold onto him more tightly than ever.

Francois stood unencumbered now, as Mrs. O'Brien bent down to his ear and whispered something only he could hear. He nodded repeatedly, as if to say yes. Mrs. O'Brien then turned to Michael, and tried to read his face as he, too, stared spellbound at the carriage descending upon them.

Expressionless, the world fell silent around Francois, and as it melted away, he heard his own slow breathing beat against the rhythm of his pounding blood. A nameless wave flooded over, rendering him vulnerable and unguarded. In the here and now, in the moments to come, he somehow knew that the answers to all his questions—to his fragmented self—were before him. He thought again of Mr. Middleton's letter, and of Bernadette's.

Prepare yourself. For unanswered questions. For heartbreak. For love lost.

How the arrival of those letters had sealed his future hopes, as small as they already were! But, now, he realized he had not read his letters well; he had missed the signs and signals sent to him from France: Signs meant to ease him slowly into a fate too good to be true, too unbelievable to believe!

For the first time in his life, as he stared at the rolling carriage, it struck him that inexpressible fulfillment might be a part of his present and future.

Prepare yourself. For inexpressible fulfillment.

Francois felt Michael's presence now, shoulder to shoulder, they held each other upward, and silently tracked the open carriage which now came up the lane of leafless magnolia, cherry, and dogwood trees leading to where they stood.

He could see her clearly now. She saw him too. She stood up in the moving carriage, her petite frame so fragile, as if she could be whisked away by a sudden gust.

Mr. Middleton pulled her down gently, saying, "For your own safety," as tears rolled over her cheeks, and she beat her heart repeatedly, calling to the boy, trying to stand again. Francois' eyes widened as he took all of her in: her youthful porcelain gaze; her sandy-blonde lockets springing from the silk bonnet ensconced around her ivory heart-shaped face; her fertile green eyes that matched his own.

Mrs. Violette Giroux Dubois saw nothing else but her son, as she raised her hand to her mouth, and howled forth deep, guttural cries—and she could no longer contain herself as she desperately pulled at the carriage door. The carriage continued forward, Mr. Middleton and Bernadette holding onto her, Mr. Middleton shouting for the carriage driver to quicken their arrival, and trying to calm her, saying, "But a moment more, but a moment….".

Even as the driver slowed, she broke free, unlatched the door handle, descending the carriage steps as the carriage still moved, and braced herself for her jump.

Sensing the chaos, the driver pulled the horses back to an immediate stop. Violette jumped out of the carriage, running to her only child as he stared wild-eyed back at her, his unsure arms now raised outward.

Francois whispered *Maman*—the word came out of him as if he had used it just the day before, though where it had come from he did not know. He hadn't known the word was there inside of him

~ 271 ~

before this moment. This was her—the woman who visited him all those years in his silence. His heart bled residual sorrow—how he longed for her all these years!—and he understood what *love lost* meant; he understood the need to prepare.

Falling to her knees, Violette grabbed Francois with untamed ferocity, shaking, embracing tightly, as she whispered though tears, "Je t'aime! Je t'ai toujours aimé!"

Francois responded, "*maman.*"

After some time, Violette looked up at the others, her green gaze stopping at Michael. With her strong accent, she called, "Michael? Come to me."

Michael, still numb and raw, walked slowly to her side. No longer expressionless, tears filled his eyes and he tried to hide his face, as Violette motioned for him to take her hand, which he did, and she pulled him into her embrace next to Francois as she thanked him in French and English and a combination of both a dozen times more, and pressed warm kisses into both their heads, held them tightly, and spoke her best English.

"For what you did for Francois, you are now my child too."

Michael, who normally recoiled from human touch, anchored into her, buried his face in her embrace, sobbed, and held onto them both.

Francois breathed in the fresh scent of his mother, and knew she was his again. And he was hers. Her lost Francois found.

The End.

~ 272 ~

37938378R00168

Made in the USA
Charleston, SC
23 January 2015